Nikki Hopeman

Habeas Corpse

BLOOD BOUND BOOKS

Copyright © 2013 by Nikki Hopeman
All rights reserved

ISBN 978-1-940250-03-8

This book is a work of fiction. Names, characters, business organizations, places, events and incidents either are the product of the author's imagination or are used fictitiously. Any resemblance to actual persons, living or dead, events or locales is entirely coincidental.

Artwork by Billy Sagulo

Printed in the United States of America

First Edition

Visit us on the web at:
www.bloodboundbooks.net

Also from Blood Bound Books:

400 Days of Oppression by Wrath James White

Loveless by Dev Jarrett

The Sinner by K. Trap Jones

Mother's Boys by Daniel I. Russell

Knuckle Supper by Drew Stepek

Sons of the Pope by Daniel O'Connor

Dolls by KJ Moore

At the End of All Things by Stony Graves

For Ward. Because everything I do is better with you.

CHAPTER 1

The brain matter clinging to the wall had that special opacity, with only a slight glisten that said, "I'm fresh, but no longer squishy."

Theo liked firm brains.

He caught himself licking his lips and glanced around to be sure no one was watching. Nope. The few remaining detectives busied themselves with paperwork, and Skeet shuffled around the body to snap pictures from every conceivable angle. The forensic technician looked ridiculous in the white paper jumpsuit, but then again, Theo supposed, so did he.

Theo stepped closer to the tempting spatter, mouth watering, and reached toward the smallest glob. It wiggled ever so slightly in the breeze from the open window.

"Ted."

He snatched his hand back as a wave of adrenaline rolled its sluggish way through his body, leaving a slight tingle in its wake. He knew from experience it would take about thirty seconds for his legs to feel weak. "What?" he snapped.

"You can start collecting evidence. The ME is on his way." The sergeant flipped through a packet of papers. "You'll assist him when he gets here."

Theo's knees wobbled. Less than thirty seconds. His circulation was good today. Maybe it was the heat. Maybe it was frustration that Sergeant Milton insisted on calling him "Ted," as if he hadn't grown up. Or died. Death really should demand a certain amount of respect from the living.

Since Theo owed this job to the sergeant, he refrained from correcting him, despite the irritation.

"Is there...uh," Sergeant Milton pointed at the corpse with his pen. "Is there any chance for this one, you think?"

Theo looked at the woman lying on the carpet. The heroin-thin limbs, cramped in the awkward positions of her death throes, combined with thick blonde hair and angular jawline, suggested supermodel looks, but the gaping chasm that was once her nose and eyes ruined the overall effect. The gray matter splattered on the wall behind him confirmed his opinion. "Nah. Not enough left."

Theo peered at the sergeant. Like most of the living, he was either too afraid or too apathetic to educate himself about zombies. No brain, no rising. But Theo didn't bother to explain. He'd rather avoid the awkward conversation.

Sergeant Milton's lips tightened into a thin line. "That's too bad. Young one."

Theo took care to paste the expected expression on his face. Sad and sympathetic, yet concerned and professional. His honest opinion? The mess of a woman on the floor might be the lucky one.

The sergeant patted him on the shoulder. "I know. It doesn't get any easier. Not really. It's always a waste."

Theo nodded gravely, another one of those expected gestures. Whatever.

Somewhere between the sledgehammer that snuffed out his first life and the indignity of rising as a zombie in only a filthy wife-beater and one red Converse sneaker, Theo had lost his own tenuous respect for death. Life was what mattered, and since he hadn't done much with his first one, he had mixed feelings about having to go another round.

"Officers." The atmosphere in the room shifted when another detective walked in. The big man filled the doorway.

Theo's flight instinct kicked into high gear. Gavahan. What a prick. The fresh-minted detective hated zombies, and for some reason loathed Theo with a rabid intensity.

Gavahan wasn't the only asshole in the department with an undead problem, but he was the most vocal. He had a knack for making Theo feel like more of an insecure geek than he actually was.

"Gavahan." Sergeant Milton nodded at the detective.

"Sergeant." An officer handed Detective Gavahan a packet of papers. The detective's gaze slid over Theo, as if he didn't exist.

"Collect what you can. Skeet's almost done with the pictures. He can check your work." Sergeant Milton strode toward Detective Gavahan, then turned back to Theo. "Tell your folks I said hi."

"You got it." Theo grabbed a stack of paper evidence bags, and with a last wistful look at the brains on the wall, bent to collect the designated items from around the room. The plastic markers went back into their bright yellow carrying case, the bits and pieces of the girl and the crime scene evidence into the bags.

He picked up a cartridge shell with a pair of tweezers, looked at it closely. Nine millimeter. Someone meant business, possibly chose the large caliber to ensure this woman couldn't rise. There were only a few ways to be absolutely certain of keeping a human down, but blowing their brains out was one of them. Decapitation and severing a brain stem also worked. Someone hated this woman.

The detectives shuffled into the hall to make room for the medical examiner. Theo placed the cartridge shell into a labeled bag and replaced it in his evidence case.

Dr. Libitin's face split in a wide smile when he caught sight of Theo. "My favorite assistant." He dropped his bag on the floor near the corpse. "I'm glad you're here."

"Hiya, doc." Theo grinned back at the ME.

"What've we got here?" Dr. Libitin's gaze swept the room before he looked directly at the corpse. Theo watched this systematic analysis of the scene at every case they worked and tried to emulate the habit as well. The doc said the place in which someone died could tell a story about the dead. Theo himself returned to the site of his death several times. He didn't think anyone would glean much information from the suburban basement where he'd hid behind a furnace, cowering for the few brief moments it took them to find him. Maybe the circumstances of the death had to be accounted for too, and Theo's demise wasn't exactly a run-of-the-mill homicide. Nothing that happened twelve years ago was ordinary.

The end came for this woman in a mostly unfurnished apartment, dirty white walls and stained tan carpet. Could be her pimp's apartment or the john's.

"Gunshot to the face. At least one direct hit from close range. Maybe four hours, considering this heat." Dr. Libitin's voice broke through Theo's musings. "We've seen more like this lately. You thinkin' the same thing I am?"

"Yeah. It's for a reason. There's no chance of rising like this."

Dr. Libitin lifted the girl's arm, flipped it over to examine the tender skin on the wrist. Theo turned his head sideways to read the tattoo emblazoned across her wrist: RISE. She'd taken the time to accent the bold black letters with a stylized sun and moon. No more sun or moon for her.

The ME peered at the tips of her fingers. "Very little under the nails, but maybe we'll get lucky. Grab the bags. Mr. Jones, did you take shots of her nails already?"

Skeet hovered behind the ME. "Let me get a couple of pictures while you hold up the hands. I didn't want to touch her, but I should get the angle."

Dr. Libitin nodded, and Theo readied his bags while Skeet took three or four shots of each hand. While Theo bagged and taped the hands, the doctor turned his attention to the rest of the corpse. He moved her legs aside, peered at her inner thighs. "Evidence of sexual activity or assault."

Theo's mouth went dry. His own death, no matter how violent, gave no insight to the disgusting things people did to one another.

"No defensive wounds." After a cursory examination of the gunshot wound, the ME waved at the body. "Huh. Either she never saw the shooter coming or she knew him. Okay, the rest will have to be done back at the morgue. Bag her."

They unfolded a blue body bag, transferred the corpse from the floor, and zipped her in. Theo helped Skeet lift it onto a gurney. The doctor waited off to one side, watching the proceedings with apparent disinterest.

Theo knew better.

He stood by, a dull anticipation rising in his chest while Skeet pulled the gurney into the hallway.

"Rigor is mild. But in this heat, with no air conditioning, I'm not surprised. Can you tell anything?" Dr. Libitin tilted his head at the wall.

Theo looked sharply at the doctor. "You sure?"

One nod was all he needed. His salivary glands kicked into overdrive, and he had to swallow or risk drooling. The glistening drop he eyeballed earlier still adhered to the wall and he reached out and gently plucked it from the dirty surface. It clung to his finger and he studied it for a moment, letting his desire grow. He closed his eyes then raised it to his mouth and licked. The texture was divine, smooth, with just a hint of graininess. He rolled the dollop on his tongue, savored it. Sweet, with the piquancy of blood. He rubbed the bit of brain against the roof of his mouth, releasing the flavor, delighting in the sensations.

Dr. Libitin coughed. Theo's eyes flew open and he swallowed. Skeet was back in the room, taking off his jumpsuit.

"Anything?" The ME's right eye twitched.

"A little over five hours is my guess." Theo spoke quietly, reined in his excitement. "The blood is flat, definitely past your four-hour window, and the brain matter is a little dehydrated. It usually stays juicier a bit longer."

The good doctor winced. "Is that too much time?"

"Shouldn't be. As long as I get to...uh...perform a thorough exam I should be able to tell you more."

Dr. Libitin stared at Theo.

"Sorry," Theo mumbled. He peeled off his own paper garment and stuffed it into the biohazard trash box near the door. "You want me at the morgue?"

"Yes." Dr. Libitin walked into the hall. He had issues with Theo's little talent, but he knew the merits. Theo usually tried to minimize his reaction to ingesting evidence, but that sample was particularly tasty.

Skeet waited in the hall for Theo. "Did you get everything?"

"Yeah, I'm sure." Theo outlined the procedure he used to collect the evidence in the room.

Skeet listened, eyes closed. "Sounds good to me, man. I don't have to check your work. You're thorough."

Theo nodded. "Thanks."

"Want me to drop you?"

"Sure." He followed his partner out to the unmarked vehicle they used for calls. "We have anything on the schedule?"

"Nah. I'll just head back to the station and wait for a call." Skeet turned the key in the ignition and pulled out of the apartment building's parking lot. "You mind if I run through the drive-thru?" He gestured at a burger joint across the street.

"Go ahead." Theo rolled his window down and lifted his face to the sunlight.

Skeet ordered two bacon double cheeseburgers, two large fries and a super-sized Coke. He wedged a container of fries between his legs, stuffed a handful into his mouth, and pulled into traffic.

They headed toward downtown Pittsburgh. Theo pulled a cell phone from his pocket and pressed a button for speed dial.

"*Clean as Death,*" the raspy voice on the line said. "Biohazard and crime scene cleanup."

"Hugh, got a scene for you." Theo read the apartment's Homewood address off a slip of paper. "I told the landlord I'd send you over."

"Thanks, man. Bad one?"

"Eh. Not as bad as some."

"All right. We'll head over now."

"Good luck." Theo flipped the phone closed and slipped it into his pocket. He turned back to the window and watched the urban fringe area transform into downtown Pittsburgh.

He tried to ignore his own reflection in the side-view mirror. His grayish complexion went beyond cadaverous, and his once bright blue eyes were now flat and lifeless. His thinning hair, arrested in the early stages of male-pattern baldness, lay flat against his scalp.

At least he didn't carry souvenirs of his death on his face, like some other zombies.

Skeet turned onto Penn Avenue and brought the car to a stop in front of the ME's office. "I'll be back for you if we get another one."

Theo nodded and closed the car door behind him. "See ya."

The Allegheny County Medical Examiner's office kept the temperature at a frigid sixty-four degrees. Theo hated it and the sluggish, sleepy feeling it caused. He stood in the summer sun, soaking in as much heat as he could before he opened the glass doors and walked into the brown concrete building.

"Hi, Theo."

The soft, girlish voice made Theo's legs go weak. "Hey, Marjorie." He cleared his throat and braced his knees. "What brings you down here?"

"One rose in the morgue overnight. They brought me in this morning, really early. I'm beat."

He studied Marjorie's face. She suffered a little decomp of the mucus membranes before she'd risen, but her beautiful eyes more than made up for it. The decomposition was a sign she'd been down a little longer than Theo before she came back, but once a zombie rose, the decay stopped. The undead didn't continue to decompose, contrary to popular theory.

Almond-shaped, light brown eyes watched him watch her. "How's it going?"

She shrugged. "The usual. They never think it's going to be so hard."

"Where's this one headed?"

"I set him up at the residence in Greentree. They're waiting for his transport."

Theo nodded. Marjorie counseled Pittsburgh's undead, helped them make the transition from one life to the next. She looked both cool and professional in tan pants and a pink turtleneck sweater. Her job was to help the recently risen adjust to their new situation. She stood, one hip cocked, a clipboard under her arm. Her long black hair swung almost to her pert little ass. Theo's circulation surged when he imagined that thick waterfall of hair cascading around his face...

"I checked him out and now I'm just waiting for Detective Gavahan to get here."

Theo's own thinning hair would have stood on end, if his metabolism hadn't been as slow as a tortoise on Xanax. Damn air conditioning. "Gavahan?"

"Homicide. You know how it goes. No good recollection yet, but hopefully it'll come back."

"That's too bad. I've got to get down to the morgue. I'm helping Libitin with a fresh one." Theo's fight or flight instincts kicked in anew. And fighting wasn't on the agenda, particularly not with an ass like Gavahan.

Marjorie actually looked sad. "Oh. Well, maybe I'll see you again sometime. Any chance with the new one?"

"Nope. Not enough left in the head." He tapped his own brow and then walked the few feet to the main desk.

He scrawled his name in the register, grabbed a visitor's badge, and clipped it to his belt. He smiled at Marjorie. "Nice seeing you."

"You, too. Hey—"

But Theo was through the set of double doors leading into the bowels of the morgue before he could hear what she had to say.

Even cutting short a conversation with Marjorie was worth it to avoid Gavahan.

Theo had been lonely during life. Death wasn't much different.

CHAPTER 2

He made his way through the familiar maze of hallways and offices to stand before the autopsy room. Dr. Libitin's voice carried through the swinging doors.

"Put that one in the freezer."

Theo shouldered his way in and shivered in the even cooler atmosphere. "Hey, Doc."

Dr. Libitin stood at a stainless steel counter, dictating into a microphone that hung from the ceiling. "She's over there."

He pointed to a cubby. The morgue recently adopted the new habit of putting curtained dividers between the slab tables, just in case someone rose unexpectedly. Sometimes the newly risen appreciated some privacy. Waking up naked with a toe tag could be a little degrading. The curtains were handy for lots of things. They shielded the body, and on occasion, Theo's special examinations, from view.

He pushed a curtain aside and slipped into the dim area around the metal slab. The white sheet was folded back to the woman's chest and he pulled it away from the body completely. The woman lay bare on the stainless steel table, breasts jutted upward at odd angles. Implants.

He gazed at her face, what was left of it, tried to reconstruct it in his mind, but fell short. There just wasn't enough left. Didn't matter.

He knelt close, sniffed at the hole where her face used to be. Closed his eyes, took a slow, deep breath. The metallic tang of blood filled his senses, quickened his pulse just a bit despite the freezing morgue. Conveyed on the undertone was the smoky scent of gunpowder. Very close range.

He bent to her neck, put his nose against her skin and licked. He tasted lust and fear. He savored the flavor of her bodily fluids and the scent of arousal before the penetrating stab of fear. He nibbled, just barely scraping his teeth across the tender flesh of her throat. Her arousal?

No. It carried the sharp jolt of testosterone and cheap after-shave, a panting excitement Theo found unique to a john.

Definitely male.

His lips twisted in distaste. Sensing another male always felt voyeuristic. His tongue raked along the line of her jaw, lapped at the blood that'd run down from the wound. He savored the tastes and sensations of sweat and blood...the salty iron tang, the bitter bite of the gunpowder. The flavors rolled around in his mouth and he continued the trail up the side of her face to the gaping wound in her head.

He placed his hands on either side of her skull and tilted it just slightly, for a better angle. Gingerly, he ran his tongue along the splintered, shattered bone until he encountered what was left of her brain. Nostrils flared wide to inhale every bit of sensory information, he steeled himself and then wrapped his lips around a blob of brain and sucked.

Images exploded in his mind and he fought to control them and understand. Her perceptions took over. Who? She couldn't comprehend what was happening. Anger and then the paralyzing terror of seeing the gun pointed at his face—her face. Their face?

She didn't know...

Who's there? Fear of the unknown. Distrust, anxiety, rage.

Black, so black.

It was fast and savage and over almost before she could think.

Confusion, fear, and pain dominated him until he jerked back from the body, a brutal return to the cold, sterile environment of the morgue.

It took effort to swallow the remaining brain in his mouth and interpret what he'd seen. As her final emotions ebbed from his body, his own flowed back into place.

"You okay?" Dr. Libitin stood next to Theo with a wet paper towel.

Theo wiped his face, and shook his head, trying to shed the final vestiges of the victim's terror. "Yeah. Not as bad as some, but definitely not pleasant."

"You get anything?"

Theo hesitated to replay the feelings. Seemed like each time he did this, the emotions felt stronger. Maybe the work was getting to him. He had more trouble leaving the world of the murdered.

He glanced at the doctor. "There was sex, but it wasn't rape. The murderer may have been the john, or maybe not. It happened a little after four this morning, couldn't have been long after the sex, because I can still taste the john. Gunshot wound at close range to the face, but you can tell that." He rubbed his temples. "It would be more helpful if she'd known her attacker. I could narrow it down somewhat. But I didn't sense any recognition."

He took a deep breath, let the sensations settle, and reiterated the facts so they were clear. "She wasn't raped. She definitely didn't know her attacker. It wasn't her pimp or the john. The cops shouldn't even bother looking at them. Someone else came in, after the sex, someone she didn't know and instinctively didn't trust."

"You can't sense anything about her rising, or wanting to rise?"

Theo frowned. "We already know she wanted to rise. It's tattooed on her arm."

The ME waved a hand in the air. "I know, I know, but she didn't think about that in her last moments, did she?"

Theo stepped back, startled. "What?"

Dr. Libitin pressed his lips into a thin line and hesitated before speaking. "Was there any indication she'd been thinking about her desire to rise?"

Theo shook his head. "No. But I've never really sensed that before, so I don't know if it's just something I can't feel." He scratched his chin and noted that his skin felt quite cold. He needed to get outside. "Why?"

The ME would not make eye contact. "We've had three others like this in the last two days, people with the tattoo, and they've all been killed execution-style, with a shot to the temple. I don't see a lot of this anymore, and I'm guessing this killer knows how to destroy enough brain matter to prevent rising."

Theo stared at the dead woman for a minute, tried to work through the chill-induced confusion that hobbled his thoughts. "Maybe it's just someone with a temple shot fetish," he suggested.

Dr. Libitin shrugged. "It's possible, but my hunch tells me otherwise. It's too much of a coincidence with the tattoos and the head shots." He gestured at the corpse. "This is the first direct shot to the face, but it accomplishes the same end result."

"You think they're somehow connected?"

The doctor followed Theo's gaze to the mangled corpse on the table. "Murder rates have decreased in the years since the Event, and they're usually crimes of passion. These are calculated killings of people otherwise able to rise."

Theo was unable to wrap his brain around the implications. "I don't see how...or why someone would target potential risers."

They stood in silence for a brief moment, and then Dr. Libitin reached out and squeezed Theo's shoulder, a rare gesture. Most of the living had a hard time touching the undead. "Thank you, son."

Theo nodded. "Sure."

The ME looked closely at him. "You okay?"

"Yeah, I'm fine. Been a long day. Maybe it's just time for a break."

Dr. Libitin squeezed Theo's shoulder one more time before releasing him. Immediately, he missed the warmth of Dr. Libitin's hand. He needed to get outside, to the warm sun.

He was halfway to the back entrance when a shadow darkened the floor in front of him.

"Theo Walker." The booming voice oozed with arrogance. "Fancy meeting the little walker at the morgue. The walking Walker. Irony at its best, isn't it?"

Theo's lips stiffened and he fought to relax the expression before he looked up at Detective Gavahan. "That joke's kind of old, don't you think?"

"It'll never get old, *Walker*." The detective pushed Theo aside and walked past. "Why do I always find you at the morgue? You looking for handouts?"

Theo stood silent, waiting for Gavahan to finish.

"You're a creepy little fucker, you know that?" He jabbed a finger at Theo's chest. "Things like you don't belong in public."

Theo watched the big man swagger down the hall. His temper simmered, which was about as riled as he got anymore.

He stalked out the back entrance to soak in the hot Pittsburgh sun. The heat helped dissipate the anger. Gavahan acted superior, always cocky. Men admired him, women wanted him. He was everything Theo wasn't. He was alive.

His cell phone vibrated in his pocket. Skeet.

"Yeah?"

"Got another."

"Okay. I'll be out front."

He slipped his phone back into his pocket and walked around the outside of the building to wait on the steps.

Skeet pulled the little hatchback up to the curb. "You ready?"

Theo slid into the passenger seat. "Where're we headed?"

"Frick Park, of all places. Barely had time to finish my lunch."

"Suck it up, man. Let's go."

The body rested chest-down in the creek in the Riverview section of Frick Park. Or rather, across the puny trickle that passed for a creek. There was so little water, the rigid torso acted like a dam and the dirty liquid puddled on one side, seeking ways under and around the mass of flesh.

Her wrists were not visible without moving the body, which Theo was not permitted to do, but he was sure they'd find the tattoo. Why else bother with beheading? If it was true someone was targeting potential undead, it would be bad.

Since the Event, zombie rights had become the next big political platform. When it was apparent the zombies weren't going away, and numbers were likely to rise over time, politicians saw the benefit of cornering the zombie vote even before they rose. They vowed zombies would never fight for their rights like women, blacks, and gays fought in the twentieth century.

Targeting zombies before they could even rise would fire up a lot of people, especially if the killer had connections.

He put the thought out of his mind and concentrated on the head.

It lay on its side about fifteen feet away, eyes open and unseeing. Could she have lasted long enough to witness her body fall into the creek? He surveyed the scene from slightly uphill and to the side.

There was very little to it. Frick Park was a popular hiking locale, and much bigger than most Pittsburghers realized. Most of the once beautifully maintained park went back to nature after the Event when priorities shifted and manpower fell short. The boundaries of the recreation area blurred, and now it stood as a mass of forest in the city. Theo found he preferred the way the park outgrew its original footprint and took over parts of the city again. Fewer people in the world meant fewer resources available for things like park maintenance. In his book, that wasn't a bad thing. He liked the less crowded environment.

Theo peered around. No spent shell casings, since it seemed clear the manner of death involved a blade. Just the head and the body as evidence. Skeet, who'd gone ahead when Theo stopped to examine the scene, was already in a fresh white jumpsuit, on hands and knees, moving slowly through the grass around the body with a headlamp and his camera hanging from his neck.

The cops stood off to one side, drawing diagrams and filling out paperwork. Gavahan appeared to be instructing them on some detail of investigation, and the other detectives hung on his every word. He didn't acknowledge Theo's presence.

Theo tilted his head and peered at the incline and the position of the body. Based on how the body lay, it seemed this was where she dropped. The absence of drag marks indicated she'd been killed right there. What footprints there were appeared to have been made by generic soft-soled shoes with no distinguishing tread pattern. It didn't appear she'd put up much of a struggle, if at all.

Her head had either been thrown or dropped by the killer when he left the scene. Was it positioned deliberately? Theo couldn't tell. A sigh escaped his lips and he grabbed a fresh paper suit from the car. He pulled it on and tugged blue shoe covers over his sneakers, then retrieved a stack of evidence markers from the big box.

He walked down the hill slowly, scrutinizing the area. The girl wore denim pants that ended just below her knees and a pink tank top. White Keds. Mousy brown hair cropped short. She carried a bit of extra weight on her, and Theo envisioned her as the girl in school who'd always stayed behind to clean the teacher's chalkboard erasers. Soft, unexceptional, and harmless.

Beginning about twenty feet from the body, he circled it in a slow spiral, scanning the ground for anything that might be considered evidence, no matter how minute or seemingly innocuous. If he thought he saw a promising item, he dropped a marker. The plastic yellow triangles stood like beacons in the long grass.

Skeet already checked the area closest to the body and only found three items worthy of a marker. Theo stayed further away, examining depressions in the long grass, and a few beer cans. The Iron City cans were rusty, obviously exposed to more weather than just overnight, so he put them aside as trash.

Theo watched Skeet photograph a purse found near the body, and hand it to Detective Gavahan. Theo sidled closer. The group of detectives crowded around expectantly while Gavahan unzipped the bag and removed the contents. He laid the items one by one on the hood of a car.

"Robbery?" Larson asked no one in particular.

"Nah," said Gavahan. "Too violent for robbery. She pissed someone off."

Theo eyed Detective Gavahan, but said nothing.

A blue tube of ChapStick, a tin of Altoids, and a purple compact joined a Hello Kitty wallet and a crumpled pack of tissues. Theo placed an evidence marker next to each item and jotted notes.

Gavahan opened the wallet and spread the contents alongside the other things. A PNC debit card, a Barnes & Noble discount card, forty-seven dollars in cash, and a University of Pittsburgh student ID made up the entire contents of the wallet. Robbery definitely wasn't the motive.

She was wearing a pink shirt and white Keds, for God's sake. What kind of fat girl wore Keds, carried a Hello Kitty wallet, and was capable of pissing someone off to this extent? The picture wasn't jiving for Theo. Violence like this meant drugs or organized crime. She didn't seem likely to be involved with either.

No driver's license, which could mean it'd been stolen. Maybe she didn't have one, but no license meant either someone drove her here or she'd taken public transit, or a myriad of other scenarios, but Theo would put his money on a driver. This soft girl didn't look like the hiking type, so what was she doing on a remote trail in the park?

"Naomi Flores." Detective Gavahan flipped the student ID over to peer at the back.

Theo glanced at Naomi's severed head.

"We'll have to go to Pitt to get contact information." Detective Brown's voice held hopeful optimism and Theo knew a stop in Oakland at The Original Hot Dog Shop, the "O," was on his agenda.

He walked toward where Naomi's body lay diverting water. Her hands were crabbed, elbows stiff, in what Theo estimated to be the final stages of rigor. Her neck pointed downhill, and it appeared most of her blood drained out and washed away with the running water. A large amount of dirt was stained rust colored, and blood spattered across the grass between the two body parts. Theo moved behind the head and positioned his own to see what Naomi might have seen in her final seconds. He spared a brief moment to wonder how long brain activity might continue after detachment.

She would have seen her own torso, the heavily forested area beyond, some trees, and a train bridge in the distance.

The fat blobs of blood on the foliage suggested an underhanded lob, a gentle toss of the head from just the other side of the creek. Or just an unconcerned heave-ho. A more forceful throw would result in longer, jagged blood splatter. These rounded, thick drops came from a head moving more slowly than Theo expected to see from a fast pitch.

What was she doing out here?

The slice across the neck was incredibly clean. The spine and esophagus—or was that a trachea?—were visible. From his vantage point a few feet away from the body, Theo couldn't see any of the rough edges indicative of a hacking, sawing cut. It would have taken some serious force to lop off Naomi's head with one swipe, but this less likely scenario appeared to be the case. Theo's brain immediately created the picture of a hulking man, perhaps someone who'd once played defense for the Steelers. Or a Samurai.

He studied Naomi's head. That spinal cord looked moist and chewy, like licorice. Surely Dr. Libitin would need help with this one. He would have to crack the skull, and the brain would be intact. His undead and professional instincts told him this one hadn't been deceased for long. Since it wasn't another gunshot victim, the entire brain would be there for him.

He looked around for Gavahan, but the big man was engaged with the other detectives.

He stamped down his desire when two vehicles bounced across the uneven ground—an unmarked cruiser and the ME's van. Sergeant Milton and Dr. Libitin climbed out of the unmarked car. He waved. Neither man waved back. They stopped to look at each item Theo had flagged.

He waited, despite a growing yearning. Patience had not been a virtue he possessed before he died, but death proved a good instructor. Worried he looked too anxious, Theo touched his chin, dabbed at this bottom lip. Was he drooling? No. Good.

Skeet's camera flash went off over and over again, documenting the contents of Naomi's purse. Theo's partner was nothing if not thorough. He made a good teacher.

The sergeant and the ME examined the body, checking various items he'd flagged and those he'd set aside as trash.

Irritation buzzed his skin like an insect. Didn't they trust his work? He brushed the annoyance aside and struggled to maintain his normal neutrality.

"Ted." Sergeant Milton gave him the standard greeting.

"It's Theo," he muttered under his breath. Sergeant Milton appeared not to have heard.

"What do we have here?" Sergeant Milton directed his comments at the detectives. Theo half-listened to the details as they were recounted, but focused more closely on Dr. Libitin. He stood back at first, just as Theo knew he would, and examined the crime scene from a wide angle. He listened to the detective's conversation, but did not move to join them.

Theo watched the ME's gaze travel from body to head and back again. He knew it would be a couple minutes before the doctor was ready to talk to him, so he walked to the ME's van.

Doug, a morgue technician, sat in the driver's seat.

"I'm going to get a bag," Theo said as he passed by the window.

"Better get two." Doug cackled at his own joke and took a drag on a cigarette.

Theo opened the back door and grabbed a blue bag. Doug still sat in the front of the van, chuckling.

"You gonna help?" Theo said.

"Nah. You and Skeet can take this one." Doug dropped his cigarette butt on the ground outside the van.

"Whatever." Like all the others. The techs never helped at the scene.

Back at the body, Dr. Libitin and Skeet examined the corpse. The ME held up Naomi's arm and Theo felt no surprise to see the word RISE tattooed on her left wrist, in tiny, delicate script. A petite, feminine tattoo.

"Another one." An unfamiliar emotion twisted Theo's gut.

"Fifth one in three days." Dr. Libitin shook his head and gently laid Naomi's arm down.

CHAPTER 3

Skeet's brow furrowed. "You think this has something to do with their undead status?"

Dr. Libitin shook his head. "I can't see how it doesn't. Most of the murders we see are simply that: murders, just killings. These people are being slaughtered, every one of them, in such a way that the means of death is also the means of being sure they don't rise. If she'd been shot, and then beheaded, I could say that someone killed her for some other reason and eliminated her chance to rise." He struggled to stand. "But these killings look to be murder designed to permanently kill. No undead rising."

"What's the connection between the victims?" Theo asked.

The doctor frowned. "I can't find one. Until this beheading, they've all come from questionable backgrounds—couple of hookers, a meth dealer—but this doesn't fit."

"Or we don't think she fits. We should reserve that judgment until we find out more about her." Theo glanced back at the head. What's your story, Naomi?

Skeet raised his camera and began firing shots again. "You want to roll her over so I can get the front of the body, then we'll get the head?"

Theo helped Dr. Libitin roll the body onto its back and perform a cursory examination for marks or other anomalies worth photographing. Her clothing was intact but stained heavily with blood and dirt.

Naomi's head showed no bruising or injuries aside from the slice across the neck. She hadn't been beaten before the final blow. Skeet slipped paper bags over her hands, despite the fact it didn't appear she struggled with her attacker.

"No other assault. She was just killed." Dr. Libitin pursed his lips.

"Estimate on time?" Theo said.

"My guess, based on ambient temperature and relative lack of rigor, is that she's been here since sometime last night. I think she died before the other, maybe even as early as last evening. That would fit with her state."

Theo considered the details. If this beheading was truly related to the hooker's murder, there would have been plenty of time between killings for the murderer to get from here to the Homewood area.

If, indeed, they were related.

"Bag her." Dr. Libitin turned to Theo. "How long until your shift is done?"

Theo peered at his watch. "Another two and half hours."

The ME pulled his cell phone from a pocket and dialed. "I'm calling Howard to see if he can spare you for the rest of your shift." He headed for the van.

Skeet's eyebrows lifted. He and Theo unfolded the body bag. "What's he want you for?"

Theo avoided his gaze. "I dunno."

His partner eyed him suspiciously, but didn't ask more. Together they lifted Naomi's body into the blue bag. Skeet tucked her feet into the bottom and Theo walked to the head. He knelt beside it and carefully turned it to face the sky before cradling it in his palms. He averted his gaze from the meaty tendrils trailing from the neck.

"Hi, Naomi." He carried the head cautiously, mindful that Detective Gavahan watched his every move. Gingerly, he nestled Naomi's head into the crook of her own arm and zipped the bag from her feet to her oozing neck.

They'd just loaded the bag into the van when Dr. Libitin snapped his cell phone shut. "Climb in, Theo. You're with me for the afternoon."

Skeet saluted him. "I'll be at the lab if you need me."

"Thanks." Theo took the seat behind Doug.

Dr. Libitin slid into the passenger seat and shot Theo a look that clearly prohibited discussing the situation. Theo sat quietly for the duration of the ride, and listened to Doug and the ME discuss an upcoming charity golf event.

The ride was a bit too long for Theo's tastes, and Doug liked the air conditioning a bit too much. When they finally reached the morgue and Doug pulled the van into the garage, Theo's torpid muscles protested his climb down from the van.

"I'm going to step outside for a minute or two." Dr. Libitin waved as he walked away. "Meet me in my office."

Two other techs entered the garage and opened the back of the van. Theo watched them lift the bag containing the pieces of Naomi onto a gurney and disappear into the building.

Three women on a smoke break paused gossiping long enough to stare at him. He didn't care. The sun shone against the side of the building and Theo leaned against the warm stone and soaked in the heat.

The gossip recommenced, only now in whispers. He ignored them, accustomed to tuning others out since even before he'd risen.

He figured he'd better head in. The women were still staring, so he flashed them his best grin. They hushed and pretended not to notice.

He took an elevator and wound his way through the morgue offices to Dr. Libitin's big corner space on the fourth floor. He knocked, and the ME's familiar voice beckoned him to enter.

Large windows offered a view of downtown Pittsburgh and a glimpse of the Monongahela River. Theo sank into an overstuffed chair in front of a giant cherry wood desk and admired the view. He'd lived in Pittsburgh all his life and so far found no reason to leave. The Steel City treated him right.

Dr. Libitin leaned back in his leather office chair and laced his fingers behind his head. "Comfortable?"

Theo experienced a moment of puzzlement before he realized a space heater was blowing under his chair. "Hey, thanks," he said.

"I'm still waiting for the report on Ms. Flores, and since Brown went into Oakland for information, it might be a while." Dr. Libitin rolled his eyes. "Brown's food obsessed."

Theo chuckled. "So why am I here?"

Dr. Libitin pushed a file across the desk to Theo. "Take a look."

He hesitated before flipping open the manila folder. "I'm not going to like this, am I?"

The medical examiner remained silent.

Theo pulled the stack of papers closer. The top sheet, a routine police report, outlined the discovery of a body beside the East Busway near the Strip District. Malia Barber, Hispanic female, aged twenty-seven, died of a gunshot wound to the left temple. Circumstances surrounding the death were unclear, but foul play was suspected. The victim was a known prostitute.

At the bottom of the report was a line that caught Theo's attention: INDICATE WHETHER VICTIM DESIRED TO RISE/NOT RISE. The word "rise" was circled.

Theo shuffled the report to the side, exposing a photograph of the dead Ms. Barber. Her injuries were every bit as devastating as the hooker he'd seen earlier today, but, in this case, the damage was done to the side of her head.

Dr. Libitin must have been following Theo's line of thought. "Gunshot wound to the left temple at extremely close range, like an execution. We think the killer is using a high caliber handgun to create the most internal damage and largest exit wound. Basically, whoever is doing this is using the right kind of weapon at just the right distance to scramble the brains and blow them out from the side. Classic execution."

Theo frowned. "That doesn't jive with the one from this morning. Her face was gone."

"She could have turned to look at him."

Theo nodded. "Possibly." He returned to the file and flipped through the additional autopsy photos of Malia Barber before finding the next report.

Another female gunshot victim. Massive trauma. A large exit wound, again to the left temple and extensive loss of tissue. Constance Updegraff, thirty-seven years old.

Theo squinted at the report. "Updegraff? How do I know that name?"

"Probably from the news. Remember the big meth lab in Bloomfield they took down?" Dr. Libitin nodded at the report. "That was her place."

Theo's eyebrows shot up. Meth manufacturing. He shifted the report to look at the photograph. The damage to her head was very similar to what he'd seen in the last photo. Again, at the bottom of the page, the word "rise" was circled.

Okay, so far he'd played along with the good doctor's theory that these were somehow related.

The next report outlined the same type of story. Alvin Krunk, African-American male, age thirty-eight, another known prostitute, found a block away from Wilkinsburg Senior High, one gunshot to the left temple, tattoo on his left wrist.

"This killer is predictable."

Dr. Libitin nodded. "And I think he's starting to realize that. Hence, the change in MO."

The final report detailed the death of Carly Harris, the woman Theo had seen that morning. "This came through fast."

"It's just the preliminary."

Theo already knew the basic facts; but the name was new information. Carly Harris, twenty-six, white female, was also a hooker, and she'd tattooed her desire to rise on her wrist.

He pushed the file back across the desk. "Didn't you say you thought Flores died before Harris?"

"I believe so."

"So why the return to the firearm after such a spectacular beheading?"

Dr. Libitin shrugged. "Beats me. Access to weapon? Environment? Time constraints? Who knows?"

Theo sat back and wiggled his toes in his warm shoes. Something about these murders bothered him, more than just the idea that some freak out there didn't want any more undead on the streets.

"So why am I here?"

"If my hunch is right, I need you. You'll have to examine every one of these until someone, one of these victims, can give you something."

"The cops are doing their part, right? They'll make a hit."

Dr. Libitin gave Theo a withering look. "Son, the people this perp is killing are the ones the cops are trying to get off the street. I don't think any of them have made the connection that all the victims were potential risers, and even if they do, it might not matter."

Theo sat unmoving. "Might not matter?"

"Come on, Theo. We've come a long way, but it's still not perfect. Many of the living are not completely okay with sharing their world with the undead. Extending affirmative action to cover zombies wasn't because people like you. They're afraid of anything different, whether it's skin color or gender. Death scares people shitless." The ME lowered his voice. "We're not so far out from the Event to have forgotten that your kind likes to eat the living."

Theo bristled just a bit, but tamped the emotion down. Dr. Libitin spoke the truth. His gaze fell on the tattoo etched on the inside of the ME's left wrist: the word RISE in classic courier font.

"My experience tells me this perp won't stop with killing risers. He's not going to get caught, and that will empower him, make him cocky. Sooner or later this guy's going to start killing undead." Dr. Libitin pushed his chair back from the desk. "You're a first gen, one of the initial wave. The undead community respects those of you who've been around since the beginning. You've seen it all. Keep your ear to the ground, listen for rumblings, and help me figure this out before it gets worse than a few killings."

Theo folded his arms across his chest. "If you're right, this could be the start of something ugly. The little trust the undead community has for the living will be annihilated. You say we're not far enough out for the living to forget that zombies like to eat them, but we also haven't forgotten how ugly your fear can be. How many zombies were killed in those first months? I would say it's a mutual distrust."

Dr. Libitin gestured for Theo to follow him and left the office. "Let's head down to the autopsy room and check out Ms. Flores."

~

Naomi's naked body lay on a stainless steel table, a core thermometer placed in her midsection. Her head was positioned above her body, held in place with rolled towels.

"Hello, Shelby. Thank you for the prep." Dr. Libitin pointed at the men's locker room. "Theo, there are extra scrubs in here if you'd like."

"Hey, Doc. I already took the photos and x-rays." Shelby, in scrubs and a surgical gown, stood off to one side, folding the denim pants and pink shirt. She placed them in a plastic bag and labeled it FLORES with a black Sharpie, before turning to him. "Hi, Theo. It's good to see you."

Theo returned the smile. "How's it going?" Shelby treated him as if he belonged at the morgue. Many of the other techs acted with suspicion, which he supposed wasn't really strange given popular culture's view of zombies, but it was nice to be treated with a little kindness.

"Same shit, different day," she replied. "Except, I guess for this." She gestured at the table.

Theo scratched his chin. "Yeah, this is a little different."

He followed Dr. Libitin into the locker room where he found a set of scrubs on the bench. Movement in a toilet stall indicated where the ME had gone.

Theo swapped his street clothes for the scrubs, slipped blue covers over his shoes, and waited on the bench. A flush announced Dr. Libitin's exit from the stall. He'd changed into green scrubs. "Ready?"

"I suppose."

In the autopsy room, Shelby held out surgical gowns. Theo pulled his on and tied it. He glanced at the naked woman on the table. "This is all happening really fast. Did you already contact the family or are you treating this as foul play and going ahead with the autopsy?"

The doctor pulled latex gloves on and tugged the cuffs up over his sleeves. "This is a clear case of foul play, and I won't allow time to degrade any evidence."

"Okay." Theo looked at Shelby. She nodded.

Dr. Libitin positioned an overhead microphone. "I'm going to record, so warn me if you have something to add that shouldn't be a part of the official transcript."

Shelby's eyebrows went up and she peered at Theo. He avoided her gaze.

Dr. Libitin began his transcript with the date. "It's fifteen hundred hours. Joining me for the autopsy of Naomi, uh..." The ME shuffled a stack of papers. "Naomi René Flores, age twenty-three, are Shelby Gusky, autopsy technician, and Theodore Walker, advisor to the medical examiner's office."

Shelby's eyebrows shot up and she squinted at Theo. He'd never been given a title before or gone on the record as an adviser. Dr. Libitin meant business.

The ME followed suggested autopsy procedure to the letter and noted distinguishing characteristics and blemishes. The only unnatural mark on her was the RISE tattoo on her wrist. She'd never even pierced her ears.

Dr. Libitin began the internal autopsy in routine fashion with the classic Y incision. He continued measuring and weighing Naomi's organs and examined the contents of her stomach.

"Looks like tuna salad and some sort of chocolate. There's a peanut." Dr. Libitin pointed at a lump of something in a metal pan. Theo couldn't tell what it might have been, but Shelby nodded in agreement and made a notation in Naomi's file.

Theo stood by, watching as impassively as he could. Despite having died once already, he wasn't entirely comfortable with the dead. His memories of his own death were of a violent, terrifying few moments and then confusion and hunger. Those first weeks hadn't been easy, but he'd do it again in a heartbeat over dying permanently. He wasn't anxious to join the girl on the table. While life had never been kind to him, the thought of the blackness facing him on the other side, was less appealing.

Dr. Libitin photographed and recorded his description of the injury to the neck, then turned his attention to Naomi's head. He began above her left ear and sliced her scalp across the crown to the right side. Shelby busied herself as Dr. Libitin peeled her scalp from the top of her head over her face and down the back, but the squelching sound quickened Theo's pulse just a bit.

The Stryker saw's characteristic burr coaxed saliva from Theo's chilled system. The engine whined when the blade bit into Naomi's skull, whetting his appetite and seducing his undead desires.

Dr. Libitin pulled the cap of bone from Naomi's head with a gentle sucking sound. He continued his verbal record of the procedure. "The skull appears intact and the dura is also intact and appears healthy." He cut through and peeled back the dura mater to expose the brain, which he carefully excised and weighed.

Theo's appetite grew.

Shelby began washing out the brain cavity when Dr. Libitin moved the organ to the side table. He prepped it for sectioning, cut a few slices, then turned to Shelby and Theo.

Shelby nodded. "I have to grab another form for this file. It'll take me a few minutes to get washed up, then I'll find the paperwork and be right back."

"Theo, can you switch off the recorder?" Dr. Libitin said.

Shelby turned away when Theo reached up and flipped the metal switch. She pulled off her gloves, dropped them in the biohazard box and left the autopsy room.

Dr. Libitin hurried to pull the curtained partitions into place. "I have to take sections of the brain anyway. The slices are over on the workstation."

Theo's brow furrowed. "What did you tell her?"

"The truth."

A wash of anxiety started in Theo's chest and moved surprisingly fast to his elbows. His hands shook. "What?"

"We'll talk about it later. It's okay. Get to work."

Theo shook his head slowly. This was wrong. No one else was supposed to know about this gift. It was an unspoken rule among the zombies not to ingest human tissue. They preferred meat raw, and they all had the urge for human flesh, but not actually giving into that urge allowed the living to accept them.

If it got out that he was not only eating, but reading the victims' last thoughts, he'd likely be murdered again.

In a new and creative way, no doubt, something designed to keep him down this time. Zombies could be killed by destroying the brain or disconnecting the brain from the body. This killer seemed to favor executions designed to prevent rising. He had no doubt that someone, somewhere, could dream up a way to make beheading really unpleasant.

As far as he knew, he was the only psychic zombie. He'd never told anyone but Dr. Libitin about his ability, and that had been an accident. He couldn't imagine that there were no other zombies eating human flesh, especially those who resisted reintegrating into society. But so far they'd managed to stay under the living radar, as he had.

"Theo, please. Get started. Shelby will keep others out as long as she can, but there's no saying how much time we have."

Theo approached the brain slices. He'd never eaten prepared brain like this, just the bits and pieces he snuck from the trash or that Dr. Libitin managed to salvage for him. He wondered if the processing would lessen the experience somehow.

He glanced over at the head on the autopsy table. The skull cavity was empty. After only a moment of hesitation, he picked it up and examined the eyes. The needle used to take samples of vitreous fluid marred them, but the deep brown irises were intact. He peered into the eyes, trying to see from behind them.

The scent of fresh blood wafted from inside the empty skull, and he inhaled deeply. The aroma went straight to the zombie in him. He lapped up a bit of the water and blood mixture from the curve of the bone and felt the fingers of his perception stretch and reach.

He held one hand out, kept his face in the skull. "Give me a piece."

Dr. Libitin took two quick steps to the workstation and picked up a chunk of brain. "Do you want gloves?"

Theo speared him with a look. "I'm going to eat it. You think I care if I get something on my hands?"

The ME placed the portion of gray matter in Theo's palm. Theo caressed it with his fingertips, surprised at how firm it was in a block like this. With his face still close to the skull, he brought the chunk of brain to his nose to inhale the blood and tissue aromas combined. He opened his eyes and studied the mottled texture of the sample. It felt slippery and soft in his grip and it excited him.

It would be so much better if it were warm...

With that thought, he brought the piece to his lips and buried his face in the skull again.

Images and emotions exploded in his mind when he sucked the brain into his mouth. At the same time he inhaled the brain, he pulled a fold of the scalp into his mouth and suckled like an infant.

Excitement...over...

Learning? There was something new happening. Someone to teach her something.

The brain slid over Theo's tongue, awakening feelings and senses he didn't know he had, didn't remember having when he was alive, but he must have, right? Or not... somehow different.

New experiences? A new place, a new life...

Simple joy, singing...something like a radio...

Theo felt his hair blow back, his hand waved in a strong breeze that stole his breath.

Laughter. I can't wait.

Freedom.

Trust, I trust you.

Expectation. Anticipation.

A pause. Questions surface.

Apprehension. What...?

Judgment.

Bewilderment. Wonder. A black wave, a scream of pain, lost.

Then nothing.

And the nothing obliterated him.

CHAPTER 4

"Theo."

Someone pulled his arm.

"Theo. Let go."

The voice wormed into his psyche and the hand massaged his arm. It was warm, but he was cold.

With a huge effort, Theo released the tension in his body. He consciously relaxed his face into a semblance of normalcy. "What happened?"

"You tell me." Dr. Libitin searched Theo's eyes. "One minute you were holding her head to your face, the next you dropped it and grabbed the autopsy table in a death grip."

They both paused at the doctor's choice of words. Theo suppressed an urge to giggle. "I need to sit down."

"You need to wipe your face." He handed Theo a warm, wet paper towel, then pulled a chair next to the table. Theo sank into it, rubbing his face with the cloth, while the doctor moved the curtained partitions back to their storage locker.

He turned on the recorder and finished transcribing his observations. "The autopsy of case 1567358-579 is concluded at nineteen hundred hours."

Footsteps sounded in the hallway just before Shelby poked her head back in. "All clear?"

Dr. Libitin nodded. "Yeah. We're done. I'm just finishing up with the sectioning and then we'll wrap this up."

"Let me help." She pulled on a fresh set of gloves before propping the head back into its place. "Want me to start putting things away?"

"Sure."

Theo noted that they both carefully avoided him. It was fine with Dr. Libitin—he knew to give Theo a little space after one of these...whatever. He guessed they'd have to figure out what to call what he did. But the morgue tech, Shelby...damn it. He'd have to deal with her. He turned so he wouldn't have to see her face.

"Shelby, listen," he began.

She put a hand on his back. God, it felt good. He fell silent, enjoying the feel of another person's touch.

"Theo, don't explain. It's okay, whatever it is. Dr. L. told me that you help him, and that you have a gift. If he trusts you, so do I."

After the crush of unfamiliar emotions and the brutality of Naomi's final moments, Shelby's kindness was almost too much for him. If he could have mustered the emotions necessary to cry, he would have. "Thank you."

She patted him and went about cleaning up from the autopsy, putting the remaining brain and skull pieces back inside the head and repositioning the scalp. If she saw the teeth marks on it, she said nothing. He carefully wiped his hands on his surgical gown.

"Did you want to try to reattach the head?" Her question was directed at Dr. Libitin.

His lips tightened into a thin line as he slid small portions of the brain into a container of formalin. "Not yet. I'd rather see what the police have in mind and what her family wants. Cover her and let's put her in cold storage for now."

Shelby nodded and continued cleaning.

Theo found a white sheet on a shelf above the workstation. He unfolded it and carefully covered Naomi's body. Her face appeared peaceful, despite the trauma, and Theo struggled to make sense of what he'd witnessed through her final emotions.

Shelby took the edge of the sheet from him and covered Naomi's head. "She's done. Leave her be."

Theo nodded. "I'm going outside." He peeled off the surgical gown and retreated to the locker room to put his own clothes back on.

Once outside, his restlessness distracted him. He needed something to occupy his hands. He settled for closing his eyes and leaning against the concrete building to absorb more heat than the evening sun alone could offer.

"You want to talk?" Shelby's voice came from somewhere to the left.

He opened his eyes to look at her. She was tall—probably taller than him—with shoulder-length brown hair. Not thin, but not fat either, so the skinny jeans hugging her legs actually looked decent on her. She'd changed from her scrubs into a pale yellow t-shirt and a pair of battered purple Converse high-top sneakers. A smile played around his lips at the sight of those shoes.

She struggled to coax a flame from a battered metal Zippo, cigarette already in her mouth. When it finally flared to life, she poked the end of the cigarette close to the lighter and dragged.

Theo sighed.

She exhaled. "So, you wanna talk?"

"I'm not really sure what I can say."

"Whatever makes you feel better."

He studied her face. She returned his gaze without judgment. For some reason, he trusted her, no doubt due to the fact that Dr. Libitin did, too.

"I can get impressions from corpses." He'd decided long ago that if it came down to admitting this to anyone, he'd play it safe. He waited to see if she'd ask how, dreading the answer.

She took another drag off her cigarette and waited, so he continued. "I kind of feel what they felt when they died. Dr. L. seems to find the information helpful sometimes."

"Cool." She nodded. "You're, like, a psychic? Or something?"

Theo pondered for a minute. "Yeah, I guess you could say that."

"See, that's awesome. You hear all the time about psychics working with the police. How lucky that they have one in forensics."

"Well, the cops don't really know. It's more of a thing between the doc and me." He tried to envision Gavahan using the services of a psychic.

"I figured as much. He told me not to say anything." She placed one finger next to her nose. "I can keep a secret."

He laughed, a rare experience for him, and she laughed, too.

She tossed the butt and ground it out with the toe of her purple sneaker. "We should get coffee sometime."

"I-I'd like that." Nervous energy jittered along his spine, a not altogether unpleasant experience.

"Do you know Marjorie Frey?"

He nodded. It was all he could do.

"She lives in the apartment across the hall from me. We go out for coffee sometimes. I bet she'd like it if you tagged along."

Marjorie. The zombie with the black, ass-length hair. Aw, hell yes.

"That would be great. I'd like that."

"So, yeah, we'll have coffee. I'll get your number from the doc, if that's okay?"

The side door swung open and Dr. Libitin poked his head out. "Theo. Come on back in. I just got the preliminary report on our Ms. Flores."

He nodded and waved before he let the door close behind him.

"I'm to give her your phone number?" Dr. Libitin said.

"Um, yeah. My cell phone number. Not the house number." He shuddered to think of his mother answering a call from Shelby. She'd invite the poor girl to dinner on the spot.

Back in Dr. Libitin's office, he settled into the chair with the space heater. He was getting spoiled and wondered what it would take to arrange a transfer to the morgue from crime scene investigation.

Dr. Libitin cleared his throat. "Detective Brown contacted me about Naomi Flores. He faxed this preliminary report from headquarters."

"That's another fast one."

"This one is cause for concern of a different sort."

Theo didn't like the way that sounded. "A different sort?"

"Despite my confidence that Miss Flores—and it is *Miss*—fell victim to our special killer, she does not fit the profile we've established for likely victims."

"How so?"

"Naomi René Flores was, by all accounts, a 'good girl.' She still lived at home and her parents are completely devastated."

"She had a Pitt I.D."

"She was a university student only insomuch as she was part of an outreach program to teach mentally disadvantaged teens basic life skills. Miss Flores was, to put it in not quite politically correct terms, mentally retarded. A mild form of retardation, but apparently she'd been starved of oxygen at birth."

Theo put his hands to his head. This was turning out to be a really long day. "Okay, so she wasn't a danger to society and the method of killing is different. She's not a victim of our perp."

"I have a gut instinct here, Theo." Dr. Libitin shook his head. "After twenty-seven years at this job, I've learned to listen to my gut."

"Then what's the connection?"

"The only connection is the tattoo. She wanted to rise. We surmise that our killer is exterminating potential risers."

"It's not enough. There's got to be something more, or there's nothing."

"I'm hoping you can help with that. What did you get from your examination?"

Theo wondered if using the clinical term "examination" helped Dr. Libitin accept what he did. Eating the brains and sucking the peeled back scalp of a dead woman didn't exactly qualify as an exam, but if it let the good doctor sleep at night, Theo was willing to go with it.

He tried to relax and slip back into the emotions he'd felt from Naomi.

"She was excited about something, I couldn't tell quite what. Lots of excitement. She was really happy, there was singing. A new life, and then apprehension, betrayal. And confusion." He shook his head, trying to give words to the emotions once again coursing through him. "But no fear."

Dr. Libitin waited patiently.

"It was someone she trusted. Could have been a woman, but I'm not sure if I'm confusing my own perceptions of her with her perceptions of whoever she was with. Her thought patterns are a little different."

"I would assume so."

Theo and Dr. Libitin sat in silence for a few moments. "I'm going to have to talk to her family myself, I think, ask them where she'd been or if she'd been planning anything in the days leading up to her murder."

"Are you going to give this information to Detective Brown?"

"No, this is best kept between us. I'll just conduct a little investigation of my own; I've done it before." He smacked the desk with his palm. "There's a connection here. We're just not seeing it."

Theo yawned and looked at his watch. It was past dinner and he'd started his shift at seven that morning. Skeet would've already gone home, so that left Theo to catch the bus. "I'm beat, Doc. Maybe if we sleep on it something will come up."

Frustration etched Dr. Libitin's face, but he nodded. "You're right. You need a ride somewhere?"

"No, thanks." Theo rose from his toasty chair.

Dr. Libitin stood quickly and thrust a hand toward Theo. "Thank you, son."

Theo reached out and took the proffered hand. Dr. Libitin didn't flinch. "Any time."

"I know the victims were alive, but I have a bad feeling about this. If there's anyone you want to warn..." The doctor's voice trailed off.

"You think this perp might start killing undead?"

"I don't know. Could be a trial run to see which method of execution is most effective." He shrugged and hung his lab coat on a hook behind the door. "Who's to say? But this is a weird one. Just be careful."

Theo nodded. "Thanks. I will."

~

He left the morgue and walked slowly to Fourth and PPG Place. A metal bench, warmed from a day in the sun, beckoned him and he took a seat a short distance away from the other people waiting on the notoriously unreliable PAT Transit.

It'd been quite a day. First the faceless hooker, then the headless girl, and Dr. Libitin seemed certain a thin thread connected them.

That thread seemed awfully tenuous to Theo. Although it was unusual, the idea of a vigilante taking out the city's criminal element was at least feasible. But the same vigilante killing a retarded girl?

Theo's mind twisted the problem over as he watched a bus come and go, disgorging and swallowing passengers.

Across the street, a wide expanse of gray stone etched with rows of names stood facing across the river, reminding him of what was before. It was one of thousands of such memorials scattered across the country in honor of those who'd fallen during the Event. He'd died, but his name was not there.

Only those who fell and did not rise were included on the memorials. No one liked to acknowledge the new population. Theo had long gotten over the bitterness of not having his name included.

The 58 pulled up to the curb and he waited patiently for an elderly woman to exit the bus. There was a time when he would have taken her arm and helped her down the stairs, but he didn't dare now. Tolerance, but not acceptance.

He took a seat in the back of the mostly empty bus and stared out the window. Could Dr. Libitin just be overthinking this? How many potential risers did he really see in a week? Three or four? Theo tried to think back to his conversations with Marjorie, who counseled the newly risen. She dealt with only a few a month, but that number didn't take into account those who wanted to rise but couldn't either because of the manner of death or the missing or defective gene.

That was the problem with the gene. There was no way to know whether you'd rise or not. Scientists worked frantically to identify the change in the human genome that allowed some people to rise and not others. If a person knew they wanted the chance to rise, their body was set aside for a few days after death to allow the gene to reanimate the body...or not. If rising wasn't their thing, they were generally cremated within the day.

The Event changed everything, right down to how people dealt with their dead. The most sacred human rituals came into question. Big changes made a lot of people very unhappy.

Theo slumped in his seat and watched other riders enter, pay their fee, and sit. A group of people got on at Meyran, leaving standing room only. People shifted to make room for more commuters, but they left Theo a wider berth than any living rider. The living, in typical fashion, were uncomfortable sharing space with the dead.

Science hadn't exactly classified those like Theo as dead. They couldn't be. Their brains still produced the patterns indicative of life. They breathed, contrary to popular fiction and horror movies. His heart beat, although more slowly and irregularly than a normal, "live," heart. His digestion was significantly slower as well, and although he still needed to eat, he required a lot less food than a living human.

Simply put, science couldn't say they were alive anymore, nor could the men in lab coats figure out how to classify them, so in the scary aftermath of the Event, the collective imagination of the people took over and decided they were undead. Zombies. A century of immersion in fabricated horror proved a hard habit to break. Even the risen had a tough time thinking of themselves as anything else at this point.

A stooped and wrinkled black woman entered the bus from the side entrance. She moved with caution, placed the end of her cane firmly on the floor before taking a step into the crowded confines of the bus. None of the living stood to offer her a seat, so Theo rose.

"Ma'am." He indicated the vacant plastic bench.

She smiled and used his forearm to steady herself on her way to the spot. "Thank you."

Theo reached for a silver pole and living people nearby moved away. He felt smaller somehow, as if the revulsion of the other riders physically affected him. He turned to face the back of the bus, put his less vulnerable side toward the people shunning him.

The old woman peered at him from under her plastic bonnet. "Don't pay 'em no attention. We been through this kind of thing before."

Theo nodded. He supposed she was right. Equality for any minority group was slow to come.

The same scientists who struggled to classify the *how* of his condition were fairly certain they'd pinpointed the *why*. Twelve years ago the planet had seen a five hundred percent spike in solar flares. The increase began slowly over a period of six months, and finally culminated in one supercharged day of radiation exposure for anyone not in a lead-lined bunker. They believed the radiation changed the human genome and resulted in some select humans being capable of foiling death at least once.

The radiation also killed millions of people; some estimates placed the dead in the tens of millions, but the true number would never be known. The resulting panic sparked the Event. Christians believed the Apocalypse was upon the world, the Jews saw the coming of the Messiah, and the Muslims prepared for Yawm ad-Din. It was the like the entire world went insane. When the dead and murdered rose again, confused, scared and lashing out at the people who'd already killed them once, or at a society trying to kill them again, all hell broke loose. The United States managed to hold things together better than most other places in the world, and still it had been complete chaos.

Theo closed his eyes against the memories.

"Overton." The driver's voice held weariness and resignation. The bus shook as passengers disembarked. A couple of seats opened up and he took one along the side. He leaned against the cold plastic and suppressed a shudder. The heave and sway of the bus combined with the chill air conditioning dulled his senses. He kept his gaze on the passing scenery so he wouldn't miss his stop.

A bright yellow house on the corner caught his attention and he shook himself to awareness. The bus lurched to a stop and he exited the side door. He jammed his hands in his pockets and walked, stiff-legged, to his parents' house down the block.

In the front hall, he removed his shoes and placed them on a tray next to the door. The television blared from the living room, and the scent of grilled cheese and tomato soup wafted to his nostrils.

"Teddy?" His mother peeked from around the corner of the kitchen. She dried her hands with a flowered tea towel. "I kept dinner warm for you."

"Thanks, Ma." He sat at the tiny kitchen table, just big enough for the three of them, and kept his eyes on the floral tablecloth. He stirred the creamy red soup she placed in front of him, agitating the unnaturally orange Goldfish crackers bobbing on the surface and dislodging the layer of raw hamburger meat on the bottom.

"How was your day, Teddy?" she said. She slid a sandwich from the stained and pitted frying pan onto a plate, which she set beside the bowl of soup.

"It was good." Theo glanced at the layer of bloody ground meat between two perfectly crisp slices of bread. His salivary glands kicked into gear and he slurped a spoonful of soup-coated meat to cover his drooling.

"How about yours?" he said because he knew his mother didn't really want to hear about his day.

"Oh, fine. The library was busy this morning." Joyce Walker volunteered at the community library on Wednesdays. "Story time is always packed during the summer."

"I'll bet," Theo responded between bites of tender ground beef and buttery bread. His mother retreated to the sink where she washed up the soup pot and frying pan. She slipped dirty bowls and plates into the dishwasher.

"Can I get you anything else?"

"No, thanks. This is great, Mom."

She smiled at him and he couldn't help but return it. "I'm going to watch TV with your father. Put your dishes in the dishwasher when you're done, please."

"You got it." He saluted her with his spoon but tucked into his meal when she disappeared around the corner. He polished off the sandwich and drank his soup straight from the bowl, scraping the last bits of meat out with his spoon. He rinsed the dishes and stacked them in the dishwasher, careful to put the utensils handle-down in the basket, just the way she preferred.

The sounds of the History Channel floated from the television. His dad, immersed in black and white footage of World War II bombers, barely noted Theo's passage through the living room.

Theo thought he'd managed an escape.

"Son, how was work?"

He turned away from the basement door to face his father. "It was busy."

"Busy? Good business for you, bad news for the rest of us." Bill chuckled at his own joke. "How's Jim?"

"Sergeant Milton is good. He said to tell you and mom hello."

His father's attention drifted back to the television. "That's nice. You tell him we need to get together for a beer. See if he wants to bring Marion for a barbecue next weekend."

"I will," he lied. Theo took the stairs down to the basement. He flipped the switch on his space heater and turned the lights on low. His clothes went in the washing machine. After adding the detergent, he shut the lid and set it to run the hot cycle, hoping the heat would kill the scent of the autopsy room.

He pulled on a pair of threadbare boxers, headed straight for his bed—a mattress on the worn shag carpet—and found the impression that matched the contours of his body. He drew the electric blanket up to his armpits and grabbed the TV remote. He flipped through channels and finally settled on the last half of *Big Trouble in Little China*.

Movement at the foot of his mattress caught his attention. "Come on, Ash." He patted the blanket beside him. A gray cat climbed onto the bed and curled next to Theo's hip. Ash butted his chin against Theo's hand and his paws began a kneading pattern.

Theo dozed off, dreamed the strange dreams of the twilight behind wakefulness and sleep, but was roused by the sounds of his parents on the stairs to the second floor. He heard the familiar creaking floorboards and the snick of their door closing behind them, and then the house fell silent.

Ash snored gently from his position against Theo's leg. Theo turned off his television and shoved his pillow into a comfortable configuration. The clock on the nightstand read one AM. He closed his eyes, ready to settle in for a nap.

A newspaper was spread out on the table in front of him. He blinked, tried to read the words, but remembered dreamers can't read. He blinked some more and could almost make out the name of the paper. It was a thin paper, not like the *Post-Gazette*, more like a *City Paper* or another small press publication.

He squinted. Is that a P? Before he could focus on the black letters, his view changed. He stood up from the table and walked to a vending machine, but it wasn't him doing the walking. A floral shirt hugged his ample belly, felt soft against his skin. He dug a dollar bill from the pocket of his jeans and fed it into the machine. It took a few tries before the bill acceptor would take it, but he didn't feel frustrated. He hummed a melody that he didn't recognize, and pressed E8 for a Snickers bar. He hated Snickers.

Someone touched his arm, a blonde woman with kind eyes and he spoke to her, but he couldn't tell what he said. He went back to the table, peered at the paper, and continued trying to focus on the letters. He unwrapped the candy and took a bite, turned a page. Another bite, his dream-self shuddered at the texture of the nougat, and something on this page caught his attention. He leaned over the paper, to read more closely. The words almost formed themselves in his mind.

Know more... No more?

Second...

A better...a better...

Something. He struggled to understand the words bouncing in his head, to read something from the paper laying mere inches from his face. Frustration blossomed and he longed to smash his fist into the laminate table, but he didn't control the hands attached to the ends of these arms.

He looked up, tried to look around to orient himself in space, in a location, but his eyes went only to the window

41

where he saw gray buildings through dirty, hazy glass. A sense of satisfaction flooded him, nearly tamping the frustration...but not quite.

The vision shifted and he stood before a pay phone. A pay phone? Where the hell would anyone find a pay phone these days? He plunked a quarter into the slot and listened to the burr of the receiving line. A woman's voice answered, but her words were garbled, nonsensical. He giggled, thanked the woman, and hung up. A kind of agreement had been reached, but he didn't know what it was. Something made him feel elated, buoyant.

A man's face suddenly entered his field of vision and his effervescent mood crashed. He felt a stalwart resolution and bitterness mixed with confusion. His hands reached for the man's pants, unbuttoned them, slid the zipper down and reached inside. Rough hands grasped his breasts, twisted them painfully, and he forced a laugh. The penis in his hand remained flaccid, so he dropped to his knees to take it in his mouth, swirled his tongue around it. He held back a gag. Hands reached around the back of his head and the man thrust his hips forward in an effort to push his dick further into Theo's mouth.

The inside of the car was immaculate, no trash or food crumbs on the floor or jammed into the upholstery. The scents of Febreze and Armor All overpowered his senses. He felt bouncy, happy, and ready to take on the world. The driver shifted the manual transmission and they flew faster down the highway. Laughter bubbled up from Theo's throat.

Hot semen spurted from the semi-erect cock in Theo's mouth. He suppressed another gag and tuned out the grunts of the man standing over him.

Wildflowers blanketed the clearing. It was beautiful. He could imagine a unicorn prancing under the tree over there.

"Shit!" the man yelled and ran with his puny dick still hanging from his pants. Theo peered at the person in the corner from his place on the floor and everything went red and black.

The scent of freshly turned dirt mixed with the distinctive odor of urine and Theo sat upright, breathing heavily, while the fear and disgust from the vision worked their way out of his system.

What the fuck? Ash, perturbed at Theo's abrupt shift, hopped off the mattress. The clock on the nightstand indicated only five minutes passed since Theo closed his eyes, but he felt as if it'd been hours.

He rubbed his face, startled to find sweat. What just happened? Since when did he dream of giving head?

Since never, that's when. And it didn't feel like a dream; he hadn't fallen asleep.

Something was seriously jacked up, and he had the uneasy feeling it had to do with the dead women in the morgue.

Theo settled back into bed, his mind replaying the images in the vision. He'd eaten too much today. First the brains, then his mom's dinner. Too much food fucked with him.

Uneasiness twitched in his soul and sleep remained elusive.

CHAPTER 5

Sweat drenched the blankets and his alarm buzzed. He swatted it into silence.

Fucked up. After a couple hours' worth of sleep, he still smelled the piss and dirt. Black shadows danced at the edges of his vision.

Ash hunkered on the small table on which the TV sat, staring at Theo with his huge yellow eyes. Theo walked stiffly to the makeshift bathroom, grabbed a towel, doused it with tepid water, and scrubbed at his face.

He peered into the mirror. His normally sallow skin had a sickly cast to it this morning and his short brown hair stuck out from his head in multiple directions. He dropped the towel on the edge of the sink and went upstairs. Maybe a cup of coffee would shake the mood. He couldn't remember if it'd ever taken this long to erase a dream while he was alive.

A half-pot of coffee waited on the counter. The sound of running water from upstairs told him someone was in the shower. He poured coffee into a mug, added cream and sugar, and sat at the table.

"Morning!"

How his mother could be so cheerful in the morning was a mystery Theo had struggled with all his life. "Morning."

"What can I get you to eat?"

"Nothing, thanks. I'm just going to have my coffee then go to work."

"Nothing for breakfast?" She sounded wounded.

"Dinner last night was great. I'm still full." She hadn't quite grasped the idea that his metabolism was so much slower. But the compliment was enough and she dropped the subject.

"All right. Your father's getting ready to head off to the marina." Bill Walker took a job as a security guard at the local river marina after he'd retired from the force. Forty-two years as a beat cop got him a commemorative watch and a nice pension. He seemed happy in retirement, and took advantage of his employee discount at the marina to berth a used StarCraft Islander. He spent many an evening fishing the Monongahela River.

His years on the force and longtime friendship with Jim Milton also got Theo his job after the Event. Theo wasn't qualified for more than the job at the video store he'd held before he died, and most retail places wouldn't hire the undead now. His dad called in a few favors, or maybe more than a few. That advantage, combined with the force's desire to be politically zombie-correct, nabbed Theo a position in the crime lab. He'd started just ordering and stocking the labs, but the higher-ups decided to make him a little more visible and let him ride along to tag evidence. They'd been relieved when he turned out to be a good observer.

Theo tried hard not to disappoint his father. The circumstance, fortunately, turned out more fortuitous than anyone could have imagined.

Theo drank the last of his coffee, rinsed the mug, and deposited it in the dishwasher. He headed downstairs and turned on the water in his tiny shower stall to scalding. His morning routine took twenty minutes.

He reversed the bus trip from the night before, but got off the 58 outside his office rather than the morgue.

Inside the break room, Skeet and Brian Hostetter played blackjack for M&Ms.

"Isn't it a little early for M&Ms?" Theo said as he dropped into a chair.

"Of course not," Skeet said from around a mouthful of candy.

"Dude, stop eating them. You're gonna need those." Brian threw a card at Skeet. "Your partner's here. I'm gone."

"See ya," Skeet said, shuffling the deck. He held it out to Theo. "You up for a hand or two?"

"Sure," Theo said, and pulled up a chair. "Nothing better to do right now."

Three rounds of blackjack and Theo's cell phone rang. "Saved!"

He grabbed the phone. "'Lo?"

"It's Dr. Libitin."

"Hey, Doc." Theo turned back to Skeet and shook the phone. "What's up?"

"Can you come down to the morgue?"

He frowned. "It's just Skeet and me here right now for the field work. If something comes in, he'll need me."

"In which case I'll personally drive you back to your office."

Skeet waved at the door. "Go, go," he whispered. "I got it."

"Okay," Theo said to both Dr. Libitin and Skeet. "I'll have to take the bus, so I'll be twenty minutes, maybe half hour."

"See you then." The line disconnected.

Theo looked at Skeet. "You sure?"

"Yep." Theo's partner dove shoulder-deep in his locker. He backed out with an iPad in his hands. "Angry Birds, man."

"Ha! All right. Call if you need me." Theo headed out the door and toward the bus stop.

Twenty minutes later, he entered the county morgue. Dr. Libitin stood at the front desk, chatting with the attendant. He caught sight of Theo and immediately waved him to the elevators.

"What's this about?" Theo said after Dr. Libitin pushed the button marked four.

"We'll discuss it in my office."

Curiosity gnawed at Theo, but his only option was to wait.

Once outside the door to his office, Dr. Libitin pulled a large key ring from his pocket and unlocked the door. Theo had never seen him do this before; it was kind of an unwritten rule that the offices were left unlocked.

The ME stood back and motioned for Theo to enter. On the desk sat a tray with two plastic containers. Fog twisted and turned inside the transparent boxes. Dr. Libitin sat in the chair behind the desk and Theo sank into the one with the space heater.

"What is this?"

The doctor's expression betrayed nothing, but Theo's stomach twisted.

"I managed to...procure samples of brain tissue from two of the other victims, Constance Updegraff and Alvin Krunk."

He unscrewed the lids from the containers and the carbon dioxide mist drifted across the desk toward Theo. He shrank back. "They're frozen."

"It's all we had. I'm hoping you can get something from them." While he talked he removed two smaller boxes from each of the plastic containers. He placed them in front of Theo.

The boxes were labeled UPDEGRAFF and KRUNK. Theo hesitantly picked up the box labeled UPDEGRAFF. "They were both shot, weren't they?"

"Yes." Dr. Libitin's gaze was on Theo's face. "Will you try?"

"I've never eaten frozen flesh. Not frozen *human* flesh, anyway."

"It's worth a try. If you don't get anything, you don't get anything. If you do..." The doctor shrugged. "Who knows? We might just be that much closer."

Theo unsnapped the flaps that held the small box closed. Nestled inside was a small chunk of brain matter, no bigger than a half-inch on each side.

"It's not all we have. There's more down in the main freezer," Dr. Libitin explained. "I just figured this much might not be missed."

Theo poked the cube. Crystals on the surface caught the overhead lighting, but just the heat of Theo's fingers was enough to melt the topmost layer. He plucked the chunk of brain from the box and weighed it in his hand; let his body heat thaw it just a bit.

He looked up at Dr. Libitin. "What if I don't get anything?"

"No harm, no foul."

Theo sighed. "Okay." He popped the brain matter into his mouth, closed his eyes, and leaned back in his chair.

The delicate tissue melted rapidly, dissolving into a velvety puddle on his tongue. The thawed brain retained none of the texture that made it so appealing to Theo, and the flavor was off. It tasted...freezer burnt.

He smacked his lips and rolled it around on his tongue. He concentrated on emotions and sensations, but other than a vague sense of discontent, he didn't get anything. No images, no strong emotions, no memories. He swallowed the tissue and opened his eyes.

Dr. Libitin leaned over the desk, staring intently at Theo. "And?"

"Sorry, nothing. I don't think so. I felt uncomfortable, but that could just be me."

Disappointment etched the ME's face. "That's okay. Constance Updegraff is the earliest victim, so it's also the oldest sample. We're pretty certain she died sometime Saturday night, but no one got to her until Sunday. Maybe we'll have better luck with Alvin Krunk's sample." He pushed the second box across the desk.

Theo eyed the box. "Another shooting victim?"

Dr. Libitin nodded.

He poked the box. "How old is this sample?"

The ME flipped through a small packet of papers. "Uh, looks like this one died early Monday morning and was found Monday afternoon."

Today was Thursday. So, depending on when Mr. Krunk expired on Monday, this sample was most likely seventy-two hours old, give or take a few hours.

Theo drummed his fingers on the desk then grabbed the box, opened it, and popped the brain between his lips. The coldness burned his mouth, so he pressed hard with his tongue to melt the flash-frozen flesh. It quickly disintegrated into the same creamy smooth liquid. He swallowed, slightly repulsed by the sensation of liquid brain oozing down his throat, and closed his eyes to await the sensations.

Nothing. Except for the vague sense of discomfort, which he attributed to eating something he found gross, he felt nothing.

He shook his head.

"Damn." Dr. Libitin sighed. "Well, it was worth a try."

"Yeah, now we know. It has to be fresh."

Dr. Libitin grunted. "Let me know if anything comes of it. Maybe it's a delayed reaction."

Theo raised an eyebrow but said nothing. The doc couldn't know about the weird waking dreams from last night. He was grasping at straws, which just went to show how frustrated he was with the cases. "I should get back to the lab."

Dr. L. nodded. "I'll drive you."

"Thanks," Theo said.

"You think Dr. Libitin is on to something with the Riser Murders?"

Skeet's question tore Theo's attention from the packing slip in his hand. "I don't know, really. I guess he might be."

"We usually only get one a week; sometimes one every two weeks. They've had five in the last seven days." Skeet returned to labeling slides and placing them in cases.

Theo considered Skeet's statement. Pittsburgh's murder rate hovered between three and five per month, on average. In comparison to the murder rate of a city like, say, Detroit, which averaged one homicide per day. Five seemingly unrelated murders in three days in Pittsburgh were well outside the norm.

Twelve years had passed since the Event that changed humanity and still the percentage of people choosing to take the opportunity to rise was only about twenty percent. That number was slowly increasing, as people came to understand the process and became more open-minded and as younger people reached the age to declare their preference. Theo imagined a day would come when the need to tattoo your intentions on your wrist would be limited to only tattooing the desire to be cremated.

With only about a fifth of the people in the city opting to rise, or at least take the chance of maybe rising, what were the odds that all five murders in a week would be risers?

He checked the expiration dates on the bottles of media already in the fridge and shoved the new stock toward the back.

What was the name of the first one? Cutter? Theo shook his head. Barber. M-something Barber.

He peeled the gloves off his hands and dropped them in the biohazard box on his way out of the physical evidence lab. "I'll be in records," he told Skeet.

He turned the corner three doors down into the records requisition office. "Leslie," he said.

The short, heavyset woman behind the counter didn't look up. "What do you need?"

Theo leaned against the counter. "I'm looking for an evidence container on a murder victim Barber. This one is recent; over the weekend, I think."

Leslie pushed her glasses up on the bridge of her nose. "That one just came in. There's a whole stack ahead of it."

"I know, but the ME seems to think this one might be related to a few others. Can I please take a look?" He flashed her a smile, knowing she tolerated his presence at best.

She narrowed her eyes at him before stalking into the metal racks, shifting three cardboard boxes, and picking one up from the floor. "Here."

Theo accepted the storage box. The label on the end, written in solid black marker, read BARBER, MALIA M. "Could you keep an eye open for a couple more?"

Leslie raised one eyebrow above her gold-rimmed glasses. "Names?"

"Uh, Krunk and Updegraff," Theo said.

Leslie might be a bitch, but she was no slouch. "What's going on?"

Theo shrugged. "Dr. Libitin asked me to help out on a couple of them. Just trying to stay on top of it. Can you set them aside for me and let me know when they come in?"

Leslie's gaze searched Theo's face. "Who is in charge of this investigation?"

"Dr. M. E. himself. This is all off the record."

She pointed a pen at him. "I'm going to check with him and if you're lying I'm telling Howard."

Theo ignored the threat to tattle to his boss. "Thanks."

"I'll remember this!" she called as he strode from the records room.

Theo turned right into the hall and walked to a door at the end. From a cubby beside the door, he took shoe covers and a surgical gown and slipped them on over his blue scrubs, then pulled the door open.

Once inside, he placed the box on a side table and pulled on a pair of nitrile gloves. He removed the lid from the storage box and placed items on a table in the center of the room. A three-ring binder, several paper bags, and a couple of plastic bags with a variety of sample tubes.

He began with the binder and skimmed through the written reports. Dr. Libitin shared the pertinent information and Theo frankly didn't care where they'd found her. He read through the information about the wound closely enough to be convinced she'd been killed in such a way as to not permit rising. A close-range bullet to the temple with a large-caliber cartridge would certainly do the trick. Preliminary ballistics estimated that a nine-millimeter cartridge was used, but more testing would be necessary to be sure. With no shell or lead recovered, they might never know.

That was a big bullet for a temple shot. Theo didn't have a lot of experience in the firearms forensics, but enough experience with firearms in general to know a close-range shot to the temple with something as small as a .22 could do the trick. These large shells were chosen for a reason.

A manila envelope held a stack of photos. He shuffled through them, looking for a specific one—a close-up shot of her left wrist. She'd tattooed the word "rise" on the inside of her wrist in calligraphy style.

He carefully examined the other photographs of the crime scene and the body, both at the scene and the autopsy photos, for any other telltale sign that this was something out of the ordinary.

Nothing.

An inspection of the clothes removed from the body gave no other information, either, and he wasn't equipped to test any of the microscopic evidence in the clean room.

With a bit of reluctance, he replaced all the items in the cardboard box.

Nothing. The crime scene evidence from Malia Barber's death offered nothing.

Theo felt frustration stir, both at the lack of apparent information and at Dr. Libitin. He owed the medical examiner a lot, but he wasn't convinced that these murders were truly related. Sometimes there was a rash of crime during the summer, when tempers flared in the heat. Murders weren't common, but there was nothing to preclude them from an ordinary increase in crime. For the last few weeks, the city had simmered in the midsummer sun. These murders could have more to do with short tempers than some sort of undead vendetta.

He tore the gloves off his hands, grabbed the box and returned it to the records room. Leslie wasn't there, so Theo made a note in the logbook and left the box on the counter.

His job was to maintain the lab and make sure everything was available for the laboratory to function. Putting the pieces of the puzzle together to make the final picture fell to the scientists and detectives, not him.

"Theo." Howard Moster's voice came from behind him "How's it going?"

"Good, thanks." Theo watched his boss walk down the hall toward his office.

He felt anger slosh in his circulatory system, and he took deep breaths to slow it down. Dr. Libitin thought he was doing the right thing. Theo would just have to tell him he couldn't do more.

And if the rest of the undead community or the Pittsburgh Bureau of Police caught wind of him eating brain matter...well, that wasn't something he wanted to risk.

Back in the physical evidence lab, Theo put on a fresh surgical gown and gloves and continued stocking the reagents. Making a decision energized him, and putting the weird murders out of his mind felt good.

He hummed while he placed bottles and boxes in their proper locations.

CHAPTER 6

Theo's locker key refused to cooperate. He jiggled it around, pushed hard and finally got the damn thing open. He made a mental note to bring some WD-40 with him the next day.

He changed quickly into street clothes and dropped his scrubs into the plastic receptacle next to the door.

Skeet sat in the break room, playing Angry Birds on his iPad again. "You done then?"

"Yep. Headed home. What are you up to?"

"Waiting for my ride. My brother is picking me up. Tomorrow is my dad's birthday, so we're taking him out for a family dinner tonight."

"Where's your car?"

"Garage. Inspection."

"Have a good time. Tell your old man I say happy birthday."

"Thanks."

Theo made his way out of the break room and down the hall toward the front door. Once outside, he stopped and lifted his face to the sun. It was setting, but still hot enough to warm his skin. July in the 'Burgh could be brutal.

Theo loved it. He hadn't loved it before. *Before* his favorite season was winter, with its frigid temperatures and annual Snowpocalypse. He'd relished the crunch of snow and ice beneath his boots and the subzero winds off the rivers.

Since his death, though, the only thing he enjoyed about winter was that his parents used the fireplace. He kind of missed sledding in Schenley Park, though.

His cell phone buzzed, interrupting his enjoyment of the heat. He glanced at the caller ID before he answered. He didn't recognize the number.

"Hello?"

"Hi. This is Shelby."

He gripped the phone. "Oh, hey, Shelby. This is Theo."

A pause. "I know. I called you."

Theo made a sound that resembled a laugh, but could have been mistaken for a donkey's bray.

Shit. Shit, shit.

She laughed back. "You're funny. Anyway, Marjorie and I are going to grab dinner. We wondered if you wanted to join us."

Speechless. He'd been rendered mute.

"Um, well, it's just really informal. We're going to Uncle Sam's in Squirrel Hill."

"That would be great." He squeaked the words out. "When are you going?"

"We're both at the morgue, so we're going to head over there now. Travel time plus parking..." Theo heard her talk to someone nearby, probably Marjorie. "Maybe half an hour?"

"I'll be there. I'm at the office."

"Okay, see you there." Shelby hung up.

The ride into Squirrel Hill seemed to take longer than usual, but he made it inside the thirty-minute mark. He got off at Forbes and Murray and ran across the street against the light to get to the sub shop. Once inside, he looked around for the girls, but they weren't there.

Uncle Sam's menu never changed. A girl with more rings in her face than Theo could count took his order of a mushroom cheese steak, rare, with extra mushrooms and an order of fries. She handed him a soft drink cup, which he filled with Mountain Dew, then surveyed the restaurant. He chose a table near the back with a clear view of the front door and moved one chair to a neighboring table.

Shelby and Marjorie arrived before his order was ready. He waved to them from his seat.

Marjorie dropped her bag on the chair next to him.

He watched them at the counter while they placed their orders. Marjorie wore jeans—the first time Theo had seen her in them. They hugged her curves in the right places and the deep red polo shirt set off the silky blackness of her hair. His blood ran a bit faster.

"Extra 'shrooms." The waiter dropped a paper plate with Theo's sandwich on the table.

Marjorie walked back to the table with her drink and sat next to Theo. She squeezed his hand. "How are you?"

"I'm good," he replied, with a return squeeze. He inhaled deeply. She smelled good, like baby powder and something fruity.

Shelby sat down in the chair across from him. "Hey, Theo."

He smiled. "How's the doc?"

Shelby wrinkled her nose. "I barely saw him today. I dragged your phone number out of him and he shut himself right back in his office." She gestured at Theo's sandwich. "Eat while it's hot. Go on."

Theo popped some fries in his mouth. "He's been working on a couple of cases."

"I know. He seems to think a few of the murders that have come through recently are related."

The waiter came by again. "Classic steak." Marjorie raised a finger. "And a jalapeno, extra meat." Shelby reached up to take hers.

Silence prevailed at the table while each started on their meals. Theo wondered at Shelby discussing work in public, but he guessed since they weren't saying names, it was probably okay.

He still glanced around the busy restaurant to see if anyone paid attention to them.

"Related how?" Marjorie said from around a mouthful of cheesesteak.

Shelby rooted through her canvas bag, came out with a bottle of hot sauce, and sprinkled the red liquid liberally over her sandwich. "Every murder that's come through in the last week has been a potential riser."

Theo's nerves, dulled from the air-conditioned interior, thudded. His gaze shot from Shelby to Marjorie, waiting for her response.

Marjorie studied her fries. "Potential risers?"

Her tone was even, almost carefully so.

"Yeah. He seems to think someone's targeting people who have the tattoo." Shelby took a bite of her sandwich, added more hot sauce. "He's got Theo working on it with him."

Marjorie shifted to face Theo. "What's going on?"

He pointed at Shelby with a fry. "Dr. Libitin asked me to help him with a couple of cases involving potential risers. He's been unable to find any correlation between the victims, though, except the tattoos."

"Why? What could be a motive for something like that?"

Theo shrugged. "I have no idea. We haven't even begun to speculate."

Marjorie's eyes narrowed. "Why are you working with Dr. Libitin? I thought you worked in the forensics lab, not pathology."

"Theo's really good at what he does. Dr. Libitin felt certain he could offer some insight."

Theo felt the beginning of nausea. He stared at Shelby, who just gave him a sunny smile.

Her foot made contact with Theo's shin under the table. Not a kick, just pressure. She hadn't told Marjorie his secret.

Adrenaline faded from his blood.

"I wondered why I saw you there the other day. It's great the ME has someone from forensics to help him out." Marjorie laid a hand on his arm.

"I don't know how much help I am, but I like working with him." Another tap on his leg made him glance at Shelby, who appeared to be immersed in rearranging the tomatoes in her sandwich. "Makes the morgue more fun."

"I don't think the morgue is supposed to be fun," said Marjorie.

"You have no idea. In my four years, I've seen some wild stuff. You have to keep it light, or you'll go crazy."

"Makes sense," Theo said. "Death isn't funny."

"So, what's going on in 6B?" Marjorie said.

The conversation at the table turned to a problem with a tenant in their apartment building. Theo listened, but didn't bother trying to follow it.

Shelby shook her cup. "Empty. I'll be right back." She headed for the soda dispenser.

Marjorie turned back to Theo. "So what's going on with the murders?"

"Dr. L. thinks a serial killer is purposely taking out potential risers."

"Serial killer?"

"We've had five bodies with the tattoo come through in less than a week."

Marjorie pressed her lips together into a thin line. "I don't understand."

"We usually get one murder a week in Pittsburgh, max. Five in less than a week constitutes a situation."

"But why does he think they're connected?"

"All but one was the result of an execution-style gunshot to the head." Theo tapped his cup on the table. "They're too similar to ignore the possibility of being related, and the fifth one to come in, while it was a different method of killing, also had the tattoo."

"Any other factors link them together?"

"All but one—the girl who wasn't shot—are all criminals of one sort or another."

"But what's the point? If someone is looking to stop people from rising, they can't hope to kill them all."

Theo looked around for Shelby and found her in a conversation with one of the waiters. He turned back to Marjorie. "To be honest, I'm not convinced they're related. Maybe the execution-style killings are some sort of gang activity, but I don't think it has anything to do with the tattoo."

Marjorie nodded thoughtfully. "I would agree. I just can't see a motive for something like that. One person doesn't have the time to eliminate every potential riser."

"Who knows what this person is thinking, or if it's more than one. However, Dr. Libitin is afraid the killings might expand into the undead community."

Marjorie's forehead wrinkled. "Seriously?"

"I'm not sure about that either, but he thinks maybe I should give everyone a heads up."

"We have a support group meeting scheduled for over the weekend. Why don't you come and just put the word out?"

Theo studied Marjorie's face. Her almond-shaped eyes held no disgust or derision; the things he was accustomed to seeing from women. "Why can't you do that?"

"I could," she said. "But it would probably be taken more seriously from someone in law enforcement."

Theo puffed up just a bit. Law enforcement. "Maybe you're right."

"We should do dinner again, too."

"Yeah. That would be great."

Shelby grabbed her bag from the back of the chair. "Hey, that was weird. That waiter works at the rink where I skate."

"You're an ice skater?" Theo barely concealed his confusion and disappointment that his alone time with Marjorie was interrupted.

Shelby punched him lightly in the shoulder. "Roller derby."

"Oh." Theo chose not to ask what exactly what "roller derby" meant.

"You ready?" Shelby pointed at Marjorie.

"Sure." Marjorie stood.

Theo quickly scraped his chair back and stood to say goodbye. To his shock and pleasure, she wrapped her arms around him in a quick hug, pressed her cool body to Theo's for a too-brief moment. Before he could return the embrace, she backed away.

"See ya, Theo." She headed for the front door and Shelby trailed behind. The autopsy tech turned at the last minute, winked at Theo and gave him the thumbs up.

What the hell? Was she trying to set him up with Marjorie? He smiled to himself.

After dropping his trash in the can by the door, he walked to the bus stop at Forbes and Murray to wait for his ride home.

Ash climbed on the bed and flopped into his usual place next to Theo's leg. Theo stroked the cat's fur and clicked through television channels without paying much attention.

He had mixed feelings about going to the support group meeting over the weekend. He'd attended a few of them when the undead began integrating, but stopped because he thought they were depressing. Either a riser dealt with their new status or they didn't. He supposed Marjorie's job was okay. He might have appreciated someone to talk him through those first frightening hours, but after that? Time to suck it up and move on.

Sitting around and talking about adjusting to life after death reminded him again of how different he was from the rest of the world, from the living, from the life he'd left behind. He preferred to move forward as if he hadn't died and make the little adjustments when he was forced. He resisted change, hated change. Dying hadn't been easy.

"Teddy, do you need anything?" His mother's voice came from the top of the stairs.

"No, thanks."

"You didn't have dinner."

"I had dinner with friends. I ate out."

Silence, then an injured tone to her voice. "You ate with friends?"

"Yes, Mom. I do have those." He rolled his eyes.

"I know, honey. Okay, if you don't need anything I'm going to bed. Your father's got a late shift at the marina."

"Night, then. I'm fine."

"Night, Teddy."

Theo listened to her footsteps go up the stairs to the second floor. He turned the lights off and shoved his pillow around for a few minutes before he finally acquiesced to insomnia.

The Xbox was a decent diversion from wakefulness. He grabbed the remote and discovered that *Call of Duty* was still in the game system. Zombie mode never failed to amuse him.

The sound of the front door opening and his father's familiar footsteps across the living room jarred his attention from the video game. He squinted at his alarm clock in the glare of the television light and saw it was almost two in the morning. Yawning, he dropped the game controller to the floor beside the bed, switched off the TV, and fell into a light, restless sleep.

CHAPTER 7

When his alarm went off at six, he was in a foul mood. He'd woken numerous times in his scant four hours, each time with a deep sense of foreboding and a feeling as though he were out of his own body. Strange dreams punctuated the short bursts of sleep he'd actually managed, but with the sounds of morning in his ears, he could not remember the details.

Uncle Sam's apparently messed with his dreams. He'd have to remember to lay off the double 'shroom subs.

He took his time in the shower, trying to shake off the loss of control. The hot water helped a lot, and he emerged feeling more like himself.

In the kitchen, his mom fried scrambled eggs and bacon. His stomach gurgled with displeasure, but he accepted a plate anyway.

"Who did you have dinner with last night, honey?" She placed more bacon into the hot pan and did not turn to look at him.

"Some friends from work." It wasn't a total lie. He kind of worked at the morgue lately.

"I'm glad to see you getting out."

"Who's getting out?" His father strode into the kitchen, a larger, bulkier version of Theo himself. Next to his retired cop-hero father, Theo felt small, in more ways than one. He knew he'd been a disappointment to them and they felt as though he wasted his potential. Dying and having the gall to come back as one of the first zombies in Pittsburgh only made an awkward situation more so.

Still, Theo knew his parents loved him. In their way.

"I did," he replied.

His dad thumped him on the back. "Wasn't Jim, was it?"

"No, not Sergeant Milton. Two people from the morgue." He glanced sideways at his father. "Marjorie and Shelby."

"Girls?" His mother turned to face him. "You didn't tell me it was girls." She clucked at his omission and went back to her cooking.

His father swallowed a mouthful of coffee. "Do I know these girls?"

"I doubt it. They're both kind of new." He didn't think Shelby had been at the morgue for long and he knew Marjorie hadn't.

His mom put a plate full of eggs, bacon, and toast in front of her husband. "I'm sure they're nice girls," she said with a smile for Theo. "Bring them here for dinner some night."

He had to get out of there. "Thanks for breakfast, Ma. I gotta go." He dropped his plate in the sink and headed for the front door and the relative solitude of his morning bus trip.

The break room was empty, so Theo walked straight through and into the locker area. He fought with his lock, kicked himself for forgetting the WD-40, changed into scrubs and dropped his street clothes into his locker before heading straight for the storage room.

Fresh supplies waited. He began checking boxes against the receiving slip and writing the destination on each. Pipettes, tubs of agar powder, bottles of DMSO, and extraction kits were set aside to go to the DNA lab. Skeet hated it, but Theo didn't mind this part of the job. Once the chaotic fieldwork was over, he found the act of turning the jumble of boxes into an orderly line of supplies therapeutic.

Skeet caught him in the hall with a dolly of boxes of ballistics gel mix.

"Yo, we're on."

"All right. Let me just put this in ballistics."

Skeet nodded and headed for the break room.

Theo wheeled the boxes into the ballistics lab, dropped them in a corner, and headed back to the break room.

"You goin' like that?" Skeet indicated Theo's scrubs.

"Yeah. Let me grab my wallet." Theo made a quick stop at his locker, cursed the lock again.

Theo grabbed a fresh evidence kit and Skeet grabbed his camera bag. They made their way to the parking garage and into the little hatchback.

"Any idea what we're headed into?" Theo said.

"Nope." Skeet fiddled with the radio. "All I know is there's more than one. Dr. Libitin is on his way."

"Shit. More than one?"

"When they called, they said 'multiple victims, ME en route.'"

Theo's stomach roiled and he steeled himself, regretting those eggs.

"We'll work together on this one. I'll be right behind you. Check my work, too. Can't make any mistakes on something like this." He put a fist out and Theo bumped it. Skeet backed the car out of the parking spot and headed for the exit.

"Where are we headed?" Theo said.

Skeet turned to meet Theo's gaze. "Frick Park."

"No shit."

"Not sure about the shit."

Theo shook his head. "This is getting strange. Dr. Libitin might be onto something here."

"At the very least, we've got a serial killer in the 'Burgh. No doubt."

They drove in silence. Skeet pulled onto an exit ramp and directed the car onto Braddock. Theo watched Regent Square pass by outside the window, mind whirling.

"Regular routine?" Skeet said as he pulled off into a parking spot. A uniformed cop directed traffic, so Skeet flashed a badge and he waved them through a dozen or so people milling about trying to figure out what was going on.

"Yeah." Theo walked around to the back of the car and popped the hatch. He opened the evidence box and grabbed a handful of marker flags and a clipboard. Skeet checked the settings on his camera and they both walked toward the police officers at the far end of the parking lot.

Detective Gavahan leaned on the hood of an unmarked car, separated a bit from the group of officers. He stared at the scene with intensity; his gaze moved back and forth from the trail to the parking lot.

A group of rubberneckers stood in a cluster, talking and staring. They pointed at Theo as he walked past them. Two female officers sat on a bench with a sobbing woman. Theo bypassed the women and made straight for the scene, which was located about thirty feet from the end of the parking lot, behind a small stand of trees. Officer Larson caught his eye and raised his chin in greeting. Theo nodded.

Gavahan turned to the new arrivals. Theo watched his face go rigid, and the atmosphere around him went cold. Bad news. Gavahan took a step toward Theo, as if to head him off, but Sergeant Milton placed himself in front of Gavahan. A few words were exchanged, but Theo couldn't hear them. Gavahan shot one last venomous look in Theo's direction, and stalked off.

Milton met him and Skeet at the edge of the scene. "Extra careful, okay? This looks to be big." His tone carried no hint of condescension.

"You got it." Theo glanced at the tangle of bodies about twenty feet off. The officers already strung police tape around the perimeter of the scene, so Theo did a careful sweep around the established perimeter to be sure they'd cordoned off a large enough area.

It looked good.

He stepped under the tape and did a quick visual pass without looking closely at the pile of bodies in the center. Nothing stuck out as obvious, so he started at the point closest to the parking lot and walked in slow spirals, dropping a yellow marker at each item that wasn't a natural part of the terrain.

He knew this would be a big one. Nothing was overlooked. Skeet moved around within the taped off area, photographing more than he probably needed. Tension and perhaps fear thickened the air. The public wouldn't like this.

His circles grew tighter, and he could no longer ignore the grisly tableau in the center, a strange mixture of anticipation and horror lapping at his emotions. He stopped walking to get a first impression of the death scene.

He heard a quick intake of breath behind him, and Skeet's voice cracked. "Jesus Christ."

Theo looked over his shoulder at Skeet to see if he was okay. He didn't appear pale, just stunned. Theo had a moment of gratitude that he remembered to stock the Vick's and barf bags. "You gonna be sick?"

"What?" Skeet wrenched his gaze from the bodies to Theo. "Yeah, no, dude. I'm all right." He gestured at the mess in the grass. "But Jesus Christ."

"Yeah, this is new. You okay taking the pictures?"

Skeet grunted and lifted his camera.

Not much rattled Theo anymore, but something was truly wrong with this scene. Even his normal undead instincts screamed.

At first glance, Theo could make out two bodies, one on top of another, lying in an area of flattened brown grass. A head lay off to one side. After looking carefully, he realized there were actually three. The third body, underneath the other two, was not as recognizable, since it, too, lacked a head.

The zombie in Theo roared, his appetite for blood and brain erupted. His nostrils flared at the scent of the mixed blood and body fluids, and he forced himself to breathe slow and deep. He scanned the area for Gavahan, desperate to avoid a confrontation in this hyper state.

Blood drenched the bodies and the grass around and underneath. The corpse on top lay face down, or chest-down he supposed, since its face was missing. The mortal injuries appeared similar to those that Theo recalled seeing on Carly Harris. He'd put money on the cause of death being close-range gunshot to the head.

Two beheadings and another execution-style shot to the temple. A chill ran up Theo's spine, and that freaked him out nearly as much as what he saw in front of him. The top body wore dirty pink sequined hot pants and a tank top with white sneakers. The pants were short enough to reveal a filthy thong and hairy ass. Theo blinked. A dude.

He couldn't quite tell the gender of the other victims, since the clothes that he could see appeared to be pants and t-shirts, and the heads gone. The body shapes seemed to be female, but he didn't want to speculate. The middle body was a light-skinned African-American.

He moved closer and squatted down near the bodies, trying to look at the wrists. He could only see one left arm dark with livor mortis. Although he couldn't quite make out which body it belonged to, he could see the word tattooed across the flesh: RISE.

His pulse increased and with renewed urgency, he continued his inspection of the space around the scene.

Theo walked in his deliberate spiral, the small, slow circles that would ensure he'd see anything left behind by a careless killer. He'd dropped only a few markers, and this worried him. The killer left maddeningly little behind, as with the other crime scenes. He wrote copious notes on the evidence pad and heard the shutter of the camera more frequently than usual. Skeet sensed it, too.

Theo gathered the physical evidence into bags for transport back to the crime lab. He meticulously labeled each item and consulted with Skeet on proper storage and placement.

He'd just packed the evidence bags into the box and put the markers away when the ME's van pulled into the lot and was waved through to the scene. Dr. Libitin stepped from the van onto the asphalt of the parking lot. Sergeant Milton met him at the curb and they stood, talking in low tones, for a few minutes before the medical examiner turned to face the scene. He did just what Theo had come to expect; he stayed back, made an initial assessment of the scene, took it in slowly.

Dr. Libitin walked toward Theo, stopping to examine each marked item. He pulled out a couple pair of gloves as he approached and handed a pair over. "Theo."

"Doc."

Dr. Libitin stopped just outside the circle of flattened vegetation to put his gloves on. "Mr. Jones, have you taken the appropriate photographs of the surrounding area already?"

"Yes, sir," said Skeet.

"Excellent." Dr. Libitin stepped close to the corpses. "Stay close, if you would, to take pictures as we move the victims."

Theo paid careful attention to the process the medical examiner went through to evaluate the remains and their condition. Skeet documented everything with his camera, including the tattoos on all three left wrists.

Theo's heart sank amid a slush of despair and adrenaline when he saw the tattoos.

Shit, shit, shit.

"Give me a hand," the doctor said and started to roll the topmost body off the pile.

Theo pulled on his gloves, stepped to the feet, and helped the medical examiner roll the cadaver off the top of the pile and onto its back. The first body, the man in the flashy pink hot pants, rolled off without much effort; apparently the ambient heat and time of death precluded rigor mortis. The second, in the deep throes of rigor, had to be lifted, and the third, past the stiffness, flipped over. The other two were female—the breasts gave it away—and the head from the bottom body lay underneath the pile. One open eye stared up at him with cloudy reproach.

"I think we're ready for some bags." Dr. Libitin looked at Theo. "Can you grab three, please?"

Theo tugged off the latex gloves and walked to the ME's van to get the bags. Doug, in the driver's seat, said nothing this time. His face hung slack and pale and his quiet demeanor told Theo the multiple murders bothered him as well.

Back at the scene, Theo pulled on a fresh pair of gloves and helped Skeet lay out the body bags. The officers attending the scene were absolutely quiet. The silence jangled Theo's nerves more than anything, and he had to refrain from cracking an off-color joke. These cops were not newcomers, these were seasoned homicide detectives and this homicide— these brutal deaths—stifled even their normal chatter.

Despite the eighty-plus degree weather, Theo felt a chill and sensed that everyone else at the scene felt it, too. He repressed the twinge of hunger that coursed through his own body. The heat and scents of death combined to bring forth the zombie. He deliberately slowed his breathing.

"Let's take a look in pockets and around the bodies for identification." Sergeant Milton tugged on gloves and searched the corpses. He found a wad of cash in the pants of the bottom body. "Theo?"

Theo retrieved a paper bag, labeled it with BOTTOM VICTIM- FRICK PARK and the date. He considered for a moment, and then scrawled along the edge: "white female, decapitated." Sergeant Milton dropped the money into the bag along with a rumpled hair band.

Officer Larson searched the middle victim, the black woman, but found nothing at all in her pockets. She wore a watch that could be used for identification. The head that lay off to the side of the pile clearly belonged to her, since the skin tone of the head matched that of the body and the other two were Caucasian. Theo placed the head at the top of the neck.

The topmost victim, the one dressed like an errant, hairy, cheerleader had an ID holder affixed to the waistband of his thong. Theo grabbed another bag.

"Jerry Cullins," Larson said. "We've got an address here."

He read the address off and Brown scribbled it in a notebook. Theo wrote the name on the bag with TOP VICTIM-MALE-FRICK PARK and the date. Officer Larson dropped the identification card and some cash in the packet.

Skeet and Theo rearranged the bottom victim's limbs into a prone position and placed the Caucasian head at the neck.

"I'll order preliminary blood tests to determine if the heads could belong to the bodies. Since they were found together and the skin tone appears to be similar, we'll assume yes, but DNA comparison will have to be done to be sure. These heads could conceivably belong to bodies not here at this scene."

"How about family identifying the face and the clothing?" Officer Larson said.

"We can try that, but we don't have an ID. I don't want to wait to make the match in case we don't ID them quickly."

Larson nodded. "Makes sense."

"I want to print them here so we can be sure of identifying them in the photos later." Dr. Libitin gestured to Theo, who retrieved three field fingerprint kits from the van. Dr. Libitin gave instructions to Theo and Skeet as they helped him fingerprint the three corpses and draw diagrams of the bodies' layout. They made several copies of the print sheets directly from the victims, and Theo slipped them into the packets with their identifying materials.

"Okay, let's bag them and get back to the morgue." The ME pushed a blue pouch closer to the bodies with his foot.

Theo's salivary glands kicked into overdrive and he had to cough to avoid drooling. He helped Skeet and Dr. Libitin transfer the bodies.

Theo grabbed the feet of one bag and Skeet the head. They carried the body to the ME's van and loaded it onto a shelf. Larson and Brown followed with another corpse and two officers Theo didn't recognize brought in the last.

When the three bodies were situated, Theo turned to look for Dr. Libitin. The ME stood off to the side with Sergeant Milton.

"You ready, man?" Skeet stood next to the car, driver's side door open.

"Let me see if the doc needs me at the morgue."

"I don't want to wait too long. This stuff needs to get to the crime lab to be cataloged. This is going to stir up some serious shit. I don't want anything coming back on us."

"I said let me see. Give me two minutes."

Skeet frowned. "Two minutes, Theo. Then we leave."

Theo resisted the urge to flip Skeet the middle finger. Instead, he walked toward Dr. Libitin and Sergeant Milton. The doc turned to him.

"Go ahead, Theo. I won't be ready for you for a little while. I'll give you a call. It might not be until tomorrow." Dr. Libitin waved him back.

Theo gritted his teeth. He didn't want to wait. Those bodies were fresh *now*. The brains would offer the clearest picture, tell him more, now than tomorrow. They would taste good, so good...

He jerked himself back. Not about the brains. Not about the brains. He couldn't let this get the better of him. Stop it now. Eating the brains served as a way to get answers, not satisfaction.

He turned back to Skeet. "Let's go."

They drove back to the crime lab in silence. Theo hoped Skeet's unwillingness to talk was a result of the scene they'd just worked and not some sixth sense about Theo's mood. He shouldn't be feeling so much agitation that he'd have to wait for his brains. No, it wasn't about the brains. He kept telling himself that. He'd have to wait for his *examination*.

He shook his head and opened his window for fresh air. The July heat, with its scent of the rivers and of rotting vegetation, smacked him in the face and increased his desire.

He closed the window, irritation rising.

"You okay, man?"

"Yeah. Just frustrated." Theo rubbed his temples.

"Looks like the doc's right, huh? These are somehow connected to the risers."

"I don't know." Theo leaned forward, braced himself on the dashboard. "I hate to think he's right."

Skeet pulled the hatchback into the lab's parking garage. "Let's get this stuff inside and logged in."

Theo grabbed the field kit from the back. "Can you get the evidence? I'm going to bring this in to restock it."

Skeet saluted. "Aye, aye, sir."

Theo snorted. "Very funny." He followed Skeet to the elevator and then into the locker room.

Once inside, they both changed into fresh scrubs, then Theo headed to the supply room with the big field kit. Skeet's back disappeared into receiving. Theo checked the supplies in the box, grateful for a moment alone in the heavily air-conditioned environment. He hoped the cold air would help his temper to simmer down and get the more base impulses under control.

The evidence packaging supplies needed to be replenished. Theo grabbed a stack of printed paper bags and a couple rolls of security tape and dropped them into the appropriate drawer. Fresh packages of nitrile gloves were followed by a handful of antibacterial wipes and sterile tweezers.

Not since the aftermath of the Event had Theo felt the urge to eat like he experienced at the crime scene. He needed to learn to control his hunger. These days, when someone rose after death, they had help, people like Marjorie, to get them through those horrible first days. The beginning wasn't really all that horrible anymore—they knew what was happening and how to handle it, not like when Theo turned.

He opened the top section of the field kit and took out two pairs of safety glasses. A good swipe with a wet cleaning cloth, and they were ready.

When he rose, he was alone. Alone with an inexplicable hunger and no way to satisfy it. Didn't understand the desire, fought it with ferocity. Now when someone turned, there were ways to placate the need, other things to eat, drugs that somewhat helped. A newly turned zombie didn't have to resort to killing...or endure the torment that went along with not killing.

He pulled the second tray out of the kit and checked the supply of plastic evidence jars. After adding four new ones, he took the black permanent marker from the groove, tossed it in the trashcan, and found a replacement.

His head pounded and he dropped into a chair behind him. The memories of those first days haunted him. He'd spent weeks in the alley and bushes behind Edgewood Towne Centre, eating from the grocery store dumpster. Nothing alleviated the hunger. He didn't know if he was alive or dead, had no idea if he could go home, how his parents would accept him. Nothing.

His wounds healed slowly and as they healed, he learned more about the Event. Many died of exposure or in the violence that followed. He discovered that he'd actually been one of the lucky ones.

It took him another few weeks to gather the courage to face his parents. In the first moments after he knocked on the door, they cried, his mother clung to him and his father stood by, watching. After the initial relief at finding the family intact, he settled into a relationship with his parents where awkwardness reigned. His mother did her best with feeding him...but Theo wondered if the newly turned managed to control the urge better than the first generation zombies did.

Theo shook himself free of the memories. He wanted to relieve the desire to feed, but not make himself melancholy. He replaced the powder brushes and scissors with sterile packs and put the dirty supplies on the autoclave tray.

He finished quickly, wiped down all the numbered markers and rulers, tidied the drawers and cases and closed up the field kit.

Time to find something to occupy his mind. Maybe Skeet could use some help checking in the evidence.

He found his partner in the computer lab, moving pictures from his camera to a lab computer. "Hey, you need anything?"

Skeet looked up from the keyboard. "Nah, I got it. Thanks, though."

Theo tipped his chin at the machine. "How many did you take?"

"Somewhere around seven hundred images."

Skeet would label each one with the case number and body number, and later label them with a name, if they ever found out who the unidentified corpses were.

Theo watched from a chair beside Skeet's workstation. The images from the scene flashed across the screen as they moved from the camera to the hard drive. Skeet assigned each image its identifying number. The images themselves didn't seem to prod at the zombie impulses, but Theo remembered the scent of blood and death and his nostrils flared.

Gotta get out.

He stood and chucked Skeet on the shoulder. "I'll be in the autoclave room if you need me."

Skeet nodded.

Theo busied himself prepping lab supplies for sterilization. He didn't want to dwell on the multiple homicides. It seemed to be bringing out the worst of him.

But he also had to admit he was anxious to get the call from Dr. Libitin. He wanted to perform his examination...times three.

CHAPTER 8

Theo shot one zombie after another, but somehow the chaos of the shooter game didn't amuse him like it usually did.

He threw the game controller at the television set and Ash roused himself enough to stare at Theo with disdain. He reached down and scratched the cat under the chin. "Sorry."

He hated feeling like this. Restless. Useless.

Hungry.

He was beginning to think eating brains created a desire for more. Maybe he should leave well enough alone and stop. Maybe all zombies could get the psychic images from ingesting the brain matter. Maybe he should ask Marjorie to try.

But that would mean admitting what he did.

He scratched the cat under his chin again.

The house stood quiet, his parents having gone to bed. A car alarm went off somewhere in the neighborhood, but was silenced quickly. Theo leaned back on his pillows, arms behind his head and stared at the ceiling.

His intuition about the murders was beginning to line up with Dr. Libitin's. There were too many coincidences to really be chance circumstances. Eight murders in less than a week, killed in ways to prevent rising...something didn't add up to random violence.

But why? Who cared if someone rose or not? Rising wasn't guaranteed, so chances of these exact people coming back again were, at best, fifty-fifty. Why kill *these* people? What was the link connecting them other than their desire to rise?

If there was no other link, then the last possibility was the only possibility. Rising remained the only common denominator.

He rolled over in bed, punched his pillow.

It didn't make sense.

He tried to envision the victims, the faces he'd seen, and the known facts. So far, the obvious links between them were their lifestyle; they all lived on the edge of society as a criminal of one sort or another.

All except Naomi. She was the unknown in the equation.

He sighed, flipped the television and light off, resolved to get some rest, at least a few hours before the sun came up.

The sound of the lawn mower woke him. The sound of his father singing opera prevented him from going back to sleep.

He pulled on a pair of sweatpants and splashed water on his face before going in search of coffee. A fresh pot sat in the kitchen and a plate of coffee cake waited on the table.

His father passed by the window, pushing the lawn mower, iPod ear buds in place. He belted out Count Almaviva's part from *The Barber of Seville*. Theo glanced around to see if the neighbors seemed bothered. No one was out.

He sat down at the table and finished off the coffeecake. The sounds of the mower and his father's singing were still going strong when he went down to his bathroom for a shower.

When he returned, his dad stood in the kitchen, gulping a Pepsi straight from the can. He mopped sweat from his face and chest with a hand towel. "Did you eat, son?"

"Yeah. The coffeecake was good."

"Be sure and tell your mother. She'll like to hear it." Bill threw the towel down the laundry chute. "I'm going to shower and head to the marina. Your mother went to the grocery store but shouldn't be long."

"Okay."

"What are your plans for the day?"

"I dunno. Thought I might go in to work for a bit."

"No plans with your girlfriends?"

Theo bit back a retort. He never said they were his girlfriends.

His intestines squirmed. He *had* promised Marjorie he'd go to the undead support group to talk about the murders. And he *did* have hopes that she might be interested in more than just dinner at Uncle Sam's with Shelby.

"Maybe tonight," he told his father.

Bill's eyebrows moved higher on his forehead. "Really? Well, that's good news."

Theo suppressed a groan. When he was living, they'd actually asked him if he was gay and promised they would love him no matter what. He was amused, but it served only to remind him of the fact he had no life.

Being dead hadn't really helped his social life at all. He couldn't even get his job at the video store back, and by the time retailers started hiring zombies, the store had shut down. Damn Netflix.

Theo watched his father walk upstairs. "Yeah, Dad. Good news."

When he heard the water run in the shower, he logged onto the desktop computer. He had to Google "undead support group Pittsburgh" to find a website.

After several minutes of ferreting out different organizations, he found the county sponsored group's site. Marjorie Frey was listed as a contact, so he knew he had the right one.

He chewed on his bottom lip just looking at the website. Support groups never made much sense to him, not even Alcoholics or Narcotics Anonymous. Why surround yourself with the very thing you were battling?

He'd been lucky enough to come back from the dead; he didn't see any reason to dwell on it. The thought of sitting around discussing his death with a bunch of strangers made him uncomfortable.

Marjorie wasn't a stranger, though, not quite. The promise of seeing her and that wash of black hair would be enough. Besides, he would be there to talk to the group about safety, not reveal the circumstances of his own death.

The schedule showed a six o'clock evening meeting with light refreshments. He jotted the meeting location on a post-it note.

The front door opened and his mother struggled in with a loaded shopping bag in her arms. He folded the note, stuck it in his back pocket and hurried to help her, silently willing his phone to ring with a call from the ME.

He was hungry.

Theo watched the digital clock on the microwave flick to four o'clock. He rattled the Yahtzee dice in the cup and tossed them onto the table. "Large straight."

His mother clucked. "You do have the luck with these dice, Teddy."

"This'll have to be my last round, Ma. I've got to get ready to go out."

"But you haven't had dinner."

His father put a hand on Joyce's arm. "It's all right. He's meeting his girlfriends."

Joyce peered at him with round eyes. "Oh," she said.

Theo didn't bother to correct the information. He waited for his parents to take their turns with the dice, then rolled four of a kind and neatly wrapped up the game.

"That's it. I'm going to go change."

"If you must," Joyce said, double-checking his addition. "I could press your jeans for you, if you'd like."

"No, thanks. I'm good." He retreated to the basement where he changed out of his sweatpants and into jeans and a dark green t-shirt. He took a moment to decide which shoes to wear, and finally settled on a pair of brown leather sandals instead of his usual tennis shoes. In the bathroom, he ran a comb through his hair and brushed his teeth.

He studied his reflection in the mirror and thought maybe the dark green color of his shirt brought out the green in his hazel eyes. Maybe.

"Bye, Mom, Dad," he said as he walked through the living room.

"Have fun, Teddy," his mother called.

His father actually winked.
Jesus.

Theo stepped off the bus at Forbes and South Craig in Oakland. He glanced at the building to his right, saw the lights on and people milling about, but crossed the street and entered the Kiva Han coffee shop.

"What'll it be?" The girl behind the counter sported pigtails high on her head, heavy black eye make-up and a ring through each nostril. Her spiked necklace squeezed tight above a worn Dead Can Dance t-shirt.

He peered at the shirt and wondered if it was for the band or a statement of undead ability. Probably the band.

"Hello? You want a drink or my shirt?"

"Key Lime Italian soda, please. Large." He dropped a five-dollar bill on the counter.

Miss Goth turned back to the soda fountain, grabbed a cup and filled it with ice. He watched her pour the syrups and cream into the cup, then fill it with club soda. She snapped a lid in place and pushed the drink across the counter.

"No change." Theo snagged a straw from a dispenser.

Her face brightened. "Thanks." She had a pretty smile, with straight white teeth; it was unexpected on such a hard-looking girl.

He stood outside the Kiva Han and surveyed the building across the street. Before the Event, it'd been a Subway, but a lot of chains went out of business and the city converted the old sandwich shop into a community meeting center. The large glass windows gave Theo a clear view of the people gathered inside.

No Marjorie in sight. He wasn't going in until he was sure she was there.

He used the straw to stir the cream into the soda and syrup mixture and took a long draw on the straw. The ice cold soda chilled him from the inside out and he shuddered, wished for a moment he'd brought a sweatshirt.

"Theo!"

He looked up South Craig Street. Marjorie walked toward him, flanked by a teenage boy and a woman.

"Hey there," she said with a giant smile. "You ready?"

He swept a hand through his hair and tried to look suave. "Sure."

She took his arm and led him across the street; the woman and teen followed close behind. Theo inhaled deeply to control his nervousness. The scent of oranges and cinnamon reached his nose from the zombie beside him. He lifted his chin and squared his shoulders.

Once inside, Theo's resolve crumbled just a bit. He stopped counting at a dozen people seated around the room, chatting quietly. Another small cluster of undead stood near the refreshments table and a few more sat near the front of the room.

He glanced at his watch. Still twenty minutes before the meeting was due to start. How many more would show? His confidence wavered. Public speaking had never been his forte, and the room was kept at a warmer-than-usual temperature, probably just for their meeting. The living wouldn't appreciate the heat, but Theo found it made his reaction time a bit faster. This was both a blessing and a curse, since it meant he couldn't bet on his anxiety being dulled by air conditioning.

Marjorie steered him around by his elbow, introducing him to attendees. He caught a name here and there, and nodded to everyone, but his nerves prevented him from retaining any information.

He'd been to a couple of these meetings back when they started, a few years after the Event. He found them to be mostly a waste of time. How could a zombie move past their death and back into the world of the living if he or she continued to dwell on death? AA, NA, and Al-Anon...he supposed they served a purpose since they focused on recovery and preventing relapse. But the undead support groups? They were all about rehashing the same things.

"I died in my neighbor's basement. Four men from down the street, people I grew up with, beat me to death with sledgehammers."

Theo would rather not remember, and he definitely didn't want to admit it to a group of strangers.

One couldn't exactly recover from dying or prevent a relapse. So what good was a support group?

Marjorie squeezed his elbow. "Theo, this is Natalie Duvall. Natalie's been running the group since its inception, back in the early years. She's a First Gen."

"Natalie, this is Theo Walker. I mentioned I would bring him along tonight."

"Walker. Your last name is Walker?" She chuckled.

He scowled. She looked familiar. He stuck out his hand. "Have we met?"

Natalie's somber gaze settled on Theo and she grasped his hand. "I think we were both at Mercy Hospital after the Event."

Theo searched his memory, studied her face for a moment before it hit him. "I remember. You were locked in a room. They said you killed a man and..."

Her expression darkened. "Those were difficult days. The transition was harder for some than others."

Theo inspected her more closely. She exhibited the signs of a violent awakening. The milky iris of one eye didn't match the rich brown of the other. Thin white scars on her face bore testament to the self-loathing that came frequently after realization. The lack of fingernails at the ends of her remaining eight fingers confirmed Theo's suspicions. Back in the beginning, before the medical establishment understood what was happening, they resorted to unethical means to render a violent zombie harmless. Theo knew of First Gen zombies with no fingernails or teeth.

Theo gave her hand a squeeze, at a loss. "Sorry. I'm glad you got better." He couldn't think of anything else to say, but she didn't seem to mind.

"Me, too," she said, and walked toward the front of the room, a slight limp apparent in her stride.

Marjorie led him around the room, introduced him to more people than he could keep straight. How was it possible that there were this many undead living in Pittsburgh? He'd no idea the numbers were this high.

And this was probably only a fraction of the total population.

"Marjorie," he put his hand on her arm to prevent her from moving to the next group. "I want to let you know before I make the announcement to the group that three more bodies were found yesterday."

Marjorie's smile faded. "Three more?"

"In Frick Park."

She put a hand to her mouth. "How?"

"Same as the others," he said. Not too much detail to scare her, but the truth nonetheless.

She fell silent, but her gaze was steady on his face.

"I just wanted to tell you so it wouldn't be a surprise."

She nodded. "Thanks."

He gestured around the room. "How many undead are in the city?"

"At last count—and we can't be sure we have an accurate number—it's three hundred seventy-eight. Another rises every month or so."

"Three hundred and seventy-eight? Really? How many after the Event? How many did we start with?"

Marjorie looked at her shoes. "We started with eighty-nine, Theo. That was twelve years ago."

"Eighty-nine." He echoed her like an idiot. "How many of the original are left?"

"All of us."

"All of us?" Theo wanted to ask another question, but Natalie's voice sounded across the room.

"Hey, everyone. We're going to get started in a minute or two, so if you want a drink or something to eat during the meeting, get it now." She pointed at the refreshments table. "Donuts are courtesy of Anne and Kerri-Leigh brought us the delicious vegan peanut butter cookies. Everyone say thanks!"

Vegan cookies for a group of zombies? Theo tried to hide his bewilderment. They stifled their zombie under the guise of the still living. The façade reinforced his opinion of zombie support groups.

The group murmured their thanks and the stragglers moved toward the food and coffee. Marjorie pointed Theo toward a chair in the front corner, so he sat with his soda, assessing the group. Maybe two-dozen zombies sat in folding chairs, sipping coffee or noshing on cookies.

In the few moments it took for everyone to get their goodies and settle in, Marjorie took a chair at the front table. She arranged several stacks of paper on the table, and then gave Theo a big smile.

His knees wobbled a bit. Damn the warm temperature.

Natalie stood behind the table. "Hey, everyone. Welcome back to our regulars and welcome to the new faces I see. We're glad you're here. I'm Natalie Duvall; I run the support center here in Pittsburgh and this is one of several meetings we hold for both established zombies and those recently turned. Since we have some new folks here tonight, I'll give my quick overview of what we do."

She gestured to the stacks of papers Marjorie arranged along the front of the table. "If you're new, please grab a contact form and fill it out. Give me an email address if you'd like to get updates or a cell phone number for text updates. Our contact information is on another sheet. You can follow us on various social media outlets to keep on top of meeting times."

Theo half-listened to Natalie give her spiel about the purpose of the meetings, which involved creating a unified undead community, providing services to zombies who'd been victims of discrimination and the like. The other half of Theo's mind raced. What was he supposed to say to these people?

"Theo Walker is here from the Pittsburgh Bureau of Investigation and the Allegheny County Medical Examiner's Office." Marjorie had, at some point, addressed the group and now introduced him. "He's got some information for us regarding community safety."

A smattering of applause followed him as he strode to the spot in front of the table that Marjorie vacated. For each zombie applauding there was one with a puzzled expression.

"Uh, hi." Theo leaned against the table and it creaked.

He stood back.

"Um, I work for the Pittsburgh crime scene investigation division," he said. After only a slight pause, he continued, "I also assist Dr. Libitin, the Allegheny county medical examiner on certain cases."

A few people shifted in their metal chairs, but no one booed.

"We've, uh, we've had a few unusual cases come through the department recently and the medical examiner seems to think they could affect the undead community."

No one shifted. Their rapt attention made Theo's palms sweat. He looked around for Marjorie. She stood at the end of the table, her gentle smile encouraged him to continue.

"Okay, yeah, so these cases have all involved potential risers, people who have the tattoo. They're all killed in, uh, such a manner as to prevent them from rising."

Zombie faces peered levelly at him. This was not a group prone to hysteria after what they'd all been through. Theo's courage swelled a bit.

"Dr. Libitin seems to think it's possible this killer might branch out into killing zombies. The victims have all died in ways that would effectively inanimate zombies as well. We're not sure if this is a trial run for killing zombies or if there's some other motive at work."

Low murmurs began in the crowd and a few people dug cell phones out of pockets and purses.

Marjorie stepped forward. "We're not trying to cause a panic, folks. This is just a public safety announcement. We do have some advocates in government, no matter what the popular view is, who are concerned with our safety. We're just saying that everyone should use caution. Be vigilant and safe. If you see anything strange, if any of your friends turn up missing, please let us know." She pointed at a stack of business cards at the table. "Some of you might not have my contact information. Take one of these. If you want to talk about this or let us know about something you see, just call me."

A blonde woman in the back of the room raised her hand. "How many deaths are we talking about?"

Theo bit his bottom lip. "Keep in mind this is privileged information. We can make tenuous connections between eight bodies."

The murmuring grew a bit louder.

"When did this start?" the blonde woman said. Theo thought briefly about choking her.

"Uh, the first body was found this past Sunday."

They weren't murmuring anymore. "Eight? Since Sunday?"

Theo held his hands up. "Please keep in mind these deaths are only possibly connected. The ME, based on preliminary findings, just wanted me to let you know so we can spread the word to be careful." The audience began to talk amongst themselves and Theo turned to Marjorie for help.

"Come on, people," she shouted. "The chances these killings are related are still slim. This is a precaution. Don't overreact. It's better to know, right? Would you rather we didn't say anything?"

The noise level receded and folks turned in their chairs to face the front again.

Theo spoke up. "Seriously. Just use common sense. Stay in groups when you can and keep me informed. I didn't bring any business cards, but if you want a direct line to me I can write my number on the back of Marjorie's card." He neglected to mention he didn't have a business card. Forensic techs weren't important enough for cards.

The rest of the meeting flew by; newer zombies introduced themselves and were paired off with established zombies in a sponsor-type relationship.

Theo had never heard anything so ridiculous.

When the meeting wrapped up, many people stepped forward to take Marjorie's card and more than a few asked Theo how they could stay in touch. He gave his cell phone number to each.

His watch showed nine before the zombies began to trickle out of the old Subway. Theo dropped his head into his hands and rubbed his face. He looked up when he felt someone press his shoulder.

"You did good." Marjorie's smile—just for him—made the entire stupid evening worthwhile.

"You think? This wasn't supposed to stir up trouble."

She shook her head. "I don't think it will. They'll react here, but once they're back outside, after they've thought it over, things will be normal. They'll be careful, and with any luck, we'll get a lead out of it."

Theo raised an eyebrow. "You have a lot of confidence in them."

"I brought quite a few of them through the transition. I know them." She gave him a tired smile and shouldered her bag. "I've got to get going. Thanks for coming tonight."

"My pleasure." Well, at least part of it.

She said goodbye to Natalie with a hug, then held the door open for another zombie before stepping through herself, that long, luscious black hair swinging behind her.

Theo looked up, face burning, when Natalie cleared her throat.

"Thanks for the warning." She pointed at the closing door. "Marjorie wasn't sure she'd get you here."

Theo shrugged. "I didn't want to come. But Dr. Libitin asked me, too."

"It's better for everyone to at least know to be careful." Natalie packed leftover papers into a Whole Foods bag. "You have a problem with us."

It wasn't a question. Theo squirmed. "Not really a problem. If it helps someone, great. It's just not for me."

"Why not?"

"I don't see the point. We're dead. It's an immutable fact. We can't relapse or recover; it's not something we can discuss away."

"No, but it's good to be around people like yourself. It's a reminder we're not alone, no matter what others might make us think." She finished packing up the bags. "To each his own, but you might be surprised."

"Maybe."

Natalie thanked the zombies who'd stayed behind to clean up the refreshments. She grabbed a bag of cookies and thrust them at Theo. "Take these. Think about coming back," she said. "We all cope in our own ways, but we owe it to each other to stick together. You don't have to approve of everything. Who knows? You might find something you like." She refused to meet his gaze as she limped from the room.

What the hell did she mean? Theo watched her exit, thoughts churning. Something he would like? What was she getting at?

Theo peered in the bag at the vegan cookies and shuddered.

CHAPTER 9

Theo jiggled his leg up and down. He sat in the storage room, behind a stack of pipette boxes, sweating.

He couldn't remember the last time he'd sweat. Crying and sweating required more of a response than his cool, slow zombie metabolism could manage. Unfortunately, drooling at the sight of human flesh was still within reason. Death loved irony.

The liquid ran down the side of his face and he swiped at it with a finger, rubbed it between thumb and forefinger, and licked it. Salty. Seemed just like the sweat from before he'd died.

Why now, after twelve years? He felt hot and antsy, too, sort of like what he remembered as being the beginning of an anxiety attack. But that made no sense, because the transition robbed the undead of the ability to process hormones and other chemicals with any speed. After he'd risen and adjusted, his once-frequent anxiety attacks, heartburn, and high blood pressure all disappeared. Hell, even his acne went away.

It appeared that death had been good for Theo's health. The irony of that statement was not lost on him.

So why the fuck was he sweating?

He spent yesterday pacing in his basement bedroom, irritated at his parents and at the cat. He ate more than usual. His mother commented she'd have to make another run to the butcher for more meat. Her statement, made off-hand and not meant to offend, further blackened his mood and by now, Monday late afternoon, his attitude was seriously shitty. Even Skeet avoided him.

He stared at his twitching knee. The leg bounce was a habit right out of his animated years, too. He pounded on his thigh with a fist, frustrated.

His cell phone rang and he fumbled it out of his pants pocket.

Dr. Libitin. Finally.

"Hello?"

"Theo, how are you?"

Fucked up. "I'm good. You?"

A sigh. "Busy. The three from last week are just adding to this mess."

Theo waited.

The doctor cleared his throat. "Can you come down for a consultation?"

A wash of relief spiraled through him. "I'll be there in twenty minutes."

"I take it there were no new bodies over the weekend?"

"None found," said the medical examiner and gestured Theo through the door he held open. "That's not to say no new murders, we just didn't find any."

Theo walked through the door into the autopsy room. He immediately saw a cubicle made from the blue cloth dividers.

"I'm not sure how you want to handle this, if you think it would be better to just do them right in a row or take a break between." Dr. Libitin busied himself at the sink behind the dividers.

Theo shrugged. "I don't know. Let's try the first one and see what happens. I'll tell you if I need a break."

"You wait here, I'll get the first." He pulled back the partition and Theo squeezed into the tight space.

He listened to the sounds of the medical examiner retrieving a table from cold storage. In only a few minutes, Theo stood aside as the doctor pushed a gurney into the cubicle and pulled back the white sheet.

The body of a Caucasian brunette lay prone on a metal autopsy table. Her head was positioned a few inches away from her neck, just above the body. Heavy suture lines in the classic Y incision were evident on her torso, along with other signs of a thorough autopsy, but her body had been prepped to send to a funeral home.

Her head, however, was not. The scalp stretched over her face, retracted to allow access to the skull, which rested on the table next to her head. Part of her brain sat in the bony cavity, exposed. Most of it was missing; Theo knew the organ underwent examination and sectioning during the autopsy.

What was left lay naked before him, a cool, glistening mass of grisly jelly. He felt his blood begin to move into the telltale swelling of an erection and his hands balled into fists.

He swallowed hard and clamped down on his excitement. This couldn't be happening. Just calm down, Theo. No way could he let the doc see him do this with a hard-on.

After a moment the surge retreated and he felt his dick go flaccid again. He turned to Dr. Libitin and tried to keep the accusatory tone from his voice. "I wondered why you didn't call me on Saturday. Or at least yesterday."

"Couldn't. The detectives were all over the place on Saturday. This is a big deal." The ME gestured at the table. "We did the preliminary autopsies on Saturday with Milton and a couple other witnesses, and the lab crew and I finished up with the paperwork yesterday. We had a full house."

Theo studied the body, his irritation dissolving just a bit. "That makes sense."

"We're just now back to the normal crew, and I had Shelby take the other techs out to lunch as a thank you for working the weekend."

Shelby. "Does she know I'm here?"

Dr. Libitin nodded. "She'll keep them out for an hour, hour and a half, at least. If we only get through one, that's fine, but I'd like to try to finish all three." He waved at the table. "Ready to get started?"

Theo suppressed a grin. "Yeah." With no small effort, he casually stepped to the table. "How much?"

"There's a cut section inside the brain case."

Upon closer inspection, he could see a chunk of brain, a generous two-inch cube rested inside the bone cavity. He felt a flutter in his stomach.

"Which one?" he said, not trusting his voice to cover his agitation.

"This is Rhonda Abraham. She was found on the bottom of the pile, and evidence shows she's been dead the longest of the three. We estimate her death to have occurred Wednesday afternoon or evening, but that's as narrow a window as we could get without laboratory testing. Those results could take a week." Dr. Libitin looked away. "I thought maybe you could narrow it down further."

Theo reached out and stroked her hair with the back of his hand, connecting with the woman laid bare on the table before him. The strands reached past the end of her neck, long and silky. Her facial features were hidden by her scalp, which was inverted to allow access to her skull. He gently peeled the scalp back to look at her face.

"She was forty-two. Two kids. Her mother had the kids but didn't bother to report her missing; figured she'd taken off with a man." The doctor's voice sounded hollow and distant.

It was a face of one accustomed to hard living. Premature aging made her seem older than forty-two, and three missing teeth accentuated her decline. Unusual angles in her nose indicated at least one break.

Theo folded the scalp back over her face, used one hand to cup her chin and the other for the back of her head, then closed his eyes and raised the head to his nose and mouth. He held the skull to his face, rubbed his lips in the liquid, parted them and sucked in the fluids.

Immediately, his sanity exploded. The tang of the diluted blood tickled the back of his throat, brought his senses into sharp relief. The smallest of sounds clanged through his body, the smell of slowly decaying tissue roused his appetite.

Saliva dribbled down his chin and he rubbed it in the bloody flesh around the edges of her skull, tantalizing himself with the knowledge that the brain matter awaited him. His nose bumped the cold, gelatinous organ and he pressed it further in, filling his nostrils. He held the tissue there for a moment before exhaling.

The smooth interior of the brain case called to him, so he ran his tongue along the sleek, wet bone. When he encountered the chunk of brain matter, he swirled his tongue around it and drew it into his mouth.

The sun shone down hot on her head and she swatted away flies. This'd better not be a sham. Her temper, exacerbated by the heat, flared, so she lit another cigarette in an attempt to chill out and drive the bugs away. She hated nature.

In the distance she could hear children playing, but couldn't make out the voices of her own. She asked her mother to keep them at the playground while she met with... whatever this was.

Theo rolled the brain around his mouth, trying to make contact with every surface, to taste as much he could possibly taste. The tissue broke apart at the edges; he smeared it across his teeth.

She took a long drag on the cigarette and tugged her tight skirt down. Rustling to her left caught her attention. Good. It's about time.

"Come with me." Whoever it was, moved off through the trees and Rhonda swatted branches away in her effort to keep up.

Theo pressed the gray matter against the roof of his mouth and pulverized it, then swallowed.

Bits of sunlight were visible through the leaves and trees. "Where the fuck are we going? Why do we have to be out here for this?"

"Just a little further now," came a voice, although he couldn't quite tell if the voice was male or female, or how close.

She pushed through a mass of branches into a tiny clearing. "What the fuck?" she managed to get out as a silver blade swung from the side and made contact with her neck.

Painless. The last thing she saw? Leaves.

She hated nature.

Theo forced his eyelids open, focused on the table below him. He'd bent forward at the waist, laid his head on the table beside Rhonda's head. Her sightless eyes would have peered at him if they'd been open.

Dr. Libitin stepped forward and grasped his shoulder. "You okay, son?"

Theo struggled to breathe regularly. "Yeah. How long?"

The ME searched Theo's face. "Fifteen minutes or thereabout. You need a break?"

"Just a minute or two. I can keep going." His dick pressed against his pants in an attempt to rise, so Theo stayed bent forward, leaned over the body, pressed his nose into her cheek, and rubbed his face on the fragrant skin between her shoulder and neck. He throbbed in places he hadn't throbbed since his death.

"Did you, uh, did you sense anything useful?"

"She went to the park to see someone. Whoever she met did this."

"Any idea why or who it was?"

Theo suppressed a surge of anger. "Not really, just that she was afraid it might be a sham. She was not happy about being in the park and hoped whatever the meeting was about would be worth it."

"Any idea of time?"

Theo replayed the scene in his head. "The light was bright and still fairly high overhead. I'd have to guess it was more afternoon than evening. Definitely before dinnertime."

"So probably toward our earlier estimates." Dr. Libitin rearranged Rhonda's head and covered the body. "I'm going to put this one away and bring the next out, okay? You sit down until I come back."

Theo sank into a plastic chair and dropped his head into his hands. His blood thumped through his veins in the irregular pattern of the undead. He felt warm and energized; both sensations were a rare treat, and he reveled in the movement of the hot, pulsating liquid in his veins.

The squeaky wheels of another autopsy table caught his attention. Dr. Libitin rolled the slab into place and folded back the sheet from the body. She had large, natural breasts, and a vee of curly pubic hair. His hands ached to massage those breasts and he kept them on the table only with effort.

This woman's dark chocolate skin lost its luster in death and appeared ashen. Her head lay several inches away from her shoulders, exposing a network of small veins and trailing meat. The corpse was old enough to have dried a little, and the red mass at the neck was just a bit congealed.

Theo's cock stiffened further and he ran his hands through his hair in agitation, his blood roared in his ears. He reigned in resentment at the presence of the ME. He wanted to be alone. He hadn't felt so alive since his death... maybe not even before. The intensity of the response left him both exhilarated and afraid.

"Name?" His throat was dry and his voice sounded hoarse. He could tell from the expression on Dr. Libitin's face he didn't sound quite right. "What's her name?"

"You okay?"

Theo nodded, a rough jerk of his head. "Let's do this."

Dr. Libitin squinted before continuing. He flipped the flap of her face back over her scalp so Theo could see her. "This is Jennifer Semuta, twenty-four. Her place of residence is listed as Robin Court."

Robin Court, a small complex of squalid, government-assistance apartments was located near the Rankin Bridge. Theo knew the area only because of proximity. Drug use skyrocketed by the general population after the Event, and Robin Court fell quickly into chaos.

"Ms. Semuta was never reported missing. She lived off and on with her grandmother, who also has custody of her son. According to the grandmother, she had a habit of being gone for a week or so at a time."

Her hair was cropped close to her head, and the short style showed off high cheekbones. Theo ran one finger along her hairline, smoothing the skin of her forehead. Pretty girl. "Same as the last one?"

"Yes, there's brain matter in the skull."

Theo folded the flap of skin back down, lifted the head to his face and breathed.

The inside of her skull smelled of metal and mold, of the tang of blood and the musk of decay. He ran his tongue along the inside of her brain case, inhaling and exhaling quickly to gather as much scent as possible.

The world moved up and down quickly, air rushed past his ears, and the voices of children made her smile. Someday her little boy would be big enough to swing, too, and she would put him on her lap and go as high as he wanted.

"Theo?" The ME's voice poked into Theo's brain, into her brain. "Theo? Are you hyperventilating?"

He tore his face from the empty head and snarled at the man who dared interrupt, fluid running down his chin. The doctor took a step back. "If you don't get ahold of yourself, I'm going to put a stop to this."

Theo focused on Dr. Libitin, gripped the head in his hands, and shook his own head. "No, no, I'm okay. Just...let me finish. I'm sorry." He tried to focus on the medical examiner's face, tried to smile reassuringly. Dr. Libitin looked entirely unconvinced, but he didn't press the issue either. Theo turned back to the skull.

A nibble off the portion of gray matter.

A quick look at the cheap watch on her right wrist showed her it was time. She hopped off the swing at its apex, smiled at a boy who laughed with her, and headed for Biddle Trail toward Fern Hollow.

Theo used his lips to wrest a chunk of brain away from the larger piece. He rubbed his upper lip and nose on what was left while he savored the glob in his mouth.

It was hot, and sweat run down the small of her back into her underwear. She squirmed a little, pressed the cotton panties to her skin to absorb the perspiration before it trickled into her butt crack.

She walked down the trail, bouncing a little, swinging her arms. It was a beautiful day for a walk, and she hoped the course of her miserable life would change today. She wanted out of the tiny apartment in the Court, away from the drugs and guns. Her boy deserved better. She would buy a house somewhere nicer, maybe even Swissvale, and move her Granny and son out of the Court. She could have a garden—fresh tomatoes like the ones she saw at the farmers' market. She'd get a tricycle at the Goodwill for Malyk.

Theo frantically rooted in the brain case for the last bit of tissue. He sucked it in greedily, chewing hard and fast. His balls tightened uncomfortably.

"Are you Jennifer?" A pleasant woman's voice came from seemingly nowhere.

She looked around, startled. "Yeah, where are you?"

"Over here. Come to your left just a bit."

Jennifer turned left and peered at the trees in Fern Hollow. "Where are you?"

A flash of black movement and shiny steel was the last thing Jennifer's eyes registered. The vision of a little boy on a tricycle was the final image in her mind.

Theo dropped the head onto the table, bent forward to hide the rock hard dick in his pants and squeeze it between his legs.

"Theo!" Dr. Libitin's voice registered shock. "Be careful. You can't drop a body part."

"Sorry," he croaked, reached behind him for the chair. He scrabbled with his hands, found purchase on the textured plastic, and sat, elbows on knees, head in hands.

"Are you okay? I really think we should stop this."

"No!" Theo almost shouted, gained a tiny bit of control, and continued in a slightly more measured tone. "I'd like to finish with these three. It seems like I get a little closer with each one."

"Closer? What did you see?" Dr. Libitin leaned forward.

"This one had a son, didn't she?"

Dr. Libitin started visibly. "Yes. You saw that? Details like that?"

"I didn't really *see* it...I could kind of feel her thoughts clearly. She was hoping to turn her life around for her son. Very clear."

"What else?"

"It was a woman's voice. When she was walking in the woods, back in Fern Hollow, she was meeting someone, someone with the potential to help her, or give her hope of some sort. That someone was a woman. She heard a female voice, then she died."

"We have a female killer?" Theo could hear the incredulity in the ME's voice. "It's hard enough to believe a man could do the things we're seeing, much less a woman."

"Either it's a female killer, or there are two people involved. Maybe a woman to lure them out."

Dr. Libitin grunted. "Could be. These are the kind of women that might not trust a man, and the type of men that might like meeting with a woman in secret."

"How are they related? Did you find something?"

"Just a hunch. All these victims are low-income, on government assistance, or criminals of some sort. Drugs or prostitution. Kind of the lowest denominator of society. To be blunt and not at all politically correct."

"Except for Naomi." Theo thought back to the mentally challenged girl.

"Except for Naomi," the doctor echoed.

Something pressed at the back of Theo's mind. His cock throbbed to the beat of the blood running his veins, bringing his attention back to the more immediate need. "Just bring the last one out and then...then I think I'll need a minute."

Dr. Libitin pressed his lips into a thin line. "I don't like the way you look, Theo. This isn't like the others."

"I think it's just because there've been so many in such a short time. I'm getting information, visions, stronger than I've ever gotten before. The next one might be the breakthrough. Please. Just bring her out." He struggled to keep the desperation from his voice, but knew he didn't succeed. "I'm just trying to help."

Pathetic. He sounded pathetic. The wash of emotion, the sense of urgency, the delicious feel of the women in the moments before their death...

"Please." He cleared his throat.

Dr. Libitin took a deep breath, seemed to wrestle with the issue. "This is, quite honestly, against my better judgment. Something's wrong with you."

Oh, no, Doc. Something's very right.

"I'm fine. It's just very emotional." Theo managed to keep his voice even. "It's hard to know I'm watching these people's last moments on earth, but I want to keep going. To help find the killer and bring this monster to justice."

That seemed to tip the balance for the medical examiner. "All right." The doctor covered Jennifer's body and pushed the autopsy table back into cold storage.

Theo massaged his erection through his pants until he heard the telltale squeak of another table being wheeled out.

Dr. Libitin pushed the final body into place in front of Theo. "You want to stay sitting for this one?"

He considered the raging boner in his trousers. "Yes, that might be a good idea."

"It's a man. Is that a problem?"

"I don't think so." Dr. Libitin could have wheeled a horse out and Theo wouldn't have been able to say no.

"This was a shooting victim, not another beheading. There wasn't much left of the back of his skull, or his brain, but I managed to save you a few sizeable pieces." The ME grabbed a clipboard from the foot of the table. "Jerry Cullins, age thirty-six. He has a rap sheet thick as a phone book for prostitution and drug charges. Shot execution style, like some of the others. The detectives seem to think he was shot elsewhere and brought to the site, since there was no splatter near the bodies."

Theo tried not to the stare at the covered form. Mr. Hot Pants Hairy Ass. "Estimated time of death?"

"Thursday night sometime." Dr. Libitin kept a wary eye on Theo and drew the white sheet from the body. "Of course, if you can narrow that down any, I would be appreciative."

Mr. Cullins's face was mostly intact, at least the right side of it. The remaining blue eye stared at the ceiling of the morgue indifferently. A strand of long brown hair fell over his shoulder. A gaping hole existed where his left ear should have been and Theo could see the metal of the autopsy table through his skull. His barrel-belly hung over a thin, flaccid penis and drooping testicles. Theo's nostrils widened at the scent of male putrescence, such a different aroma than from the women.

Above what was left of his head sat a small plastic container, with several globs of tissue inside. He opened the container and placed it next to the man's ruined head.

Theo barely maintained control despite the fact a male body lay before him.

A groan escaped his throat and he knew he had to hurry. He fumbled with the container of brain matter, didn't bother to go slow. He emptied the contents into his mouth and sucked frantically.

He sucked hard on the dick in his mouth, wanting to turn this trick as fast as possible. He seemed like an okay guy, but his personal hygiene habits left a little to be desired. He twirled his tongue around the cock and squeezed his balls.

"I'm gonna..."

He released him and the john ejaculated onto the ground. He drew a cloth handkerchief from a pocket to wipe sweat from his brow and Jerry fought back a fit of the giggles. Who carries a cloth handkerchief these days?

"You're good, baby." The john panted.

"That's why you keep coming back." He caressed the money in his thong and watched the man slip around the corner of the building toward the tennis courts. Jerry would give him the usual five minutes to be well away before he walked to the bus stop. He tugged the sequined pants down over his ass cheeks and perched on the curb.

"Hey."

Fuck. Someone had seen them. He whipped his head around to face the voice. "What do you want?"

"Are you always so disgusting?"

Jerry peered into the dark trees, trying to figure out where the voice was coming from and who spoke. Cop? He considered his chances of outrunning the speaker.

A slight form emerged from the shadows, thin, with a black halo. "I asked you a question."

Definitely not a cop. "Bitch. Mind your own fucking business."

And the world exploded.

Theo pitched forward onto the floor as Jerry's brain blew out the back of his head. He felt a hand on his shoulder and struck out. Metal crashed on metal and Theo squeezed his legs together tightly against the pain in his crotch. Urgency compelled him to open his eyes.

Dr. Libitin rose to his feet. "Jesus Christ, Theo, I was trying to help."

"A minute, give me a minute alone. Please." Theo struggled to his knees.

"What's the matter? Maybe I can help." Dr. Libitin took a step toward Theo.

"No! Fuck!" Theo pulled his hair to take his mind off the orgasm threatening to overtake him "Please, just a minute. Go!"

Fear registered on the medical examiner's face and he backed out of the examination area.

Theo fumbled with the button and zipper on his jeans, cursing. He yanked his cock out of his pants and frantically began stroking. He jerked himself off in a matter of seconds, gray-green ejaculate shooting onto the linoleum floor.

He remained on his knees, panting, cock, still hard, hanging out of his jeans.

"Theo, I don't know what happened, but something isn't right. We have to get you out of here before my staff comes back." Dr. Libitin's voice came from the other side of the divider.

Jolted into reality, Theo stuffed his penis back into his boxer briefs and yanked his zipper up over the erection. He grabbed a handful of paper towels from above the sink and wiped his mess off the floor. He dropped the towels into the biohazard disposal box, sure no one would search it.

"I'm sorry, I'm okay now. Come on in."

Dr. Libitin's face was red with fury and an angry red welt swelled below one eye. "What the fuck was that?"

Theo shook his head. "I don't know. I just...it was all really intense. I just needed a minute to collect myself."

"Bullshit, 'collect yourself.' You were out of control."

Theo hung his head, shamed. "I'm sorry."

"I don't think this is a good idea anymore."

Panic struck him like a train. "No, no! I can control it. Maybe we just don't try for three at a time again. I'm sorry."

Dr. Libitin replaced the cover on Jerry Cullins's body and dropped the plastic container into the biohazard box on top of the paper towels. He glanced down into the box and looked back at Theo with reproach. "I do hope you got something from that."

"I did. The shooter was definitely a woman."

Finally, a familiar glimmer in the doctor's eyes replaced the reproach. "You're sure?"

"Absolutely." Theo willed his heartbeat to slow and blood to settle back into its normal flow. "She attacked just after Mr. Cullins turned a trick."

Dr. Libitin nodded and pushed the body toward cold storage. "We'll talk more in my office. Meet me up there."

CHAPTER 10

He stopped in the men's room to clean himself up and splash cool water on his face. His metabolism was cooperating once again and calming down. The simple ritual of washing his hands and face settled his mind as well. His thoughts returned to the autopsy room.

He'd never felt sexual gratification from ingesting brain matter before, but then again, he'd never eaten so much in such a short time. Until this mysterious serial killer, he only had a nibble here and there, never more than a tiny bit every few weeks, if even that. This amount of brain in his system in a week was unprecedented.

He didn't know any other zombie that ate human brains to ask if this reaction was normal. When zombies integrated back into society, the act of eating of human flesh became a serious taboo. Living people were understandably nervous about the possibility of being eaten. Once that chance was eliminated, people and the undead seemed to settle back into the old routines.

He ran his hand through his hair, stared at his reflection in the bathroom mirror. His skin shone clear and pink, lit from within. He looked...alive. And he felt better than he had in years. Blood pumped through his veins in an almost uncomfortable way.

He also witnessed a man get a blowjob. Okay, he'd vicariously given it. After twelve years without sex, indeed without even an orgasm, he was both surprised and not surprised he'd reacted physically.

Could the simple act of eating human flesh change him so drastically? Is this what he'd missed by not feeding in those first days? How did the other First Gen zombies resist the pull to continue eating?

He thought back to the short conversation with Natalie. He wouldn't have to approve of the ways others might cope with their new lives.

Were they all abstaining? Or were they giving in? He wouldn't approve of that... or he wouldn't have approved of it before half an hour ago. Would he now?

He watched his eyes widen in the mirror, the dark brown irises reflecting the overhead fluorescent light. He smiled at his sparkling counterpart.

The door behind him opened and he stepped away from the sink. He gave a brief nod to the tech who'd entered the bathroom, then exited. He walked the short distance down the hall to Dr. Libitin's office and claimed the upholstered chair in front of the desk.

He'd tried since his death to get it up. Sure, he'd tried. A few fumbling experiences in life with the odd girl here and there made up the entirety of his sex life. After death his luck only got worse. He couldn't get it up at all.

None of them could.

Doctors surmised this was a natural response to the slower blood flow and transmission of the necessary hormones and chemicals responsible for sexual performance. Apparently, no zombie guy could get it up and female zombies were unable to orgasm, either by masturbation or other forms of stimulation. It frustrated some zombies, but he didn't care one way or the other, since it hadn't changed anything for him.

Until now.

Theo succeeded in getting it up, it stayed up, and he finished the job.

Not bad for a celibate zombie in his early-thirties.

What the fuck was happening to him?

He sat forward in the chair, rested his elbows on his knees. Confusion battled with excitement.

He could have a sex life again. Or for the first time. But what triggered this?

A light tap on the door caught his attention. He turned to watch Dr. Libitin stride into the office and take the seat behind the desk. Theo shifted his chair slightly to face the medical examiner.

"What was that?"

Theo had to strain to catch the doctor's low voice. "I'm not sure." He shrugged, helpless to explain what occurred and not sure he wanted to share the sensations.

Dr. Libitin studied Theo's face. "I've seen risers just after they turn, just after they awaken. They're vicious, unpredictable...almost inhuman."

Theo snapped his gaze to the doctor.

"I saw that in you today."

He wanted to protest, mentally turned over reasons to tell Dr. Libitin he was wrong, but his mouth wouldn't speak the syllables. No, no, no, that's not how it was.

But that would be a lie. He'd felt a primal, basic fire stoked by eating the brains or maybe by the psychic experience of dying again and again.

He dropped his head back into his hands. "I'm sorry."

"Just tell me what you saw. Hopefully we can salvage this somehow."

Theo resisted the urge to ask Dr. Libitin if he would allow him to continue. Never eating again, never experiencing the final moments of a life. It was too much to bear.

"This is a female killer. Or at least a woman is involved and does the killing some of the time."

The ME's brow furrowed. "I can't imagine a woman being strong enough to take a head off in one stroke. It must be a team of killers. Maybe the woman just does the shooting?"

"But why?"

"Why does anyone kill? Who knows?" Dr. Libitin shrugged and shuffled through paperwork on his desk. "The woman killing thing doesn't surprise me, it's the ferocity."

"Didn't you say you found a connection between these victims?"

"Just the demographics and the tattoos."

Theo pinched his bottom lip. "Except Naomi."

"How many times can we rehash this? She's the enigma. But there's no doubt now she's a victim of this killer. The latest beheadings tie her in."

Theo shook his head. He was missing something. "My experiences tell me that most of these victims—at least out of those I've sampled—were expecting something from the person they were meeting, likely also the one that killed them." Theo paused, tugged on the crotch of his jeans.

"Keep going."

His mind whirled in overdrive; the stimulation of the past few hours was just too much. "There's something more, but I can't nail it down."

"What else did you see?"

"The first one—Rhonda, right? She was impatient and she hated being outside. She heard a voice; she assumed it was the person she was meant to meet, so I felt the assumption, too. I couldn't tell if it was a man or a woman's voice. Maybe because of the time since death? Maybe the fresher they are, the better picture I get?"

Dr. Libitin maintained eye contact with Theo.

"The second one was happier. She thought something good would come out of the meeting. It was a woman's voice, then the flash of what I know to be the weapon, and nothing."

Theo rubbed his face. "Do you have any water in here?"

"I'll get you some." The doctor walked out of the office and Theo listened to his footsteps retreat down the hall. He reached inside his pants and repositioned his now flaccid penis.

Dr. Libitin reappeared with a cold bottle of water. "I'm sorry, all we have is cold."

"That's okay, I think I want cold water right now." He twisted the cap off and chugged down half the bottle before placing the bottle on the desk in front of him. The icy liquid trailed a path down to his stomach, a sensation he remembered from before he died. It felt wonderful, like life again.

"How was the last one different?" The sound of the doctor's voice brought him back to the problem at hand.

"Mr. Cullins wasn't meeting anyone. He was turning a trick behind the building by the tennis courts at Frick Park. It was dark. He finished, waited for the guy to walk away and someone called to him. I got the impression of a slight person walking from the trees and shooting. It was a total surprise." Theo skimmed over the details of the blowjob, wanting to keep that to himself for later consumption.

"So we potentially have a killer who both plans their marks and is opportunistic." Dr. Libitin poked a finger on a stack of papers. "But how does Naomi fit into this? Her family is solid middle class. The only distinguishing factor about her was the retardation."

Again, that niggling feeling at the back of Theo's mind. "You said the others all lived at the lower end of the socioeconomic scale. Naomi doesn't fit that, but because she was retarded she may not have been perceived as contributing anything to society, either. Maybe not a criminal, but flotsam. A non-entity."

Dr. Libitin frowned. "That's hardly politically correct, Theo."

"Neither is murder."

Theo eyed the man smoking the cigarette with envy. He wasn't a smoker, never had been. It just seemed like it would be nice to have something to do with his hands while he waited for the bus. His mind continued to wander back to the incident in the autopsy room.

Zombies could still get lung cancer.

"Hi, Theo."

The voice came from just over his shoulder and he stepped sideways in surprise.

Marjorie giggled. "I'm sorry. Didn't mean to startle you."

"Hey." Theo leaned against the bus shelter, tried to look nonchalant. "What are you doing here?"

"I'm finished for the day, but I drove in with Shelby this morning and she's still at the morgue. Figured I might get home faster on the bus than if I wait for her."

Theo watched her mouth form the words but barely heard them. Her pale lips pressed together and separated. "Uh huh."

She tilted her head to one side. "Are you okay?"

"Um, yeah." He refocused his gaze on her eyes, her almond-shaped eyes, so dark brown they were almost black. "You're taking the bus this evening."

"Yes. I do sometimes. It's relaxing. I can read while someone else drives."

He felt a jolt of adrenaline and decided to take a chance. "You hungry?"

"Kind of. You want to grab a bite?"

"Yeah. Let's stop in Oakland at Fuel and Fuddle."

"Sounds good."

The hiss of air brakes interrupted further discussion and they squeezed onto the bus along with the few other people at the stop. Theo sat near the back of the bus and watched Marjorie claim one closer to the middle. She turned and smiled at him before pulling a book from her bag.

Something in his midsection turned over in a very pleasant way. He'd actually asked her to dinner. Just Marjorie and him. He peered over the people seated between them at the back of her head. Butterflies fluttered in his stomach, but she appeared cool, and tucked her hair behind her ear.

The ride to Oakland took longer than Theo could remember it ever taking before. Finally, the bus lurched to a stop at Forbes and Oakland Avenue. He pushed his way through the crowd and took Marjorie's elbow as she rose from her seat.

"Ready?"

She smiled and they stepped off the bus before the commuter crowd could shove their way on. On the sidewalk, as they wound their way through the folks waiting for another bus, Marjorie slipped her hand into the crook of his elbow.

Those butterflies threatened to turn his stomach inside out.

They walked the short block from the bus stop to the corner of Forbes and Oakland Avenue. Theo enjoyed the feel of Marjorie's hand on his arm, and was almost surprised when a voice called out near him.

"Spare change? You got any change?"

He hesitated and looked down at the speaker. Crazy Betty. Oakland had its fair share of panhandlers, and it seemed like Betty had been around forever.

She raised a filthy arm and pulled her sleeve back to show a crude *riser* tattoo. "Help out someone who will be like you someday."

Marjorie pulled a couple bills from her coat pocket and handed them over. "Get something hot to eat." She patted Betty's shoulder, then pulled Theo away, her hand back on his arm.

"That was nice," Theo said.

"Betty's harmless." Marjorie's tone sounded stiff, and Theo studied her profile, but could see no hint of tension.

At the restaurant, Theo held the door for her, and she removed her hand. He was almost disappointed, but the knowledge she was his for the next hour or so made up for it.

"You want a table or a booth?" The hostess wore a black apron over loud purple jeans and a green turtleneck.

Marjorie turned to him. "Booth?"

"Sure."

They followed the hostess to a booth near the back. Plenty of privacy and little light. Theo slid into his side and shrugged off his coat while Marjorie pushed her bag across the opposite bench and took her seat.

He couldn't stop looking at her.

"Jen will be your server." Purple Jeans dropped menus on the table and retreated.

Marjorie peered at his face through the low lighting. "You look great, Theo. I'm glad we decided to do this."

Theo tried to control his reaction. He didn't want her to see him blush. "Thanks. You look pretty fantastic yourself."

She smiled and grabbed a menu. "I haven't been here in forever. What's good?"

Theo scanned the menu for his standard fare. "I always get the same thing."

"What's that?"

"Rosemary's Breasts."

Marjorie giggled. "I love the names. I think I'll have the Chubby Buddha."

Theo relaxed in the warm room, unsure if his energy came from the atmosphere, the company, or was a remnant of his earlier activities. He didn't care. He was alone with Marjorie.

The server came to take their orders. Marjorie asked for hot tea, into which she stirred a packet of sugar. Theo watched her movements, feeling as though her presence were food enough for him.

"So, do you come here a lot?"

"Actually, not too often. My folks don't like to drive into Oakland."

"Your folks?" she said over the rim of her mug as she blew across the surface.

He mentally smacked himself and floundered for an explanation other than "I'm past thirty and still live with my parents." "Uh, yeah," he said. "I eat out once a week with my parents. You know, the family thing."

She nodded. "That's nice. My family lives in San Diego. I see them once a year, for the Chinese New Year. It's a big tradition with us. My parents moved to the US from China."

"They're in San Diego? How'd you end up in Pittsburgh?"

"Came here for college, just never left." She shrugged. "I like it here."

"So is this where you, ah," he stumbled to complete his sentence. Theo had never broached the topic of turning with Marjorie. He wasn't sure if it broke some rule of undead conduct he didn't know about, and mentally smacked himself for giving up on the support groups. "Um, is this where you turned?"

She shook her head. "No. I turned in San Diego and came out here for graduate school. No one knew the old me here. I thought I could start over, you know?"

Her gaze held his. He did know. It was intoxicating, the thought of going somewhere no one knew the old Theo, the live Theo, and building a life based solely on who he was now. The temptation hung in the air before him all the time, but he had nothing to take with him, no skills with which to get a job, no possessions, and no money.

It was something out of his reach.

But she'd done it.

His attraction for her swelled.

The server put their meals in front them, the rosemary encrusted chicken breasts in front of him, and the teriyaki chicken over rice for Marjorie. Conversation centered on menial things while they ate. Marjorie seemed to avoid certain subjects. Maybe he overstepped when he asked about where she turned. His palms started to sweat a little, and he wiped them on his napkin, hoping she didn't see. He wasn't sure what she'd make of sweaty palms.

"I think Mel Gibson is the absolute worst choice to direct a movie about the Event. I mean, look what he did to Jesus and then all that anti-Semite stuff he was in the news for. I'd like to see someone younger and more open-minded direct the movie. How about Shia LaBeouf?"

Theo tried to drag his attention back to what Marjorie was talking about—what the hell was she talking about?—but he struggled to focus. "Um, yeah, sure I think he'd be good."

Marjorie gave him a satisfied grin. "See? No one else agrees with me."

"Well, I do." Theo reached across the table and laid his hand on Marjorie's.

She didn't pull hers away and his pulse quickened.

Their server appeared and started piling dirty dishes one on top of another. "How about some coffee or dessert?"

"I'd love another pot of tea." Marjorie peered across the table at him. "If you're not in any rush."

"I'm definitely not. I'll have coffee."

She turned her hand over underneath his and squeezed. "Good. We have more time."

Theo was afraid he turned transparent and she could see the desire rippling just under his surface. He made himself back off just a notch; fear of rejection tempering his enthusiasm. This one would really hurt; he liked Marjorie a lot.

"So," she said when a fresh pot of water sat in front of her and Theo poured cream into his coffee. "You're from Pittsburgh?"

He nodded, grabbed a couple packets of sugar. "Yep. Born and raised Yinzer."

"Died here?"

He stopped shaking the packets briefly, then ripped them open and emptied them into the mug of coffee. "Yeah. Died here, too."

"How did it happen for you?"

Theo sipped his coffee and considered the question. He studied her eyes, but could find no derision.

He decided to take a chance.

"I don't usually talk about it," he began.

Her expression turned to one of embarrassment. "I'm sorry. I should have known better than to ask. When I work with a recently turned undead, and even in meetings, it's something we get out in the open right away, so no one wonders and no one steps on any toes. I apologize."

He squeezed her hand again. "It's okay. I don't usually talk about it, but I think it's okay to tell you."

Her chest rose and fell in a big inhalation and exhalation. "Whew. I thought I made a mistake."

"No, you didn't." And, over coffee and tea, he recalled the night he'd been chased by a mob of his childhood neighbors, who were scared witless and panicked into murder by the solar radiation and the stories of the dead rising. How he'd sought refuge behind a furnace in a house a couple blocks from his parents' home and been found and beaten with broomsticks, sledgehammers, and mallets. No amount of pleading, of crying, or of trying to convince them he wasn't dead stopped the violence. His screams fell on ears deafened by fear, by a sudden, irrevocable change in the world and in the rules they'd all taken for granted throughout time.

They'd beaten him to death behind the cold furnace, and it was in that same spot he'd woken, wedged between the machine and the cinder-block wall.

He'd never been sure exactly when or how he'd lost his clothes, but all he wore when he crawled, days after his death, through the shrubs between the backyards of his neighbors was the filthy white tank top and a pair of red Converse sneakers. The sneakers were his. He couldn't remember ever owning the wife-beater shirt.

"How did you handle the beginning?" Marjorie's hands were wrapped around her mug.

"I didn't really. I was locked in the neighbor's basement for the first few days. It wasn't until I started to come around, back to my senses, that I realized I would have to break a window to get out."

And he'd slipped through the tiny ground-level window, leaving trails of his own flesh, a testament to the gore he left behind in the basement when the anger and horror ravaged him. At least his scars were easily hidden.

"So you didn't feed?"

Theo slipped a couple twenties into the check folder and left it at the end of the table. He considered how much to divulge. When most of the undead rose, they battled a horrible need to feed, generally on human flesh. In the beginning, this had disastrous results for human-zombie relations, obviously. Now there were ways around the frenzy, which Marjorie employed in her capacity as a counselor.

There weren't other humans in the basement where he rose. "No, I didn't."

Her gaze swept over his face, examining the details. He knew what her next question would be and dread threatened to bring Rosemary's Breasts back up. The humiliation of those first days...he was loathe to relive it and desperate to not admit it to Marjorie.

"How were you able to control it?" Marjorie's expression was one of confusion. "Even the ones we help now need so much sedation. It's hard to imagine turning and not wanting to feed." She whispered the last word.

Theo steeled himself. "I didn't really have the opportunity."

"Hey guys!" A voice carried over the din of the restaurant.

CHAPTER 11

The words Theo didn't want to speak died on his tongue as Shelby approached, smiling. She wore an outfit nearly as loud as the hostess's—tight green pants made of some kind of stretchy material and a striped shirt. Her hair was pulled back in a loose ponytail. A smile tugged the corners of his mouth at the sight of the purple Converse sneakers.

Thank God. And Theo didn't believe in God.

"Hey, Shelby," he said with an exhale of relief.

The morgue technician slid onto the bench with Marjorie, playfully shouldering her out of the way. Marjorie held her tea mug in the air to avoid spilling it and laughed. "Your ass takes up too much space, Shel."

Shelby feigned hurt and lifted one butt cheek off the seat. "Aw, you hurt its feelings. Kiss it."

Marjorie rolled her eyes. "Look at this, Theo. See how she treats me?"

Theo, both happy to be included and jealous of the friendship between the girls, smiled at Marjorie.

"What are you doing here?" Marjorie mopped tea off the table.

Shelby poked her chin in the direction of a group of people just pushing in their chairs. "Morgue tech night out. Poor servers." She shook her head sadly. "I think they draw straws to see who has to wait on us."

Theo chuckled. "I bet."

"You guys done?" Shelby swiped the receipt holder and peeked inside. "Looks like it. You need rides home?"

"That would be great." Marjorie stuffed her wet napkin in the empty mug.

Theo's heart fell. There went any chance of Marjorie inviting him back to her place. "Sure," he said. At least he wouldn't have to get back on a bus.

They followed Shelby out of the restaurant and to her car. She'd found on-street parking for her tiny hatchback just down Oakland Ave.

Marjorie opened the passenger door, pushed the seat forward, and climbed in the back. She pulled the seat back in place. "Shotgun, Theo, since you'll get out first."

He dropped into the bucket seat. "Okay."

Shelby wielded out a mass of clanking key chains. She fished through the assortment of University of Pittsburgh emblems.

"Pitt fan?" Theo said.

"Alum. Got my bachelor's there. Working on my masters." She found the car key and saluted him with it. "Not just a fan. It's a way of life."

He laughed, still feeling revitalized by his extraordinary day, and Shelby started the car.

"Where to?"

"Do you prefer the parkway or back roads?"

"At this hour? Parkway."

"Okay, head east and get off at Swissvale."

Marjorie and Shelby's chatter bounced off Theo. He stared at the Pitt logos, the panther, the tiny front page from *The Pitt News*, and the rubber replica of the Cathedral of Learning, on Shelby's key ring. They swung against her knee with the motion of the car, highlighted by the dashboard glow against the green of her pants.

Something about the Pitt logo rattled him. There was something so familiar about them, aside from the fact he'd grown up in the shadow of the university.

A memory tugged at his brain...was it his memory? Or was it something he'd seen through someone else's eyes? He shook his head, tried to remember, but suddenly found himself outside.

He ran his fingers through his hair and felt surprise when he realized the ends reached past his shoulders. Missing teeth were conspicuous in their absence when he smoothed his tongue along his lips.

Sunlight shone through the heavily leafed tree branches and warmed the top of his head. A little boy sat in a walker, reached his hands out to Theo beseechingly. His latte-colored skin glowed in the sun. He stepped toward the boy, but almost bumped into a man standing before him, who wordlessly handed over a twenty.

"The usual, babe?" Theo's lips mouthed the words. The man nodded, a mute. The tennis court net swung a little in the breeze.

Theo slipped on wet pine needles, just catching himself. The man and the tennis courts were nowhere to be seen. His skirt rode up his thighs, and he hitched it back down, cursing. A black shadow to his right caught his attention. He reached out with his mind, tried to grab an impression.

Negativity, no, not just negativity, a sense of great evil rolled off the black shadow. It flitted through the trees, lithe, like a cat's tail, and Theo's awareness flickered again.

The little boy giggled. Theo knew he liked being tickled just there on his leg. Fuck his father. No need for him. Theo would make this boy's life better by himself. A sudden wave of protectiveness took him off-guard and he leapt off the swing. It didn't matter how. He would do it.

He swatted at the branches in front of his face, impatient with his surroundings. Why'd they have to meet all the way out here anyway? Fleming's sat just around the corner—a perfectly good bar. Back to nature bullshit. He tried to keep track of the black thing jogging parallel with his own track, but he blinked.

The cock in his mouth tasted foul, like body odor and shit. He wanted to breathe through his mouth to avoid smelling the sweat and nastiness, but could only grab breaths between thrusts. He wrinkled his nose and braced his hands on his knees.

He sensed the blackness before he saw it, sensed the negative fog encroaching. He kept pumping on the dick with his mouth, aware only in the corner of the mind that was solely Theo. He struggled to turn the head to the side, to get a better view of what came from the trees, but the other part of the mind concentrated only on finishing the blowjob before the smell overpowered him.

111

He really should start charging more.

The old growth area of the park kept visibility to a minimum. He could still sense the evil, see it dart among the trunks, but only caught glances. Dammit.

Metal flashed among the trees, the evil moved in quickly. Sunlight glinted among the green leaves and showed him another vision of the coffee-skinned boy, pushing a tricycle with his feet. He laughed, hope tugged at his heart, another flare of black and silver from the side caught his eye.

The sequins on his hot pants rode up into his ass crack when he sat, and Theo's brain screamed.

"Mind your own fucking business," he said, oblivious to the danger approaching. He squinted into the darkness, tried to see the black apparition clearly, and focused all his will on the black specter in the trees, until a blast took his vision.

A newspaper swam before his mind, a newspaper on a keychain. It bumped Shelby's knee as she drove and laughed. He caught her stealing glimpses of him when she pretended to change the radio volume. He sat quietly, considering the implications, and watched the newspaper key chains bounce.

"Theo?" Shelby reached over to tap his knee.

He jerked his leg back, slapping at a bug on his cheek. His hand came away wet. He was drooling.

"Sorry! You okay?"

The radio played Pink Floyd, the scent of pine air freshener hung in the air. The car was stopped. Theo shook his head. "What?"

"Are you okay?" Shelby's face peered at his, backlit by the interior car lights.

"Why are we stopped?" He sat up. When had he slid to the floor?

Marjorie touched his cheek and he braced himself from withdrawing. "Because you had a seizure of some sort. Are you okay?" she said.

"Uh, yeah." Shit, shit, shit. More visions. "Rosemary's Breasts must be a little off tonight."

"The food did that to you?"

His face burned, and he hoped he hadn't actually turned red. "What did I do?"

"You slid out of your seat, hit the floor, and started talking in tongues or something. Do you need the hospital?" Shelby's forehead sported deep wrinkles of concern.

Jesus, no. "I'm okay now. Sometimes if I eat something that disagrees with me, that happens."

Both faces stared at him, doubt written in their furrowed brows and narrow eyes.

"Really, I'm fine." He opened the window, took a few deep breaths. "See, I'm fine now. How long was it?"

"Just a few minutes. Long enough for Shelby to pull over."

"Okay. That's fine. I'll just get home and rest. Be fine by morning. Really."

"It goes against my better judgment as an undead counselor to not get you some medical attention." Marjorie's worry was apparent.

"I'm sorry. I promise I'm fine. If you could just drop me off, I'll be fine."

"Will you be alone?"

Shit, shit, shit again. "No. I have...roommates."

"Okay. If you're sure."

"I am. Carry on." Theo waved at the road.

Shelby sat back down in the driver's seat and merged into parkway traffic. "Race Street or Braddock?"

"Braddock." He gave her directions to his parents' house as she drove past the darkened Edgewood Town Centre.

His parents' house.

Goddamn it. He'd planned on keeping his living arrangements as quiet as possible to avoid the certain humiliation that would come with admitting he still lived at his parents' house.

He sighed.

Shelby turned onto his road. "You can pull over there, in front of the yellow house."

She whistled. "Nice pad."

"Thanks." He got out of the car and hitched the seat up so Marjorie could get out. He offered her a hand, and she took it. Her hand was cool, soft.

She maneuvered out of the vehicle and Shelby fiddled with the radio.

Marjorie did not release his hand. "Are you sure you're all right?"

"I'm positive. Cooked meat does that sometimes," he lied.

"Raw is definitely better."

"It is. I hope you enjoyed dinner, anyway."

"Thank you, Theo. I had a nice time."

Warmth spread through his limbs. "Me, too. We should do it again."

A sweet smile brightened her face and the corners of her eyes crinkled. When she smiled like that, the slight decomposition around her eyes disappeared. Theo's heart threatened to thud out of his chest.

"I would like that." Her gaze held his—did he dare to think *expectantly*?

Shelby turned the radio up.

Theo leaned forward, watched Marjorie's eyes close as she lifted her face toward his. He pressed his lips to hers and took her other hand in his. She slid her hands out of his and wrapped her arms around his waist at the same moment she opened her mouth and deepened the kiss. Theo felt his dick respond to the body contact.

And quickly broke the kiss. He didn't want her to know about his...newfound ability.

Marjorie stumbled forward just a bit and he grabbed her shoulders. "I'm sorry."

"It's, it's okay. I guess the street isn't the place for this anyway." She turned back to the car. "Thanks again, Theo. I'll see you soon."

Marjorie dropped into the passenger seat and Theo closed the door for her. He leaned through the open window. "Thanks for the ride."

Marjorie turned to grab her purse from the back seat and Shelby gave Theo a big wink. "You're welcome. Now go take care of yourself." She jerked her chin toward the house.

Theo spun to see what she gestured at and saw his mother's head in the living room picture window. He just barely resisted dropping his face into his hands.

"Talk to ya later, Theo," Shelby said, smiling, and pulled the car from the curb.

He gave one last wave, just in case Marjorie still watched.

"It's better this way," he mumbled as he walked toward the front porch. "She can't know."

The front door opened before he could touch the doorknob.

"Teddy, who was that?" his mother eyed him.

He tamped down his temper, reminded himself he was probably still feeling the effects of his earlier snack. "No one."

"That didn't look like 'no one,' Theodore. It's not polite to court a lady in the street. Bring her in next time."

"I'm not 'courting' her, Mom." Theo struggled to check the volume of his voice. "She's a friend, and after she figures out I still live here, I'm sure she'll stay that way."

He shoved past his mother and down the stairs into his basement room. After closing the door quietly—no sense inviting more arguing with a slam—he threw himself on the bed and tried to convince himself it was better he couldn't go home with Marjorie.

Point one: zombie men couldn't perform, or at least the ones not indulging in elicit brain-eating activities. It wasn't as if she had sex on her mind, anyway. Even if they'd ended up together for the night, nothing could have happened because he couldn't admit to her what he'd done, and there was no way she'd accept that he could do something no other zombie could. She dealt with the newly turned every day, and led the support groups. If someone managed to get it up, she'd be the first to know and she would share the information.

Point two: their conversation at dinner took an uncomfortable turn. Theo avoided support groups and other communal zombie activities because he had secrets. The circumstances surrounding his rising were one and the fact that he received psychic images from ingesting brain matter was another.

And now he knew of a side effect of eating, one that could pose serious problems in the continuing struggle for undead integration. If zombies knew that eating brain matter could solve their physical problems—including sex—no human would be sure of their safety.

Of course, he was making the giant assumption that other zombies didn't already do this. And he wasn't so sure of that anymore.

Point three: he couldn't risk another round of visions while with her. Drooling and speaking in tongues? Fuck. He'd have to be careful everywhere.

He rubbed his nose. Ash stared at him from the foot of the bed, tail twitching.

"What?" Theo said to the cat, who sauntered up next to Theo's thigh.

He couldn't socialize. It was definitely better this way, no matter how empty the knowledge made him feel.

Theo struggled to relax in the pitch-black room. His limbs ached with cold—they were leaden, stiff and uncooperative. He rolled over painfully, mind reeling.

Why did he hurt so much? He grappled with his arms, tried to get them to function. So cold.

He'd never turned on the space heaters or electric blanket. Fuck.

He inched to the side of the bed and fumbled with the controller for the blankets. He'd stay here in bed long enough for his muscles to loosen, then get up and turn on the heaters. He double-checked the lights on the controllers to be sure they were set on high, then laid back in bed to wait for them to warm up.

Leaving the heaters and blankets off overnight was not typical for him. Maybe the vision in the car rattled him more than he'd thought.

Maybe the effects of eating the brains lasted longer than he could have imagined. A stab of fear in his midsection was followed by exhilaration. Just a few cubes of brain left him able to forget about the problems inherent to being undead for an entire evening. If he could get his hands on brain matter at each meal...it was feasible he could live an almost normal life again.

He couldn't remember feeling cold last night or even thinking about being cold. Usually, no matter what was on his mind, the sensations that went along with being cold trumped his other problems. His body temperature dictated his mood, and nothing else mattered when he was cold. Once he raised his temperature to a normal range, his mind could focus on other things.

Like he focused on Marjorie last night.

Until, of course, he flopped to the floor of the car like a neurotic fish.

He pulled the blankets around his shoulders and rubbed his thighs. The little alarm clock on top of the TV blinked two thirty-seven.

Not time to get up. What woke him? He didn't think it was just because he was cold. He closed his eyes, tried to put himself back in the frame of mind he had when he woke.

His limbs began to thaw a bit as the heat from the warming blankets loosened his muscles. He flexed his fingers and breathed deep. The blankets quickly heated to maximum temperature and he pulled them over his head to breathe the warm air as well.

After a few moments in the heat, he poked his head and an arm out and switched on his bedside lamp. His gaze fell on the floor next to his mattress, where the *City Paper* lay.

Shelby's keychain. The little *Pitt News* figured prominently in the vision. He'd been looking at her keys just before it hit.

What the fuck?

He closed his eyes and shifted back under the blankets. What had he seen? The killings. The setting was the same as the visions he'd gotten earlier that day, but the stories were slightly different, and all mashed together.

He remembered the little boy, the boy with the beautiful brown skin. One of the victims he'd sample earlier was a mother. Theo pinched the bridge of his nose, trying to summon the vision.

Jennifer Semuta. She had a kid; she'd thought of him before she died.

He dreamt of the blowjob, and swallowed hard at the memory of the smell. That must have been Jerry Cullins. And the other one...Rhonda Abraham. Missing teeth.

It made sense to have the visions since he'd eaten from them just hours ago. Less than a day. But these new visions were not of things he'd seen while eating. Was his mind filling in blanks and inventing more of their stories or were these delayed visions more psychic remnants? Did something jog his psychic ability?

He'd never experienced delayed episodes after eating brains before. Had he? He sat up, careful to keep the heated blankets tucked close to his body. Had he?

Something happened a few nights ago...he thought he'd been dreaming, but never feel asleep. What the fuck was happening?

Newspaper print flashed before his mind's eye. Something about second chances and more information. Rising. A pay phone. Unicorns. Happiness and sunshine and wind through a car window...then red and black death.

CHAPTER 12

The other visions flooded back in a rush, frustration at not being able to read the newspaper, happiness, more dick.

More dick? Why the fuck was he thinking about so much dick?

Because he'd been eating the brains of prostitutes, that's why. These visions had to be remnants of the victims' memories. He had these psychic connections to their living selves; the extra information must come across when something prompted it, like the Pitt key chains on Shelby's ring.

A surge of excitement propelled him out from under the blankets and to his desk. He rummaged in the top drawer for a pen and notebook, and then took the few steps back to the warm haven of his heated bed.

He jotted notes, just words that entered his brain. Penis, trees, newspaper, happy, candy.

He paused at "candy," scratched it out and wrote Snickers.

He hated Snickers. What else? Car, pain, hatred, unicorn, red, black, death.

When had he seen these? And what the fuck did a unicorn have to do with all this?

He grabbed the tiny datebook he kept in the nightstand drawer and began writing in the dates he'd ingested brain matter compared to the dates he remembered dreaming from someone else's head.

The first two examinations were on Wednesday. He'd seen the newspaper on Wednesday night or Thursday morning. He ate the frozen samples on Thursday.

What about on Thursday night?

All he remembered about Friday morning was that he'd woken in a pretty foul mood and couldn't remember any dreams. He blamed the sleepless night on the double 'shroom sub from Uncle Sam's.

Could the lack of psychic impressions be because the samples were old? Maybe he needed fresh flesh to get impressions.

Nothing again until tonight in the car...and he'd fed today on fresh brain. More than he'd ever eaten before. The delayed visions hit him hard.

He'd eaten samples before for Dr. Libitin, but never more than one at a time and usually just tiny bits. Not frequently either; he'd considered himself lucky if he got one a month.

Suddenly, the offerings were plentiful. Eight in six days.

There had to be a connection between the frequency of feeding, the quality of the samples, and these crazy visions. He felt certain they were a continuation of his psychic impressions, not just him reliving the initial experience.

Theo jotted a few more items on his list: missing teeth, boy, more dick, black shadow, body odor, black specter, newspaper on a keychain (Shelby?).

He circled the keychain entry. Something about that niggled at his brain. In his dream, he'd seen Shelby's laden key ring. What were the dangly bits? All Pitt emblems. Why would his mind turn to Pitt key chains and newspapers?

His gaze fell to the week-old *City Paper* on the floor. The University of Pittsburgh ran a college paper. *The Pitt News.*

In one of his dreams, he'd been looking through a paper trying to read something. What if that paper was *The Pitt News*?

Theo felt stirrings of excitement. A lead.

He threw the blankets off and shoved his arms into his fleece robe. He heard nothing upstairs, so he walked silently up the basement steps and cracked the door open. The first floor lay dark and silent.

As quietly as possible, he padded across the floor to the computer and switched it on, praying his father still had it muted. The start-up screen appeared but no noise accompanied it. Whew.

Theo waited for the geriatric machine to wheeze into life, and then accessed the Internet. He typed "University of Pittsburgh student newspaper" into the search engine and pressed enter. "*The Pitt News*—Daily Student Newspaper of the University of..." was the first return. One more click took him directly to *The Pitt News*.

He chewed on his bottom lip. Now what? A variety of options faced him. He scanned through the first page of the website, perusing the articles about student life, sporting events, and the police blotter. He clicked the last link.

The dates in the police blotter went back a week. Nothing recent. When would Naomi have been looking at the paper? No way to tell how old the memory of reading the paper might have been, and the entries in the blotter weren't ringing any bells for Theo. From last Tuesday:

> 3:57 p.m. — Police received a report of a woman acting suspicious at Forbes Library. The area was checked, and the person was gone upon arrival.
>
> 4:17 p.m. — Police received a report of a theft of a wallet from a backpack at Litchfield Tower A. An investigation is pending.

He shook his head. This didn't seem right. It was all very innocuous college crap. Back on the home page of the newspaper, he peered at the links. Classifieds?

Nearly a hundred classified ads scrolled before his eyes. He sighed and began reading. Most of them were for apartment rentals. The population of the city, of most cities across the country, declined after the Event and housing wasn't nearly as hard to find in and around Oakland as it had once been. Based strictly on the number of ads and the lower prices, it seemed like the property management companies were desperate.

He waded through the housing offerings, job offers, noted with mild interest that Alex's Flowers was still in business, and then scanned the research study announcements. Finally, at the very bottom of the page, he read a few short lines that brought excitement bubbling to the surface.

> WONDERING ABOUT YOUR CHANCES OF RISING? Do you have the tattoo? Maybe you don't, but you're curious as to why you should. Sick of your current life? Stuck in a dead end situation? You CAN be different. Die and rise. For more information contact user #16-39845.

He read the ad three times, and felt his nausea grow with each reading. The ad reeked of manipulation and evil. Rising was not a guarantee, even for those who wanted it. No one knew if they would rise until they died. If he read this ad right, someone promised a new life through rising.

Impossible.

Ash jumped up onto the desk next to the computer and Theo stroked his back.

Not only could rising never be guaranteed, it certainly didn't improve your life. Maybe back in the beginning someone could have made that claim. Theo even had his fifteen minutes of fame, since he belonged to the First Generation, but now? No way. Public fascination dwindled quickly, replaced by a wary acceptance.

Being undead only complicated life; it didn't improve it. Most zombies lived the exact same life they'd lived before, with a healthy dose of caution.

Ash settled down next to the keyboard, front paws tucked to his chest. Theo rubbed the cat's chin absentmindedly.

So what to do with the ad?

He could contact user 16-39845 himself or he could take the information to Dr. Libitin. He clicked the link to contact the user just to see if he could find any identifying information, but found himself on a page with a form email. Any queries probably went to a mailbox associated with the newspaper and user 16-39845 logged in with his or her own password to retrieve the queries and contact the interested parties. The setup was a good way to protect the privacy of everyone involved. Only those interested in the ad responded, and the advertiser only had to contact those that he or she considered genuine.

So Theo would have to give out his own name and number in order to be contacted by the advertiser.

Visions of the bloody crime scenes flashed through his mind. Nope. He'd take this to Dr. Libitin. *The Pitt News* would no doubt give up the identity of user 16-39845 to the police.

He squinted at the tiny numbers in the corner of the monitor. Not quite four o'clock. He still had a couple hours until his alarm would go off and his Dad would be up soon to get ready to go to the marina. He jotted *The Pitt News* user number on a piece of scrap paper, shut down the computer, and made his way back into the basement.

He stepped over the *City Paper*. He blinked at the paper at his feet, then grabbed it and climbed into bed. From inside his cocoon of heated blankets, he perused the classifieds.

On page twelve, he found what he sought: a near-exact duplicate of the ad from *The Pitt News* promising a successful rising and improved life situation. The placer of this ad was protected in much the same way as by *The Pitt News*: with a user ID number and anonymous mailbox. Theo circled the ad with a wide red marker.

This killer advertised for victims.

Two very long hours later, Theo took a quick shower, and ate a breakfast of scrambled eggs and rare bacon. When his mother entered the kitchen, he handed her a fresh mug of coffee and half a grapefruit.

"Theo, you didn't have to do this." He surprise was tangible, and he felt a twinge of guilt.

"Sure I did, Ma. I'm sorry I snapped at you last night." He kissed her on the cheek.

"That's all right." She patted his arm. "Are you off to work already?"

"Yeah, I thought I'd catch the early bus and get some deskwork done." He tucked the *City Paper* under his arm.

"Okay, have a good day, then." She sat down at the tiny table and shook open the *Post-Gazette*.

Theo blinked. "Hey, Mom, can I see the classifieds for just a second?"

"Sure." She pulled the section from the stack and set it aside.

He grabbed it and flipped through, looking for the miscellaneous services. He scrutinized those ads with no luck, then sat down to scan the rest of the section.

No ads at all about risers, rising, or improved life, with the notable exception of a psychic who promised to reveal your future. After reading the psychic's ad a second time, Theo realized it was a woman in Chalfont whose business was actually well established. Nothing foreboding there.

He refolded the paper and handed it back to his mom. "Thanks."

"Nothing interesting?" she inquired as she sprinkled sugar on the cut surface of the grapefruit.

"Nothing interesting." He closed the front door quietly and made his way to the bus stop, the *City Paper* in one hand.

The morning was warm and dry already, and promised to be a scorcher. At the bus stop, Theo pulled out his cell phone and dialed Dr. Libitin's office.

"Hello?"

"Hey, Doc."

"Good morning, Theo."

"I have some information to share."

"Oh? What's that?"

"I'd like to discuss it in person."

Silence.

"It's not about what happened yesterday. Well, I guess it kind of is, but I think I may have found something that supports your theory."

"Really? Okay. I'll be in my office."

The bus pulled to the curb. "I'll see you in a bit." Theo found a seat and kept to himself for the duration of the ride.

Once downtown, he hopped off the bus about a block from the morgue and walked the remaining distance, letting his body soak in the heat.

He signed in at the front desk and took the elevator up. The door of the ME's office stood wide open, but Theo still knocked on the wall beside the door.

"Come on in, Theo."

Dr. Libitin sat behind his desk, so Theo dropped into the upholstered chair opposite. The ME's eye sported the shadow of a shiner. Shame washed through Theo.

He put the *City Paper* on the desk in front of the doctor. "Page twelve."

Dr. Libitin's brow furrowed into a web of wrinkles. He opened the *City Paper* to the page Theo indicated and read the ad circled in red permanent marker. He squinted at Theo. "And?"

"And I found an identical ad in *The Pitt News*." He went on to describe his delayed visions, the connection he'd discovered between his "examinations" and his psychic constructions, and the deceitful nature of the advertisements.

During his lengthy explanation, perhaps the most Theo had ever spoken in one sitting with the doctor, the ME's expression went from skepticism to utter disbelief.

"You really have a feeling about this?"

Theo nodded. "Yes, I do."

"Do you think this is our killer?"

"I'm almost positive. The person who placed this ad is flushing out people who want to rise and making them think it's a sure thing that will change their lives. It certainly wouldn't be the first time someone took advantage of a person's desire to start over."

"But our killer seems to choose only a specific kind of person."

Theo shook his head. "Maybe this is part of a screening process, to weed out the ones who don't fit the killer's profile."

Dr. Libitin leaned forward. "This is excellent. If I can get Chief Niemic to okay a request for the information connected to the ads, we'll have a place to start."

Someone behind Theo cleared his or her throat. He turned in his chair.

Marjorie. His heart flipped over and back again, in that slow, familiar way. The side effects from his diet of brains had worn off. He swept aside the disappointment and stood.

"Hi, Marjorie."

She smiled at him, just for him. "Hey, it's nice to see you again so soon."

He grinned, sure he looked like an idiot, but was powerless to stop it.

"Dr. Libitin, I'm here for..." she consulted her clipboard. "For Edwin Nessing."

The ME nodded. "He's down in the holding area. Michael is with him; he'll sign for the release and help take him to the van."

"Thank you." She disappeared around the corner, but peeked back around. "See ya, Theo."

"Okay." Theo turned back to Dr. L. "Someone turned?"

"Yes. He was hard to contain this morning, so we had to put him in holding and sedate him. She shouldn't have any trouble with him now; he's really out of it." Dr. Libitin still stared at the advertisement. "You're sure these visions of yours are connected?"

"I'm sure. I'm seeing more from the victims' point of view, hearing more of their thoughts. Some of it I can't account for, but I just know it's connected."

"What, for example, can you not account for?"

Theo thought. "Well, I saw unicorns. That makes no sense."

The medical examiner chuckled. "I guess there's no accounting for taste."

Theo gave Dr. L. a mock glare.

"I'm not convinced we should continue these examinations. This is good information, but..." Dr. Libitin gently prodded his black eye. "You scared me, Theo."

The beginnings of panic and anxiety wound their way through Theo's chest, constricting his throat. So slow. Not like the waves of emotion he'd felt last night.

He said nothing, not trusting himself to remain calm.

Silence stretched between them.

Finally, Dr. Libitin sighed. "Will you tell me what happened yesterday?"

"It's overwhelming, seeing the visions. I feel the emotions of the victims." Theo weighed his words, not wanting to risk his chances of being cut off from his supply. "Perhaps the escalated violence of these crimes makes the visions more powerful."

Dr. Libitin's gaze was steady on Theo's face. "Go on."

"I...that's all."

"That can't be all. You've eaten from murder victims before and never had a reaction as strong as what happened yesterday. What was different?"

Oh, gee whiz, Doc, maybe the amount, the freshness, the frequency.

The orgasms.

"I'm not sure," he finally said.

Dr. Libitin seemed ready to push the topic, but his phone rang, followed almost immediately by Theo's phone. They looked at one another.

"I'll take mine in the hall." Theo strode from the office.

Forty minutes later the morgue van wound its way through the narrow streets of Oakland. Doug neatly parallel parked the big white vehicle beside an abandoned lot on Melwood Avenue. The building on the lot must have once been a decent place—probably full of college students year-round based on proximity to Pitt.

But now it stood empty, the glassless windows stared at the packed dirt yard full of trash and debris. The city earmarked funds for restoration and rebuilding after the Event, but apparently North Oakland fell outside the focus.

No great loss, really.

Patrol cruisers and several easily identifiable unmarked cars lined the street. Theo walked the short distance to the abandoned house, past a green Civic with the driver's side mirror taped on. Skeet's red car sat in the alley beside the decrepit building, hatch up, evidence box open. Theo grabbed a paper jumpsuit and stepped into it on his way inside.

A uniformed officer pointed at the stairs. "Third floor, apartment eight."

Theo nodded his thanks.

The other cops, smears of Vicks VapoRub glistening above their upper lips, studiously ignored him. Theo sniffed the air, and caught the distinctive whiff of death and some other rancid scent, which increased in intensity as he climbed the stairs. The air shimmered with heat on the top floor.

The door to apartment eight hung open. Theo entered what was an efficiency apartment, one large room with a stained mattress on the floor. Wallpaper hung in strips from the walls and Big Gulp cups and food wrappers blanketed the floor. Squatters.

"Hey, man." Skeet peeked from around a corner in the back left of the room. He wore a paper dust mask striped with Vicks.

Theo walked across the room into a small alcove that must have functioned as a kitchen. The appliances had been stripped out at some point, and all that remained were the cabinets. Doors hung askew off hinges or lay on the floor. A few yellow evidence flags sat near objects of interest. Too few of them.

"Not much here," Theo said, and peered around for anything Skeet might have missed. Piles of feces decorated floor and counters. He nudged a blob with his covered shoe.

"Cats everywhere," Skeet said. He moved around a pile of black plastic on the floor, taking photos. "We must've scared off twenty of them."

Theo nodded at the plastic covered lump. "What's this?"

Skeet leaned down and lifted a corner. Theo bent forward.

Wide, brown eyes stared back at him above a mouth that gaped open. Lips stretched back over gums, revealing crooked, yellow teeth.

Theo started. "I know that person."

"Everyone knows that person. That's Crazy Betty."

"Holy shit. You're right." He tilted his head sideways to get a better look at the facial features, but the contorted expression made definite recognition impossible. "I saw her yesterday. Marjorie gave her money on our way to eat last night. That's insane."

A tangle of gray hair lay beneath Crazy Betty's head, the straight strands at odds with Betty's tight black curls.

"Is there someone else under there?"

"Just another head. Pretty sure it's Cheryl, the panhandler who works the 7-11 with Betty." Skeet paused in snapping pictures. "The gray-haired one, real quiet. You know who I'm talking about?"

"Yeah, I think so. Always holds the door for you."

"That's the one."

"Just the heads?" Theo looked up at Skeet.

"Just the heads. I know, I know." Skeet shrugged. "The bodies are out back. I did a preliminary pass, but take some flags and see what else you can find. Take the fire escape down. Let me finish taking these shots and I'll be down."

Theo glanced at Crazy Betty's death grin one more time, then grabbed a stack of flags. The sign for the fire escape pointed him toward the back of the building. The hinges on the swinging screen door screeched when he pushed it open and stepped out onto the metal staircase. He descended carefully, mindful of the heavy rust.

Dr. Libitin stood in the pathetic dirt square passing for a backyard, talking with Detective Gavahan. More black plastic covered another mound. Theo could guess what lay underneath.

He entertained the idea of going back upstairs to work the head scene with Skeet, but instead decided to just pretend Gavahan didn't exist.

He started his customary spiral at the corner of the building closest to where he stepped off the fire escape. He kept his gaze on the ground, hesitating occasionally to examine an object and either dropping a flag or not. He kept his ears tuned to the conversation between Gavahan and the ME.

"I don't see why you keep him around." Detective Gavahan's voice carried.

Dr. Libitin remained silent.

"He's a liability. If something goes wrong, he'll be the first one blamed."

"I don't really think that's the case."

"Come on, Doc. He's weird. I can't put my finger on it, but there's something not right about him."

Theo glanced up. Dr. Libitin stared at the ground.

Detective Gavahan's voice hardened. "I don't want him affiliated with the department."

Theo's insides twisted slightly and he felt the stirrings of anger.

"Detective, that's not a decision for you to make. Mr. Walker is employed by the crime unit, not by the Bureau of Police or by my office. If you'd like to file a complaint, you'll have to file it with Howard Moster. I suggest that you be sure you have solid grounds for a complaint, since Mr. Walker does fine work for the forensics unit." Dr. Libitin walked away from the detective toward the front of the house.

Theo continued his slow spiral, as if nothing happened. A flash of metal near his feet caught his attention and he crouched to inspect it. He used the edge of a flag to move grass away from the metal object.

Could be a piece of a blade. He dropped the flag beside the item and knelt closer to the ground for a better look. One sharpened edge, one blunt. Could absolutely be a piece from a knife or sword, and a blade seemed to be the killer's weapon of choice for beheadings.

A pair of shiny brown wing tip shoes entered Theo's field of vision.

"I'm sure you heard every word I said, zombie."

Theo rose to his feet.

"I will find a way to get you out of the bureau."

Theo swallowed hard. "I've never done anything to you."

Gavahan's eyes narrowed and he jabbed one finger into Theo's shoulder. "You exist, zombie. That's enough. Your kind shouldn't exist. And you sure as hell don't belong on the police force."

Theo felt his bowels clench in a slow spasm. His brain registered anger, but his body struggled with a lethargic flight response. The effects of eating the brains definitely had abated. He couldn't speak.

Gavahan barked a laugh. "Can't defend yourself? That's because you're dead. Dead men don't belong with the living."

Theo watched him stalk from the backyard into the alley alongside the building.

"Don't listen to him. He's an ass."

Theo turned to see Skeet standing on the last step of the fire escape.

"A world-class ass," Skeet said. He walked to Theo. "I don't get his problem. I know there's competition between the detectives, but it's not like you could take his job. He's full of shit."

"Thanks." He mock punched Skeet in the arm. "I could take your job."

Skeet laughed. "I know it."

"Did you see this piece of metal?" Theo pointed down.

Skeet frowned and knelt. "I missed this." He pushed the overgrown grass aside for a better look. "Part of a knife?"

"Or sword." Theo indicated the sharp edge. "This side is sharp, this side is blunt. I think it's too thick to just be a knife."

Skeet grunted. "Grab the collection kits. I'll finish the photos then we can start gathering the items from down here."

"You processed the kitchen already?"

Skeet answered in the affirmative, so Theo made his way to the car and managed to avoid the troupe of detectives.

Back at the scene, Dr. Libitin and Doug removed the black plastic from the bodies and Skeet snapped pictures. Theo walked the remainder of his spiral, searching for more evidence before he began collecting items.

He finished with the evidence and stacked the packages in the big yellow case before the ME and Doug tucked the bodies into body bags. Skeet stepped into place beside Theo.

"Did they get the heads already?" Theo said.

His partner nodded.

"Skeet, Theo, would you mind helping Doug put the deceased on the gurneys?" Dr. Libitin gestured to the stretchers off to one side.

After the bodies were strapped onto the gurneys, Doug pushed one toward the street. Skeet grabbed the other.

Theo and Dr. Libitin stood in silence for a moment. Theo looked at the place in the grass where the bodies had lain. Dark with wet gore, it would have to be cleaned up. Couldn't leave that kind of biohazard in a yard in Oakland.

"What did you do about the outdoor scenes last time?"

Dr. Libitin shrugged. "I think they brought a fire truck into Frick Park to wash it all away. I don't know what they'll do here."

"You want me to call *Clean as Death*?"

"Ask the sergeant. I don't know how they would get reimbursed for this one, since there's no property owner."

"Okay." Theo scuffed his boot in the dirt. "Hey, uh, thanks for what you said to Gavahan."

"Theo, lately I'm beginning to agree that maybe you shouldn't be part of the force, but it's certainly not for the bigoted reasons he spouts."

Theo felt as though Dr. Libitin punched him. After all the time they'd spent together, after all the information Theo had been able to give him...

Anger bubbled thick and unpleasant through Theo's body. "I'm sorry you feel that way."

"Did you find anything unusual down here? There was nothing of interest upstairs."

Theo considered. "Did the bodies have the tattoo?"

"Yes."

"Both of them?"

"Yes, both the bodies had the tattoo." Exasperation colored Dr. Libitin's words.

"Then, yeah, we found something." Theo described the piece of blade they'd discovered.

"You bagged it?"

"Of course."

Dr. Libitin nodded, looked out at the scene, no doubt recreating the vision in his mind. "The wounds are consistent with the last victims—decapitation with a large blade. Maybe our perp broke the weapon."

"My thoughts exactly."

"I'll talk to Milton about putting some weight on knife dealers and pawn shops in the area to keep an eye out for people buying anything big enough. It could lead to something."

"That's a good idea."

After a few moments of silence, Theo couldn't resist asking. He tried to keep the anticipation and apprehension from his voice. "Will you need me at the morgue?"

Dr. Libitin turned to look at Theo's face. "No, I don't think so."

Theo suppressed the urge to argue with the doctor. "If you change your mind, let me know. I do feel like I'm getting good information. The visions are getting clearer."

Dr. Libitin's lips pressed into a thin line. Theo's nerves began to fire under the doctor's scrutiny. Finally, he nodded and walked back to the alley.

Theo shook off the anxiety attack threatening to take root. Maybe there were benefits to not eating brains—he could better control his emotions this way.

"You going to the morgue with Dr. Libitin or are you coming down to the office with me?" Skeet's voice came from the other side of the house.

"I'm coming with you." Theo turned his back on the messy scene in the yard. "I need to ask the sergeant about cleanup."

"He's out front."

Theo found Sergeant Milton at the front of the house, looking over notes on a clipboard. He asked about cleaning up the mess on the third floor and in the backyard.

"I'd appreciate it if your friend could handle it. The department will reimburse him. Give him my number." Sergeant Milton tipped his hat at Theo. "Thanks, son."

Theo called Hugh and relayed the message. "If you do a good job here, I bet the department will keep your number."

"That's awesome! Thanks, man, I owe you one." Theo pulled the phone away from his ear. Hugh's appreciation came through loud and clear.

"No problem."

Theo and Skeet hopped in the little red hatchback and headed in the direction of the crime unit headquarters. Theo's mind replayed the vision of the heads they'd discovered upstairs. They were intact. Brain matter would be available.

Dr. Libitin seemed convinced that these killings were related to the victim's RISER tattoos. If his theory had merit—and Theo was beginning to suspect he was onto something—then he needed Theo's help.

He would call.

Skeet's phone rang, interrupting Theo's thoughts.

"Yep, got it." He dropped the phone into the center console. "We've got an attempted murder over in Verona."

After stopping to get fresh supplies and drop off the evidence from the Melwood murders, Theo and Skeet spent the rest of the afternoon working the attempted murder. The victim scored a ride to Presby in the LifeFlight chopper, and it looked like he would live. The cops already had the suspect. The crime appeared to be gang related, and it was the first death in a week where Theo saw no connection to the Riser Killings.

The crime scene was big, since the victim ran from his attacker, and Theo used extra care in processing the evidence. It would help send the perp to jail and it kept his mind off the Melwood murders.

He waited for a call from Dr. Libitin, but his phone remained silent.

His focus wavered between the tasks involved in cataloging a large crime scene and his base zombie desires. He recalled the conversation he had with Dr. Libitin not long ago when he said he didn't want to be involved in the Riser Killings any longer.

What had he been thinking?

To hell with the risks of getting caught. Brain matter seemed to be the only way he could live an even semi-normal life. He'd risk it.

A sharp whistle caught his attention. Skeet gestured him over. "I can't quite get the ruler to sit flat here. Can you hold it in place while I take the picture?"

Theo knelt beside a shell and put his fingers on either end of a plastic ruler.

"You okay?" Skeet said. He hunched over to put the camera lens close to the ammunition waste.

"What do you mean?" Theo looked at the back Skeet's head. "I'm fine."

"You just seem preoccupied." Skeet sat back on his knees.

Theo handed him the ruler and labeled a bag. "Yeah, I guess. Just thinking about those killings in Oakland." He picked the shell up with a pair of tweezers and dropped it in the bag.

"Doc thinks they're related?"

"Yeah. They both had the tattoo."

Skeet scratched his chin. "Seems kind of incredible, you know? Why would someone kill people just for wanting to rise?"

"I've been trying to figure that out for days." He wasn't sure how much he should say to Skeet. "I'm connecting the dots between the victims, and there's nothing really convincing."

"I don't know. The hookers, the drug dealers, and now panhandlers. Sounds like someone's on a crusade to clean up the streets."

Theo stared at Skeet.

"Don't it look that way to you?" Skeet rocked back on his heels and stood up. "Anyway, I'm just saying. It looks like this killer—what'd you call it? The Riser Killer?—doesn't want these kind of people on the street."

Or maybe he doesn't want those people to rise. Is he cleaning up the streets or cleaning up the undead population? Maybe it was less about preventing anyone from rising and more about preventing a certain kind of person from rising.

Skeet looked at his watch. "You ready? I think we're about done here and we're going to hit the worst of rush hour at this point."

"Yeah, let's go."

Skeet turned the radio up and let Theo wallow in his thoughts all the way to the lab.

He'd been free of anxiety since he died. His indolent system just didn't seem to be able to drum up the effort required to move anxiety hormones through his body. It was one thing about being alive that he didn't miss one bit.

But he felt the stirrings of anxiety when he thought about not eating...eating... Why couldn't he say it? Or even think it? Brains. He wanted brains. Not cow brains or pig brains or monkey brains. Human brain matter. When he thought about not eating brains ever again, the old tightness in his chest, the shortness of breath fluttered like wisps through him. His old frenemies.

He had to ensure a supply of brains. The best way to do that was to get back on Dr. Libitin's good side. If he could help solve these Riser Murders, the medical examiner would see the benefit in his continued involvement. As long as his talents were useful, he could eat.

He needed to get samples from the latest victims, the Oakland panhandlers.

"Dude, we're here."

Theo looked around and realized they were in the parking garage underneath the forensics lab. "Whoops."

Skeet chuckled. "Man, whatever is on your mind must be some major shit."

"You could say that."

Dr. Libitin's words rang in his mind: "I'm not convinced we should continue these examinations."

Theo would just have to convince him.

He stepped off the bus at Forbes and Bigelow and made his way into the William Pitt Union. A computerized sign in the lobby told him *The Pitt News* office was on the fourth floor. He waited impatiently for an elevator, not trusting his plodding circulation to get him up the stairs.

The door to room 434 was closed. He turned the handle, found it locked. A sign on the wall indicated the office closed at five.

Damn.

He knocked anyway, not expecting a response, but the door swung open a couple inches.

"Can I help you?" A preppy kid in a pink polo shirt squinted through glasses at Theo.

"I hope so." Theo offered a smile and the kid recoiled. "Is there a way for me to find out the name of someone who placed a classified ad?"

"Our policy is to keep names confidential. I can't give you that information."

Theo dug his technician's identification card out of his pocket. He held it up quickly, then put it away again. "I'm with the police."

Pink Shirt squinted again. "Let me see that."

Theo pulled the card out of his pocket, held it out. Maybe his name and photo on the PBP card would be enough and the kid wouldn't ask for a badge.

"That's not police."

Frustration swished through Theo's midsection. "I didn't say I was an officer, I said I'm with the police." He pointed at the label on the ID. "I'm with forensic investigations." It wasn't a complete fabrication.

Pink Shirt seemed to mull this over. "Why don't they send a cop over?"

"Because this is my specialty. I'm collecting evidence."

"Okay." Pink Shirt opened the door.

"Thanks." Theo put his hand out. "I'm Theo. Pleased to meet you...?" He let the question hang.

Pink Shirt stared at his hand and put both of his in his pockets. "Yeah, okay. I'm Blaine."

Blaine. Of course. "Thanks, Blaine."

"Do you know which user you're looking for?" Blaine said as he dropped into a chair in front of a computer and pulled the keyboard toward him.

Theo looked around the office, spied a stack of *The Pitt News*, and grabbed one. He flipped through to the classifieds.

"Here." He pointed at the article about rising. "I need to know who placed this ad."

"Number 16 dash 39845." Blaine tapped the numbers into the computer and hit enter. Theo tried to stay nonchalant and not crowd him.

"Um, so this ad was placed online by Alice Smith. The user opted to have all correspondence go to an email address." Blaine blinked at Theo.

"So anyone interested in contacting Ms. Smith would send an email to the user's account and all those messages would be forwarded to her email?"

"Uh huh."

"Is there a record kept of the messages that are transferred?"

"No. That would be against our privacy policy."

Theo chewed his bottom lip. "Any other contact information for Ms. Smith?"

"Not that I'm giving you without a warrant." Blaine looked Theo up and down. "You're not a cop and I'm not losing my job. I can give you the email address and you could contact her that way."

"Doesn't sound like you're interested in the safety of your readers."

Blaine shrugged. "It's up to the reader to decide whether or not it's safe to make contact with an advertiser. Not our problem." He poked at the newspaper. "There's a disclaimer."

Theo shook his head. "Can I just have that email address?"

Blaine scrawled a Livenet address on a piece of paper. "Here."

Theo stood up straight. "The Pittsburgh Bureau of Police thanks you, Blaine, for your assistance."

"You're welcome." Blaine cracked a smile. "Just don't tell anyone where you got that."

Back at home, Theo found a note from his parents. They'd gone out to dinner with some of his father's friends from the marina. He had the house to himself for the evening. His mother left a container of rare cooked ground beef in the refrigerator. He grabbed the beef and threw it in the microwave for a few seconds to take the chill off, then sat down at the computer desk with his dinner.

He typed the email address into Google. No results.

He searched for Alice Smith. Over a million results.

Alice Smith and Pittsburgh reduced the results to ten percent of the million, but nothing definitive turned up. Lots of obituaries, but then again, most names returned obituaries, lots of them from the Event. A few links to memorials, and a prayer chain request came up with Alice's name as well. Plenty of folks wanted to see a global holiday announced, lists and statues, like the United States had done after 9/11, but with the scale of loss during the Event, it was nearly impossible. No one could be sure who died during the Event and who was killed in the subsequent panics, or even if they'd risen and died a second time. Information was scattered and semi-accurate at best.

The last twelve years had been more about maintaining some semblance of society and not allowing the power and resource infrastructures to be crushed under the weight of loss and need than about memorializing the billions that died.

He searched for Alice Smith 101, A. Smith 101, and a myriad of other combinations of the name and numbers. He threw in "University of Pittsburgh" and *"Pitt News."* His searches returned nothing that looked even remotely useful.

He scooped a spoonful of beef into his mouth and chewed, thinking.

Clearly his next move was to email Alice Smith. He'd need an alias of his own, preferably something that didn't give away any personal details at all.

He opened Livenet and created his own pseudonym-inspired email account, then began to type.

> Hello Alice,
> I saw your classified ad in the Pitt News.
> I'd like to meet you to discuss information on rising. Please contact me at this email address.
> Regards,
> Pat

He clicked send.

CHAPTER 13

Theo retreated to his basement den and turned on the space heaters. He undressed, pulled the comforter over his shoulders and turned on *Call of Duty* to kill some zombies. Ash splayed on the rug, close to one of the heaters. Theo went through the motions of the video game, but his mind was at the morgue, on those heads from Melwood Avenue, the complete brains, still wet and succulent.

Sweet... Those brains were waiting for him. Waiting for him to gorge himself on their ambrosia and unlock their secrets.

He grabbed his cell phone from his pants pocket and checked for messages or missed calls.

Nothing. He flipped the phone over in his hand, then made a quick decision.

He dialed Dr. Libitin's work phone number. The medical examiner always carried his work phone.

"Libitin."

"Hey, Doc. It's Theo."

"What can I do for you?"

Theo plucked at a loose string on his comforter. "I was wondering if you needed me at the morgue."

Exasperation came across the phone line. "No, Theo. I'm not at the morgue."

"Oh." Theo scratched his head. "Where are you?"

Silence stretched into minutes.

"Theo, what's going on?"

"I just want to help you solve this case. Listen, I went to *The Pitt News* this evening—"

Dr. Libitin cut him off. "I don't buy the philanthropic angle, Theo. Something else is going on. You didn't see yourself when you...you ate those brains last time. It was like seeing a recently turned zombie. It's not right."

Theo's ire swished around. "Are you saying you won't need my help any longer?"

The ME paused. "I'm not sure. I have to give it more thought."

Theo tried to be patient. "Well, when? When will you be done thinking?"

The silence on the line turned cold. "I'll call you tomorrow."

And the line went dead.

Theo waited for the wash of anger and could only note that it took a long time to reach his midsection. His mind told him he was furious, but his chemical responses were definitely back to normal. Zombie-normal, that is. He wanted the instant response, the wave of emotion that required living circulation.

He needed information for Dr. Libitin. Needed to convince the medical examiner his examinations were worthwhile, necessary.

Back upstairs, he logged into his brand-new email account as Pat Jones. Nothing. He supposed it really was too much to hope Alice was sitting in front of a computer. He clicked refresh a couple of times out of boredom and a vague sense of desperation with no results.

The sounds of car tires on the gravel driveway and his father's voice forced him back downstairs. He switched off the television and retreated under his blankets so his parents would leave him alone.

His brand of misery wanted no company.

He rose the next morning after a sleepless night, feeling empty. He went through all the necessary motions to satisfy his mother that everything was just fine, and caught a bus to the forensics lab. The pipets in the analysis lab needed refilling, he had requisitions to submit for new fingerprinting supplies, and the DNA isolation kits came in. Busy work, but it occupied him, along with checking his phone every thirty minutes for Dr. Libitin's promised call.

Lunch came and went. Skeet offered to bring burgers back, but Theo's appetite waned. He spent his lunch hour in the supply closet. The sounds of Skeet and Brian playing blackjack for candy in the break room reached his ears, but Theo remained impassive. When the other technicians started the afternoon shift, Theo resumed his work counting boxes of powdered agar.

"Yo, we're up." Skeet pounded on the doorframe.

He followed Skeet through the break room and into the locker room. Skeet changed out of his street clothes and into scrubs and Theo followed suit.

"What's the job?"

"Convenience store hold-up. The owner shot the perp in the face. Point blank."

Theo cringed. "Lovely."

Skeet made good time getting out of downtown despite the lunch rush, and they wound their way east on the parkway toward Wilkinsburg.

The parking lot of the CoGos in Braddock was jammed with cars. Theo and Skeet parked near the street and unpacked the field kit from the trunk. Just outside the car, they each donned a white paper suit.

"Fucking circus." Skeet peered toward the convenience store. Reporters and cameramen stood four and five deep outside the front of the store, yapping into microphones and jostling elbows.

"Must be a slow news day."

Theo followed Skeet toward the store and chuckled at his partner's enthusiasm in pushing the news crews out of his way.

"'Scuse me. Pardon me. I'm sorry, did I shove you? Oh, that's gonna leave a mark."

The crowd dispersed for Skeet but backed away farther when Theo walked through.

Inside, an elderly African-American gentleman sat on a stack of beer cases, tears streaming down his weathered face. Detective Gavahan knelt close, speaking to the man in tones so low Theo couldn't hear his words.

"What's he doing here?"

Skeet glanced over at Gavahan. "I don't know. Maybe because he's homicide?" Sarcasm edged its way into Skeet's voice.

Theo glared at Skeet. "No need for that."

"Don't be stupid. Here—take these flags and start marking. There shouldn't be much to find." Skeet turned to photograph the body.

Theo dropped flags next to items that looked like they might be important and labeled bags with a description and flag number. He kept one eye on the big picture window for the medical examiner's van.

"Looking for your ally, zombie?" Gavahan's voice came from close to Theo's ear. He jerked away from the bigger man.

"Keeping an eye on the scene," Theo said.

"No need. That's what I'm here for." The detective pointed at the body. "You only have to pay attention to that. Or is that what you want?"

Theo spun to face Gavahan. Did he know something? The smirk on the detective's face caused Theo's nerves to sputter in a slow fire. Gavahan laughed and returned to the store owner.

Theo did his best to ignore Detective Gavahan, despite a rising feeling of unease. Compounding to his discomfort, he'd spent forty-five minutes cataloging evidence and the ME didn't show. Unusual.

Theo grabbed the tweezers and began collecting evidence for transport back to headquarters.

The flash of a white van in the parking lot caught his attention and Theo felt a slight relief of the tension he'd been carrying. Finally he would get to talk to Dr. Libitin and he would see Theo's point and his usefulness. They would go to the morgue and Theo could eat. He could eat sweet brains. He felt his salivary glands swell and release.

Doug came into the store with a blue body bag. "Hey, Theo."

"Hey. Where's the doc?"

"Didn't come in this morning. Dr. Baler is here."

Theo blinked and waited for the anxiety to return. He wasn't disappointed. "Didn't come in?"

"I've got an echo. That's what I said." He unfolded the body bag and placed it beside the corpse.

"But the doc never misses a day. That can't be right. Something's wrong." Confusion flooded Theo's mind, and realization began to dawn that this meant he would not eat.

"Well, he's missing today, Sherlock." Doug walked back outside.

Theo's mind scattered in a million directions. One thought rose to the surface. He would get no brains. His gaze landed on the ruined man at his feet, his face laid open, brain cavity and its contents exposed.

Theo's vision narrowed to the pulpy red matter in the skull. Brains. He saw nothing else, knew it could be his only chance to feed for a long time. He dropped to his knees beside the dead man, all his senses focused on the food laid bare before him. He dipped a finger into the mass of red muck jiggling inside the cavity, swirled it gently in the gelatinous ooze. A line of drool crept out the corner of his mouth, and when it dripped into the brain and blood, Theo swirled the liquid and tissue together.

Black shadows blended with the red liquid before him, faces came and went in the mélange of fluids. A flash of pink sequins, brown eyes, and Hello Kitty. The voices of the dead beckoned to him, pulled him further into their memories, whispered their secrets. They promised life.

Blood and brain matter screamed his name.

Skeet's hand on his shoulder kept him from leaning forward and burying his face in the dead man's skull.

"Theo? Theo? Theo!" Skeet shook hard and squeezed viciously, bringing Theo's awareness of his surroundings into sharp relief. He removed his fingers from his mouth.

Dr. Baler, pretty, blonde, and petite, knelt on the floor opposite Theo, staring at him. Her jaw hung open, disgust clear in her eyes.

"I'm sorry," he mumbled. "I can't..."

"Get him the fuck out of here." Gavahan's voice boomed from behind Theo. "Now."

Theo sat back and looked around, humiliation foremost in his brain, but the sensation not yet in his body.

Gavahan stood with the shop owner. "I knew you'd be a problem, Walker. We'll deal with this later."

Skeet jerked back hard on Theo's shoulder. "Let's go." He thrust the field kit into Theo's arms. "Out to the car, now."

They were on the parkway before Skeet spoke again.

"What the fuck, man? Really. What the fuck?" He hit the steering wheel, caused the car to jerk to the left. "Jesus H. Christ. What the fuck were you thinking?"

Theo dropped his head into his hand. "I don't know. I don't know. I'm sorry."

"What were you doing? What the fuck were you doing?" Skeet's voice sounded shrill and high-pitched, like he was holding back panic of his own. "Just what the fuck, man?"

Theo could hardly blame him. If his body were functioning normally, he would be freaking out. Instead, he just felt his typical numbness.

"I just got lost in thought. I wasn't going to do anything," he lied. "These Riser Killings must be getting to me."

"Do you have any idea what I go through every day because you're my partner? Do you know what they call me?" Skeet shrieked, his voice too loud in the confines of the car. "Necro lover. Brain donor. Gangrene groper. Stiff sucker!"

Theo stared at his partner. "I didn't know."

"Of course the fuck you didn't. You don't know anything. You don't see anything except your own fucking misery. You're a selfish bastard." Skeet pulled into the garage, screeched the tires into a parking spot and wrenched the door open. "You know what, Walker? When you died, you stayed dead. You've made no effort to come back. Maybe it's because you never were human, not even when you were alive." He slammed the door and tromped toward the stairwell.

Theo knew those words would hurt if he were capable of feeling. All he felt was a supreme emptiness. Nothing.

The fact that he was even aware of the emptiness was merely a reflection of the life he felt after he ate. He hadn't missed emotions in the last twelve years.

Was he better off without them? His panic attacks and anxiety left him an outcast in life. How many fourth graders ended up in the corner, teacher holding a paper bag to his face just before a math test?

Only one in his class. The other kids treated him like the freak he was, and kids don't forget. Not even when they're adults. His social life, or lack thereof, was dictated early in life by his inability to control his emotions.

Life without them had its perks.

Theo made his way into the lab, dragging the field kit with him. He dropped it on the table in the supply room, and collected and packaged dirty instruments for autoclaving. He sorted through the contents and restocked where needed. He went through the motions woodenly, unable to drum up enthusiasm.

Why didn't Dr. Libitin go to the crime scene? Why wasn't he at work? Theo needed to find him. He'd promised a phone call.

At six o'clock, Theo changed back into his street clothes, checked his phone to see if he missed something. Nothing. He rode the bus home alone, ignored the fact that despite the crowding, no one would sit in the empty seat next to him. His parents were gone again, something Theo was grateful for. His mother would shove food on him again, and he had no appetite.

Why didn't Dr. Libitin call?

Theo turned the shower to scalding and stepped under the spray. His skin reacted slowly to the heat; circulation picked up and a pink color gradually returned to his flesh. He hadn't realized how gray his complexion had become over the years. He scrubbed vigorously with a green bar of soap, trying to drive more blood into his dermis.

He scoured himself from head to foot, soaking in the heat of the shower until he was deep pink.

The only thing that surfaced was the blood. No emotions. He knelt down in the tub, and after only a moment's hesitation, grasped his dick. He closed his eyes and stroked, fantasizing about Marjorie's face, her black hair, and that silky, thick ripple of midnight. He imagined her dark lips on his, undressed her in his mind to see her small breasts tipped with areolas the color of her lips and the thick tangle of curls between her legs. He stroked faster and imagined parting those curls with his tongue...

But his dick stayed flaccid. Nothing. He couldn't get it up, couldn't even really feel the desire, no matter how hard he tried. Nothing.

He shut the water off and shoved the shower curtain aside. His towel felt cold against his heated skin, and he watched in the mirror as his complexion drained and went from the hard-won pink color back to the now-familiar gray.

Anger. He wanted to feel anger, rage, anything, at this inability to feel. Had the experience of death robbed him of the desire for emotion? The last twelve years were full of nothingness, and he hadn't questioned it. Consuming brain matter reminded him of something he'd been missing, and now although, he couldn't drum up the actual emotion to care about its loss, his mind knew the emptiness should not be. His brain, not his heart, told him this lack of conscience was simply wrong.

What could he be capable of with no conscience? He moved through each day doing what was expected of him without reacting. He'd been raised right, given the right tools and knowledge to do "the proper things," and his actions over the last twelve years reflected only that, not a true desire to be good.

He blinked at his reflection in the mirror. His gray eyes took in the mousy brown hair, the shadow of stubble, the square jaw and crooked nose. He had his mother's chin and his father's brow. His family's history was written in his face, a history that ended with him.

He was nothing.

He should have stayed dead.

~

Theo looked at his clock ten minutes before the alarm went off. He stared at the red lights in the darkness of his basement room for those ten minutes, waiting for the buzzer. The numbness he'd felt the night before remained.

When the blare of the alarm startled Ash from his place against Theo's thigh, he shut it off. His cell phone registered no missed calls. He stepped into a pair of clean jeans and a navy blue t-shirt and walked upstairs.

His mother stood in the kitchen, light pink robe atop her floral nightdress. "Eggs?"

"No, thanks. I ate kind of late last night."

She kissed him lightly on the cheek. "Okay, then. I'm going to get showered. Have a good day, dear."

"Thanks, Ma." He watched her walk up the stairs, then sat down at the computer desk to check his Livenet identity. Aside from offers to increase his manhood—that he sincerely doubted could help him—he had nothing. Either Alice didn't check her messages often or she was onto him.

Dammit. He'd really been hoping to have something to give Dr. Libitin today. He had to convince him the eating was for a good cause.

The sun warmed his back on his walk to the bus stop. He peered around his neighborhood, the neighborhood he'd grown up in. Each house on the street had a story, most of them unpleasant. He'd been held down behind the tree house in that yard and force-fed dog shit. In the basement of the yellow house, he'd been beaten up at least twice. The man who lived in the white house on the corner coached his Little League team and never once let Theo on the field.

Why did he stay? There was nothing here for him.

He stepped onto the bus when it finally arrived and took a seat near the front. He held his cell phone in his hand the entire time so he wouldn't miss a call.

It never rang.

CHAPTER 14

Theo spent the morning mixing reagents for the labs and running the autoclave. He didn't see Skeet, and none of his coworkers bothered to include him in conversation. His phone remained silent, taunting him with the promise of opportunity. Lunchtime came and went and Theo kept mixing. The lab wouldn't need more media for quite a long time. Theo wondered if today would be one of those rare days that didn't require a field visit. He would welcome one of those slow, anonymous days. He didn't think he was in the right frame of mind to work another murder case.

A knock on the door of the autoclave room jarred Theo. "Come in."

Skeet cracked the door open.

The slow adrenaline jolt from Skeet's knock worked its way through Theo's legs, but petered out before it reached his midsection.

"Could you come help me catalog some of the evidence from yesterday?" Skeet's gaze would not meet Theo's.

"Sure." Theo set a timer for the autoclave run and hung it around his neck. He and Skeet retreated to the physical evidence lab to catalog and check-in the remaining hair and fiber samples from the convenience store. They worked in silence for the better part of an hour, until Skeet's phone rang.

"'Ello?"

Theo half-heartedly listened to the one-sided conversation. Skeet flipped the phone closed.

"We're up."

Theo's nerves rattled like they'd remembered they were supposed to do something in situations like this. "*We?*"

"Yes, *we*. Apparently your little stunt at the CoGo isn't enough to warrant taking you out of the field." Skeet shook his head. "Or someone called in a favor."

"Who would do that?" People didn't call in favors for Theo.

"I did, you fuck." Skeet's voice had hard edges. "I told them you're one of the best field agents we have, that the Doc likes working with you and that I could control you." He jammed a finger at Theo's chest, but the pain didn't register. "Now don't dick this up."

"Hey, I don't know how to thank you…"

"Then don't. Just don't make me regret this. You ready?"

Theo took a deep breath. "Yeah. What's the call?"

"Search warrant in Blawnox. The officers found physical evidence that might link this guy to a rape and murder. They want it handled right."

Theo perked up. "Murder? The Riser Killings?"

Skeet rolled his eyes. "Not all the murders in Pittsburgh are related to your Riser Killer."

Theo blinked. He should be mad at Skeet's condescending tone. Instead, he shrugged. "Okay, let's go."

Once they got a look inside, it seemed pretty clear the homeowner had something big to hide. Skeet and Theo cataloged and photographed box after box of pictures of the perp's target—a pretty teenage girl whose naked, battered body floated up the river nearly into Ohio before she'd been fished out. They found several cell phones, all registered to the guy in the living room with only one phone number in the call log. "Souvenirs" were taken from the closet, including a stained pair of pink Victoria's Secret panties, a plastic bag full of blonde hair, a tiny box of fingernail clippings, and a gold locket with pictures of two Chihuahua dogs.

The man sat in a La-Z-Boy recliner in the living room, sobbing. He'd confessed to raping and killing the girl, said he loved her and she drove him to it by ignoring him. Skeet made sounds of disgust throughout the entire process and called the perp foul names under his breath.

Theo did his job and wondered if the girl's brain survived the soak and what it would taste like.

His phone never rang.

CHAPTER 15

Theo moved through the next two days without really experiencing them. Every so often he stopped to consider how he felt, but the only answer he found was numb.

It didn't seem to matter much.

Friday afternoon, Theo collected the dirty glassware from the fluids lab and prepped it for the autoclave. He'd just set the timer on the big oven when Skeet tapped the door.

"We've got a body."

Theo flipped the switch to start the glassware cycle and followed his partner to the garage. "Where are we headed?"

Skeet unlocked the car doors with the remote. "Savannah Avenue."

"In Edgewood?"

His partner nodded and dropped into the driver's seat.

"Isn't that real close to Frick Park?"

Another nod.

Something fluttered in Theo's stomach, faint and slow. "Is it a Riser Killing?"

Skeet hands tightened around the steering wheel. "I don't know."

Tendrils of unease coiled in Theo's stomach. "I'm surprised they're letting me back out with you after... well, after what happened at the CoGo."

Theo watched a muscle in Skeet's jaw clench and unclench. "Gavahan agreed to let it go."

"Why?" Theo choked out the word.

"I don't know. He just never said anything. Like it never happened."

After a moment of incredulity, Theo dropped it. "Hey, have you heard from Dr. Libitin lately?" He kept his tone as neutral as possible. For the first time in a week, he was grateful for the lack of emotions.

"No, you?" Skeet's hands relaxed a little. "Kind of weird. He usually calls for lab results a couple times a week."

Skeet pulled off the parkway and made his way through the back roads of Edgewood to Savannah Avenue.

The sawhorses set up as barricades prevented Skeet from pulling the car close to the scene. Theo caught sight of the white ME van parked at the other end of the blocked section of road and his stomach squeezed just a touch.

"I'll move them." Theo got out of the car and shifted the sawhorses far enough for Skeet to pull through, then put them back in place.

A uniformed cop approached Theo. "You're not permitted in here."

Theo slipped his badge from the pocket in the scrubs. "Forensics."

The officer's gaze swept over Theo with a familiar, contemptuous look. Once again, Theo acknowledged he should feel gratitude that he couldn't be offended. It didn't matter. He shook the ID. "I'm with forensics."

The officer stepped aside wordlessly and Theo followed the little red hatchback. He helped Skeet grab the field kit from the back and they walked through the overgrown grass to an area marked off by yellow tape. He kept one eye out for Dr. Libitin, but didn't see him. Gavahan, however, stood on the sidewalk, talking with a woman in a blue housedress and writing in his notebook. He did not acknowledge Theo's arrival.

"You take the perimeter." Skeet handed him a stack of yellow markers. "I'll start photographing."

Theo began his survey of the scene, as he'd seen Dr. Libitin do so many times before. The body lay crumpled in the midst of the untended lawn, more weeds than grass. From his vantage point he could see the cause of death clearly—a shot to the temple.

There went that flutter again.

He strained to see the wrists, but the body lay on its side, arms underneath. Skeet shot him a look and returned to his camera.

The heavy vegetation slowed his work. Possible evidence hid under brambles and thistles. Theo pulled on a second pair of gloves.

Movement at the ME's van caught his attention. Doug pushed a gurney; Dr. Baler walked behind him. The assistant medical examiner glanced over at Theo, then looked away. Theo couldn't blame her after what happened at the CoGo's.

Still no Dr. Libitin. Disappointment began in Theo's chest and trickled weakly through his abdomen. He started toward the body to help the ME and Doug, but Skeet waved him off.

"No, Theo. Collect the physical evidence."

A twitch of irritation flicked at Theo's mind, but he kept searching. Gavahan joined the group at the body and joined a discussion held in tones too low for Theo to eavesdrop.

Doug and Skeet bagged the corpse. Theo watched, tried to catch a glimpse of the wrists, but only determined that the victim was a man with artificially red hair. He glanced at Gavahan, the detective met his gaze with his own stony one.

He headed to the car to grab bags and a marker while Skeet moved from flag to flag, photographing the items Theo deemed worth investigation. He kept his gaze on the ground, trying to remain vigilant for any article of interest.

"Hey."

Theo lifted his head. Doug and Gavahan stood next to the car. He nodded to Doug.

The technician and detective exchanged a glance. Doug spoke. "You heard from Doc lately?"

Theo frowned. "No. Has he said anything about needing me at the morgue?"

Gavahan's gaze pierced Theo. "He hasn't been at the morgue."

"Not at the morgue?" Theo echoed, trying to process the information.

"When was the last time you talked to him?" Gavahan's voice sounded strained.

Theo thought. "Uh, Tuesday night, I think. I talked to him on the phone for a minute or two Tuesday night."

"I saw him last on Tuesday," Doug said.

"Are you sure you haven't seen or spoken to him since Tuesday?" A note of urgency tinged Gavahan's words. "We figured you might be the one to keep in touch with him."

Theo noted concern etched on the detective's face. "No, I swear. We didn't... um..." He thought back to the way they'd parted. "No. I don't think he would contact me."

A muscle in Gavahan's jaw twitched. He walked away without a word.

Theo and Doug stared at each for a moment before Doug spoke again. "I'm worried."

"Yeah." Theo couldn't say the same with honesty, but his mind puzzled over the medical examiner's absence. "He hasn't called in sick or anything?"

"Nothing. No communication with anyone. He's not answering his work phone or his personal phone." Doug shifted from one foot to the other. "He's never done this before."

Theo chewed his lip. "Has anyone checked on him yet? Gone to his house?"

Doug inhaled and exhaled noisily. "That's the next step. I guess I'll do that today. Don't want to let it go over the weekend."

Theo studied Doug's face, saw the signs of worry and stress in the tightness around his eyes and mouth. He worked closely with Dr. Libitin, had to be feeling his absence. "I'll go with you."

"He's coming here to pick me up after he logs the body in. Said his shift is about over, anyway," Theo told Skeet. They'd driven back to the lab and Theo explained Doug's concern over Dr. L's absence.

Skeet agreed. "It's not like him. I don't know if I've ever gone to the morgue and not seen him there. Did the man take a day off?"

"I don't know." Theo shook his head. "We worked together a lot over the past couple of months, but I don't know anything about his personal life, except that he lived alone."

"As soon as Doug gets here, you leave. I'll finish getting this stuff in the system."

"Thanks." Theo paused. "Skeet?"

Skeet didn't look up from unpacking evidence bags. "Yeah?"

"Did he have the tattoo?"

Skeet continued moving the bags from the field pack to the table. Silence hung heavy in the air.

"Come on, man. Did he have the tattoo?"

Skeet sighed, pressed his lips together. Finally, he spoke. "Yeah."

"The Doc was on to something. You know it, I know it. These Riser Murders are real. And this is another one. Someone has to tell Baler and Gavahan, get them to see." Theo spoke in low tones.

"And what? What then? There's no real evidence. If Libitin doesn't come back, Baler will have to take a look at the evidence from the other cases, and sooner or later, the cops will start piecing it together."

"How many more people will die before someone eventually 'pieces it together?'" Theo felt anger lick his ribs. "I don't think anyone wants to put it together. No one cares that these people are dying, that potential undead are being killed, and when this killer starts to target zombies, no one will care about that either."

Skeet hit the table with his fist. "What do you want me to do, Theo? There's nothing conclusive tying these deaths together."

"The manner of death has been consistent—either execution-style shot to the head or beheading. Ballistics should be able to link at least some of them to the same gun. There's that and also the socioeconomic class of most of these victims. The only outlier is Naomi."

And his psychic visions. But he couldn't tell Skeet about those. That information would remain useless unless he could prove the things he'd seen.

"Just please, mention it to someone," he pleaded. "Gavahan. Or Baler. Tell Baler to look at the records."

Skeet dropped into a desk chair. "Fine. I'll say something when someone comes for this evidence."

"Thank you." Theo laid a hand on Skeet shoulder and noted the slight recoil. "This killer is picking victims she thinks no one cares about. We have to prove that wrong."

Skeet frowned. "What do you mean 'she?'"

Tiny fingers of panic massaged Theo's brain. "Uh, just a slip. I'm going outside to wait for Doug."

Skeet's frown followed Theo through the door. He made his way to the front of the building and sat on the concrete steps to soak in the summer heat.

He felt limber by the time Doug pulled up in a blue sedan.

"Ready?" Doug called.

Dr. Libitin lived on the North Side. The red brick-front building was sandwiched between its neighbors. Doug pulled up to the curb and Theo followed him to the porch.

The lid on the mailbox hanging next to the door was propped open by overflowing mail. Doug and Theo exchanged a look.

"Do you think we should just go in or call the police?" Theo peered at the windows, but the curtains inside were drawn and prevented him from seeing the interior.

Doug held up a key. "He left a key at work in case we ever needed somewhere to crash."

Theo raised his eyebrows.

"Yeah, he's that kind of guy. Always said we're welcome." He inserted the key in the lock and twisted.

"Hello?" Doug led the way into the house.

The front door opened directly into a dimly lit living room. With all the blinds tightly drawn, the only light came from a floor lamp in the far corner.

"Doc?" Doug's voice rang through the house. "Hey, Doc! You here?"

Nothing. Theo stood just inside the front door, hesitant to invade the privacy of a man he counted as a friend.

"We've got to check the house. He could be in trouble." Doug walked to the stairs. "I'll check upstairs. You check this floor and the basement."

Theo walked silently on the thick beige carpet toward the hallway. As he passed the sofa, he peered behind it and beside it, afraid to see Dr. Libitin on the floor.

He opened a door just off the living room and found an immaculately clean powder room. A crisp white hand-towel hung from a brass ring and even the soap was clean and dry.

Dr. Libitin took pride in his home, just like he did in his job.

The putty-colored tile in the hall extended to the kitchen. Theo flipped a bank of light switches, illuminating both the kitchen and the dining room. A coffeemaker and a bowl of apples and bananas sat on the beige countertop. The bananas sported brown spots, obviously just past their prime.

He opened the refrigerator and found the basics: a grapefruit half, still fresh, various condiments, and a bag of coffee beans. A loaf of bread in the bottom drawer looked fine.

Soiled dinner dishes and a rinsed coffee mug filled part of the dishwasher. Not enough to run it, but only one meal's worth.

Theo heard footsteps on the floor above, a door clicked shut. Doug's voice carried from upstairs, calling for Dr. Libitin.

Theo ran his fingers inside the kitchen sink, found it dry. It was clear the kitchen hadn't been used in some time.

He opened a door, flipped the light switch on the wall and peered into a well-lit basement. "Doc?"

Down in the subterranean room he found a boiler and a spotless workshop area.

Dr. Libitin's house reflected the man—neat to a fault and arranged with precision—but with no apparent sign of the man himself.

Theo went back upstairs and found Doug standing at one end of the hallway, scratching his head.

"Nothing up here. The bed is made and the towels are dry." Doug frowned. "I don't think he's been here."

"But he hasn't been gone long. Everything looks like he just walked out this morning."

"So what the fuck is going on? We've been trying to contact him since the first day he didn't show up. Dr. Baler came out here, obviously he didn't answer the door. We've been doing everything we could think of to find him. This was our last resort."

Theo wandered into the bedroom, trying to connect with the home's occupant. "Why didn't someone call me sooner? Do the police know?"

"You're not popular at the morgue." At least Doug was straightforward. "Of course the police know. They say he's a grown man and we don't have any reason to be alarmed yet. Emphasis on the yet."

Theo continued his search. Everything appeared neat and in its place.

"Did you check for his cell phone?" Theo said.

"I didn't open anything."

Theo strode to the side table and opened the narrow drawer. One cellular telephone rested in the drawer, plugged into a cord running through a hole drilled in the back of the drawer.

Theo looked back at Doug and pointed at the phone. Doug walked wordlessly to Theo's side.

"That's his work phone." He leaned over and looked further into the drawer. "There's another charging cable here, looks like an iPhone adapter. That would be for his personal phone."

"Did you see it anywhere?"

"No," Doug said and pulled his own phone from his pocket. He dialed and they both waited, listening.

Nothing.

"It's not here. And he's not answering it." Doug shoved his phone back in his pocket, frustration creeping into his voice. "Fuck me. I honestly thought we'd get here and find him in the house, drunk or like the 'I've fallen and can't get up' lady. We'd buy him a Life Alert as a joke for the office Christmas party."

Theo swept his gaze around the orderly bedroom, taking in the open closet door and the potted ficus in the corner. A feeling of dread slowly settled in his stomach.

"Something's very wrong."

Doug nodded. "What do we do?"

"We have to call the police." Theo closed the closet door, feeling as if he should honor the tidy order of Dr. Libitin's personal space.

"I think this might go beyond a call to the police." Doug paced at the foot of the bed. "We should go see Gavahan."

A sour taste bloomed in Theo's mouth. "Gavahan's homicide. Why wouldn't we go to someone in missing persons?"

Doug seemed to consider this. "Gavahan is just as concerned as we are. He's been asking around since Wednesday. And this isn't just a 'missing person.' This is a missing medical examiner. You have any idea how many people out there curse his name? He's put murderers behind bars, man, or at least his autopsy evidence has. Besides, I don't know anyone in missing persons. I'm a morgue tech. I only work with homicide detectives. We should go to Gavahan and ask him for a name of someone in missing persons. He's going to want to deal with this himself, though, based on what I've seen from him already."

Theo followed Doug back to the front door. Almost as if an afterthought, Doug changed course into the kitchen and began opening drawers. He fished through several before he brought a notepad and a pen out. Theo watched from the opposite side of the counter while Doug wrote a note to the doc that they'd been in the house and to call if he got in. Doug hesitated before adding "you've got us worried" to the end of the note. He met Theo's gaze. "So he knows we're here and knows he needs to call. I'm not jackin' around."

Theo nodded. "Good idea."

Doug brought the mail in and left it on the dining room table. Theo studied the interior of the house, looking for clues to the doctor's whereabouts, but saw nothing. The house seemed like someone left for work, expecting to come back at the end of the day.

Doug locked the front door when they left.

"I think we should go straight to Gavahan." He shifted the sedan into drive and headed back toward the parkway.

Theo remained silent, letting Doug talk.

"It doesn't make any sense that Doc's missing. He wouldn't just go on his own. He loves his job, he loves the city. He's really involved in a big case; he just won't say what it is. I'm pretty sure it has something to do with the recent killings. Maybe he's getting too close."

Theo winced as Doug merged into the neighboring lane, a little too close to the car in front.

"Do you know anything about those cases, Theo? You've been spending time with the doc."

Theo winced again. "He asked my opinion a couple times." How much did Doug know?

"Just asked your opinion? Do you have some kind of experience with this stuff?"

"Not exactly. I guess he thought I might have new insight since I died, too."

"Oh." Doug fell quiet for a minute. "I hadn't thought of that."

Doug steered the car around a corner in downtown Pittsburgh. "How did you die, Theo, if you don't mind my asking?"

Theo cleared his throat and opened the passenger door. "I was murdered."

"Oh."

Thankfully, Doug remained silent for the walk into the bureau headquarters.

Theo stood near the door, ready to make a quick exit if Gavahan got shitty. He'd figured out the closest bus stop and knew which bus would take him home. He almost felt uncomfortable under Gavahan's gaze.

The cubicle-slash-office was sparsely furnished, with only one chair opposite the metal desk, so Theo didn't even have to make an excuse to keep his distance. One wall sported framed certificates—firearms training, police academy diploma proclaiming Decebal Gavahan a graduate with honors, and various seminars and certifications. Gavahan was clearly a good detective, if one could overlook his asshole attitude.

His name was Decebal? Theo suppressed a giggle.

"We're sure he didn't just go on vacation?"

"Come on, Dec. We've been through this over and over since Wednesday."

Theo shot a look at Doug. Since when was he on a first-name basis with Detective Gavahan?

Doug continued, "You know him better than that. His work phone was in his nightstand. He wouldn't have left his work phone." Doug's tone carried a hint of panic.

"We should have gone in his house days ago. I should have listened to my gut." Gavahan assessed Doug. "Any signs of a struggle?"

Doug turned around to look at Theo, who shook his head. "No," Theo finished for him. "There were not."

The detective propped his feet on his desk. "I get the feeling there is something you're not telling us, Mr. Walker. Now would be the time to spill it."

Theo felt a spike of panic. "We were collaborating on a situation together that he is invested in."

Gavahan leveled his gray-eyed gaze on Theo. "What situation is that?"

"The recent Frick Park killings." Theo couldn't call them the Riser Killings without knowing what Dr. Libitin might have shared with Gavahan.

The detective leaned forward in his chair. "Why did the medical examiner involve you, a forensic technician responsible for merely cataloging evidence, in these cases?"

Theo paused. "I think my background led him to believe I could offer a unique perspective."

"What perspective would that be?" Gavahan shoved a pile of folders across the desk and several glossy photos of ruined corpses fell out. "It's clear you weren't decapitated or shot in the head because you wouldn't be standing here now. So what exact circumstances would lead Dr. Libitin to think you would be of any use at all?"

Theo smelled a trap. "I guess because I died already he thought I might have some empathy for the dead."

"Empathy? Why would the medical examiner care if you had *empathy* for the thing on the table? Everybody has empathy for victims of violence, but that doesn't mean shit in a homicide investigation." Gavahan smacked the desk.

"Something's going on with you, zombie. I will find out what it is."

Doug looked from detective to zombie, astonishment clear on his face. He remained silent.

"I'm outta here, Doug. Call me if you find out anything about the doc." Theo slipped through the door, walking as fast as the air conditioning in the bureau would allow.

Theo took a seat in the back of the bus, away from the small group of commuters riding near the front. He leaned his forehead against the seat in front of him.

Again, he acknowledged a certain relief at the fact he couldn't feel emotions. Anxiety would once have crippled him in Gavahan's office.

Dr. Libitin didn't share the details of his involvement with Gavahan, or anyone other than Shelby. Theo was confident of that. If he'd been questioned about Theo's presence in the morgue, he would have had a ready excuse, but Theo couldn't imagine who would question Dr. Libitin about his actions in the morgue. Without Dr. Libitin to maintain the wall between him and the rest of the force, morgue officials included, Theo would have some serious explaining to do.

He had to find the medical examiner.

Certain Dr. Libitin's disappearance was connected to the Riser Killings, he took the train of thought to its logical conclusion: finding the killer.

A burst of laughter from the front of the bus drew Theo's attention. He raised his head and watched the group of college kids joke and laugh.

He didn't have the kind of friends he could joke around with. Dr. Libitin came close, along with Skeet and possibly Shelby and Marjorie now. Shelby didn't seem to judge him for what he did at the morgue; she seemed to see the value in it, but he had no doubt Skeet and Marjorie would have a problem.

Especially Marjorie. He broke a zombie code, one they shared.

He had to find Dr. Libitin and make this right.

It took two hours of killing virtual zombies in his video game before Theo even dozed. In the hazy half-sleep, Theo dreamt of unicorns, little boys, and pain. Black shadows punctuated his dreams, and the scent of gunpowder hung heavy in his nostrils.

Each time he began to reach consciousness, he willed himself back into sleep, desperate to see the psychic visions that would offer insight or lead to an answer. Nothing worked. The visions were devoid of emotion. He needed more brains, needed to feel closer to the dead, to ingest their lives and their memories.

Finally, he gave up. Theo scratched behind Ash's ear, eliciting a purr from the cat. He extricated himself from the burrow of blankets he'd made on the mattress and walked upstairs.

The ticking clock punctuated the silence of late night. His father worked the overnight shift at the marina and wasn't due home for another couple hours and his mother went to bed.

He pushed the button on the computer tower, pulled out the rickety wooden chair, and waited for the glow of the monitor to illuminate the room. A few clicks of the mouse took him to the site for his fake email account and he entered the password.

The spam filter failed to weed out the offers to enlarge his penis and news of an inheritance from a long-lost uncle in Nigeria, but in the midst of the junk, one message stood out.

Alice Smith.

Theo clicked on the link for the message.

> Hello Pat,
> I would be happy to meet with you to discuss your rising. Let me know what day is good for you and we'll make the arrangements. I am located on the east side of the city.
> Sincerely,

Alice

Theo blinked at the screen, a mix of emotions bubbling gently in his gut. He quickly tapped out a reply:

Alice,
I can meet any time you're available, the sooner the better. The east side is not a problem. Did you have a place in mind?
Pat

He read through it twice, trying to be sure he didn't say anything extra between the few lines. Once satisfied, he clicked send.

There would be no sleep for him tonight. The bit of adrenaline the email produced would make sure he stayed up. He paced the first floor. The sound of his mother's bedroom door opening halted him in midstride.

"Teddy? Are you up?"

He sighed. "Yes, Mom."

She picked her way down the stairs. "Do you need to me to make you something? I can get you a bowl of ice cream."

She meant well. He knew that, and tempered his response with her intentions in mind. "No thanks, Ma. I'm good."

"Well, I'm up now. I might as well get you something."

Shit. He'd never get any peace. "I'm actually heading out, Ma. I've, uh…" He ran through possibilities. "I've got some late work."

"Oh. Well, okay. I didn't realize." She patted his arm then settled into his father's recliner and pulled a bodice clutcher novel from the side pocket. "Okay, then, honey. Be careful."

He watched her get comfortable, realizing that now he was committed to going out.

Great. Where the hell could he go at this hour? He'd have to get out of the neighborhood or she'd wonder what he was doing.

Theo grabbed his jacket and locked the front door behind him. He made for the bus stop through darkness of night.

The bus carried no passengers when Theo boarded. The driver nodded. "Where you headed?"

Good question. Theo took the front passenger seat. "Frick Park." Maybe the killer left something the cops missed. He might as well be useful.

He had the bus to himself for the entire ride and almost found himself fidgeting. He noted his restlessness with detached observance, and switched his focus back to the task at hand.

At the park, he thanked the driver and made his way toward the small information stand near the head of the trails. The dim streetlights made looking at the trail maps difficult, and Theo regretted not bringing a flashlight.

The head of the trail to Fern Hollow loomed large and dark in front of him. He looked around the trailhead, saw no other people, no one to follow him. He took a step into the forest.

The night closed in around him, the claustrophobic feeling comforting. Maintenance of the park fell by the wayside during the chaotic years following the Event, and he thought it was for the better. Before the Event, the trails had been manicured and kept clean, the perfect wilderness experience for the urban dweller. Now city resources were tight and manpower short, parks and recreation budgets weren't the priority. For the first time in Theo's thirty-odd years in Pittsburgh, he felt like the park was being reclaimed by nature. He loved it.

A deer path zigzagged off the main trail, toward Falls Ravine, and Theo took it. He'd be less likely to meet up with the random junkie sleeping off a trip or couples looking for privacy.

He walked to the site where Jerry Cullins, Jennifer Semuta, and Rhonda Abraham's bodies were found. Someone had washed away the gore, because all that remained was a large, damp area on the ground. Theo went to the center of the area, knelt, put his hand to the ground. He concentrated, trying to feel sensations, something, anything, to connect him the deceased.

All he felt was cold and foolish.

His psychic powers didn't extend to wet grass.

Sounds reached his ears, noises as if someone were struggling. He pushed through the brambles, thorns scratching his hands. New trees battled older, established behemoths for sunlight here in the woods and Theo just managed to wedge through.

A bit of moonlight filtered down through a break in the canopy, illuminating two people sitting against a rock. A man struggled with a woman's arm, pulled at it, hit her twice. Her sobs barely reached Theo's ears. He moved as silently as possible through the trees, approaching the pair. His heart beat a bit faster, and he found a large stick before he moved closer, ready to defend himself.

The snap of a twig gave him away, and the man looked up. "Who's there?"

Theo held still.

"Cocksuckers! Get the fuck away!" The man went back to twisting the woman's arm.

Theo watched, puzzled, until he realized the man was just trying to find a vein to shoot the woman up. Those were not sounds of fear coming from the woman, they were the sounds of a desperate junkie.

He moved quietly away from the couple, back to the clearing where the Riser Killer left his victims. He stood, peered around the small clearing, tried to get a feel for why the killer chose this spot to dump the bodies. Aside from the fact it was secluded, he could see no logical explanation for the choice. He turned in a slow circle, examining the ground and trees.

When he reached a hundred and eighty degrees, he saw a small opening in an otherwise dense growth of underbrush, just big enough for him to squeeze through, if he was careful. He approached the area, inspected the break in the vegetation, went through, and followed a crude trail.

The lights from South Braddock didn't have a chance of reaching this far back, but the half-moon hanging in the sky offered enough light for Theo to see his steps. Nine Mile Run split into smaller creeks throughout Frick Park, the waterway topography changing along with the rest of the park.

Theo heard running water ahead and to the side of him and made for the loudest. Maybe sitting near running water would help him think clearly and bring some insight—the kind of insight and empathy only Theo could experience.

The trail opened into a small clearing where Nine Mile Run spilled from a rock outcropping and formed a small pool before trickling downhill. The moonlight brightened the space and Theo could see better here than in the trees. Pretty amazing spot.

He squinted at the rocks around the waterfall, scoping out a spot to sit and think. Closer to the water, he poked at the rocks with his stick, checking which ones would hold his weight and which wouldn't be safe to stand on.

Near the waterfall, he saw it would be feasible to sit behind the water flow, so he surveyed the larger rocks for a way across the pool. He moved across two rocks and judged the distance to the second, before taking a test hop to be sure he'd have the leverage necessary to make it to the next.

He hopped once, hard, and pushed forward when the rock gave way underneath him and he went into the pool, scrabbling the whole way down. Dark shapes emerged from behind the waterfall, and flew close over his head, shrieking the entire way.

Great, just fucking great. He couldn't get on the bus to go home if he was soaked through with run-off.

The water was only a few feet deep, but he'd dislodged the flat rock and it stood on end, propped by something underneath. Theo put a hand down to the silty bottom to push himself to his feet, and brushed something rubbery. His foot slipped out from underneath him and tossed him off balance. He flailed, looking for something to right himself, and ended up grabbing the thing under the rock.

It felt strange, whatever it was, not smooth. Tentacles? He frowned and tugged on it, trying to dislodge it from under the rock. He had to wrestle a little and shift the rock to just get a bit of it above the surface and into the moonlight to get a better look.

As he wrenched it back and forth, he noted a pale color contrasting with the dark of the pool bottom. His curiosity piqued, he braced his feet against the rock and yanked, hard. Finally, the rock toppled on its side and gave up its hold on the object. Theo sat in the muddy water, watching the object emerge through the murk.

It was a hand, connected to an arm. Theo watched, removed from the moment, feeling no emotion, as a bloated body floated up from beneath the rock.

CHAPTER 16

Theo knelt in the chilly water, and stared at the body still wedged in the muck under the rock. The silt kept its hold on the left side, from the waist up. The right arm bobbed in the gentle movement of the water created by the falls, waving at him.

It took several minutes for Theo to absorb what lay in front of him. His first instinct was to grab the arm and shove the rock off the body, drag it to the ground and check for a heartbeat, but thankfully, he thought it through. Instead of ruining what appeared to be a crime scene, he gingerly grasped the hand again, flipped it over and checked for a pulse in the wrist. He felt in a couple different spots, held firmly, but could not find any sign of a heartbeat. The hand was gray and very cold, sleeved in a dark sweater of some sort, and Theo knew the person was gone.

He stood, working the stiffness from his knees and waded slowly out of the water. With his back to the corpse, he rubbed his temples, trying to force his brain to function. The night sounds of the park captivated him for a moment, and he listened to the hoot of an owl not far from where he stood. Rustling in the underbrush caught his attention and he watched a light colored cat, low to the ground, run from behind one tree to another.

The blare of a car horn, probably from Forbes Road, brought him back to reality. He shook his head, knowing the loss of body heat from sitting the cool water was affecting him. He turned around to the body, and realized he needed help. His cell phone had stayed dry in his pocket, and still held a dial tone. He pressed nine-one-one and waited for an operator to answer.

"Allegheny County nine-one-one, what is your emergency?" A female voice came across the line.

"I found a body," Theo said. Blunt, but effective.

"Sir?"

Theo swallowed. "I found a dead body."

Silence hovered on the line.

"I'm sorry, to clarify, you found a body, is that right?" the operator said.

"Yes."

"What is your name, sir?" The operator maintained an incredible monotone.

"Theodore Walker."

"Are you sure the individual is deceased, Mr. Walker?"

"Yes."

"What makes you think that?"

Theo looked back at the body. "Most of it is underwater and the arm and leg I can see are not moving. I work for the forensics department."

"What is your location?"

"I'm in Frick Park. I walked back Falls Ravine, but took some deer trails or something. I'm near a small waterfall on Nine Mile Run."

"You started on Falls Ravine Trail?"

"Yes."

"Okay, I'm dispatching someone to you. Please stay on the line with me until we get someone there. Do you have a flashlight or some other way to signal?

"No. Just my phone."

"Okay."

The operator paused for a minute or two. "You said you work for the forensics department?"

"Yes. Howard Moster is my boss."

"Okay, Mr. Walker. They'll start yelling when they get a little way down Falls Ravine, so if you would just yell back to lead them to your location, that will get them to you. They're about five minutes out. Would you like to stay here on the line with me or hang up?"

"I'll go ahead and hang up. I can wait here for them."

"Okay, Mr. Walker. You have a great morning."

"Thanks," Theo replied, and as an afterthought added, "You too." He clicked the off button to end the call.

Morning? He checked the time on his phone. Yep, almost three AM. He found a dry spot on the bank of the pool and sat. The hand continued the gentle bobbing, waving at him from underneath the dirty water.

It mocked him. He tried not to look, but the white flesh shone like a beacon in the moonlight.

He couldn't just sit there until the crew got arrived. He'd do his job.

Theo stood and inspected the scene, as he would for work. Mimicking Dr. Libitin, he stood back from the center of the scene, in this case the corpse, and took in the bigger picture. The bright moon didn't afford him quite enough light to do a thorough inspection, but he'd do his best. His concentration faltered because of the lower body temperature his wet pants brought on.

Footprints marred the scene, but most of them were probably his. He'd have to give up his shoes to forensics. The waterfall began at an outcropping about ten feet above the pool of water, not a big fall, and not a huge volume of water, but enough to have carved out a deeper pool than he'd originally thought. There could be a lot of things hiding in that water.

More bodies, certainly.

Several deer trails wound their way to and from the little clearing. Again, lots of prints, so unless footprint evidence from the Riser Killer existed from a crime scene he didn't know about, these would most likely be worthless. He walked slowly around the pool, noting the locations of discarded gum wrappers, condom packages, several syringes, and even an old blue towel.

Once he'd made his way to the edge of the water, he peered at the corpse. Any evidence on it would be rendered useless by the time submerged, unless the victim managed to stash away his or her killer's driver's license.

Stranger things had happened.

"Hello?" A voice carried through the forest.

Theo called back. "Here!"

"Keep calling. We're coming."

He repeated the word several times before he saw lights bobbing. "Right here," he repeated one final time before the clearing was filled with uniformed officers and detectives in suits.

"Hey, Walker." Detective Brown stepped next to Theo. "You okay?"

Theo nodded. "Yeah."

"This is weird, huh?" the detective said. "So where's our stiff?"

Theo pointed to the pool. "Under that big rock there."

The crew immediately began setting up portable spotlights, centered on the pool. Theo stepped to the side.

"Your partner was right behind us when we left the parking lot. He should be here shortly." Detective Brown clapped Theo on the back and walked to the edge of the pool, inspecting the scene.

Theo watched the path the others appeared from, and in just a few minutes, Skeet shoved his way through the crowd, dragging the big kit from the back of the car. Howard Moster trucked along right behind him.

"Boss." Theo stepped forward to take some of the supplies from Skeet.

"Theo." Howard nodded to Theo. "Kind of unusual for one of our own to find a scene."

"I guess so." Theo unlatched the kit and grabbed a stack of flags.

"You can't work this one." Howard held his hand out for the flags.

Theo relinquished them, confused. "Why not? I've been here for almost a half an hour already. I've canvassed the scene. I can tell you where everything is."

Theo watched as Skeet and their boss exchanged a look. "Protocol," said Howard. "You'll have to be questioned."

"Questioned? But I just found it..." Theo waved at the pool, looked from his partner to his boss, saw the resolve on both faces. "I examined the scene already. I'll show you where the items of interest are."

"No, you need to stay available for the detectives. We'll look with a fresh set of eyes." Howard gestured for Skeet to start working the scene. Skeet assembled his camera equipment without looking at Theo. "Start with pictures of the pool, Skeet. They're going to want to get that body out of the water."

Theo watched his partner and his boss pull on hip waders and perform his usual job duties with the now familiar sense of detachment. He knew the situation should provoke him somehow, but it didn't. If he were alive...if he'd fed lately...maybe it would.

Skeet took shot after shot of the rock and the area where Theo fell into the water then climbed out.

Maybe it was better he couldn't feel.

"Looks like someone used a tool on the rock over here. It's got scratches in it." Skeet pointed at the bottom edge of the rock, facing away from Theo.

Theo's boss walked to the side of the pool to examine the marks. He and Skeet spoke in quiet tones, pointed at the rock. Theo couldn't hear them.

He continued observing the activity around him, but did not make another attempt to help. Some sort of self-preservation instinct told him to just stay out, and he almost felt gratitude when Detective Gavahan entered the clearing.

"What do we have here?" The detective's voice boomed through the clearing, not diminished at all by the sound of flowing water.

Dr. Baler and a morgue technician followed Detective Gavahan out of the woods.

Howard pointed at the pool. "Body under the rock."

"Witnesses?"

"Just one." Howard turned to Theo. "Mr. Walker found this one."

"Did he?" Gavahan's eyes narrowed. "What were you doing here at this time of night, Mr. Walker?"

Theo thought for a minute. "Taking a walk."

"A walk?" Gavahan grinned. "Is strolling through dark parks in the middle of the night a habit of yours?"

"Not exactly."

"Then what—exactly—were you doing out here?"

"Thinking."

"We've done all we need to document the scene," Howard interrupted. "It's safe to move the rock."

Gavahan nodded. "Then by all means, move it. Let's get the body out and see what we're dealing with."

Skeet and Howard shifted through the mud and silt to the body. Dr. Baler and the morgue tech unfolded a body bag next to the pool, ready to collect the waterlogged corpse.

Skeet grabbed one side of the rock, Howard the other, and they heaved back on it. Both men stumbled back, seemingly surprised at the ease with which they tilted the big rock. A wet sucking sound echoed in the clearing.

"It must have originally been standing up." Theo's boss brushed his gloves on his waders. "It slipped right back into a crevice underneath."

Indeed, the rock seemed to settle back into a spot under the water. Howard and Skeet rolled the body over onto its back. The corpse was stuck fast in the mud, and the men pulled hard on it. Theo couldn't help but move a step or two closer.

A murmur rippled through the assembled law enforcement officials in the clearing when Skeet and Mr. Moster lifted the body free of the muck.

The corpse lacked a head.

The upper body, clothed in a sweater of indeterminate color, dripped dirty water. Dark slacks stuck to the legs. Rigor looked to be minimal, but the fact the corpse had been submerged for some time made the issue of rigor a questionable one.

A flurry of noise escaped the people gathered around the pool. Skeet and Mr. Moster lifted the body by the legs and shoulders and shuffled sideways with their heavy burden. They laid it out next to the pool. Skeet moved back to the area where the body lay and used a metal pole to root around in the mud for more clues.

Theo's attention turned to the body. Something seemed off, but he couldn't quite put his finger on it. The thick layer of mud on the body prohibited identification by clothes or other features.

"I need to take this one to the morgue," Dr. Baler said. "We'll have to clean it up before we can even attempt an ID. The body does appear to be male, based on proportions and shoes."

Everyone's attention was drawn to the feet, which were clad in brown loafers. Theo's brain fired, but failed to make the connections. He knew he was missing something.

"Ah, guys. We have the head." Skeet's voice came from behind. "It was jammed under the rock."

Dr. Baler pointed at it. "I know this is a little unusual, but go ahead and try to wash some of that mud off."

Skeet's eyes bulged a little, but he knelt down and swiped at the face with gloved fingers, at the bald scalp. A hawkish nose came into view, followed by clear blue eyes.

Theo felt the stirrings of agony in his midsection. "Dr. Libitin."

Adrenaline still trickled through Theo's system hours later. He sat in an interview room at the bureau headquarters, waiting for someone to come and chat with him. He'd recited his version of events over and over again and each time it sounded ridiculous, even to his ears.

He'd been out walking. Walking. Right. He didn't believe himself.

What sick facet of karma put him in the exact place to find Dr. Libitin's body? It made no sense. No amount of rationalizing could explain away the extraordinary coincidence, and Theo didn't believe it was one.

Somehow the killer did this. He'd been set up to find the doc.

But how? He made the decision on his own to go walking. He didn't leave his parents' house at anyone's suggestion. He'd chosen to go to Frick Park of his own accord. Walking at night was not his habit.

The image of Dr. Libitin's face emerging from the layer of muck would not leave him. Every time he blinked, he saw the blue eyes, unmoving under Skeet's ministrations, the tears rolling from Skeet's eyes onto Dr. Libitin's face.

He dropped his head into his hands, despair gnawing at his soul.

He lost the best friend he had in this post-Event world, and his only true ally.

His only source of food.

He rubbed vigorously at his face, trying to force the emotions from his system. He felt incapable of dealing with them.

Time crept by. Theo estimated he'd been in the little interview room for an hour, hour and a half by the time Detective Brown cracked the door open and stepped in the room.

"Walker? You doing okay?"

"Yeah."

"You need anything?"

"To get out of here."

Detective Brown's forehead crinkled. "Can't do that yet. You found the decedent. Gonna have to answer a few questions."

"Who's going to ask them?"

The detective's gaze dropped to his shoes. "Not sure yet. We're working on writing up the preliminary report so we know what to ask."

Theo nodded.

"That was a tough break back there, finding the doc. I know you were friends with him. I'm sorry you had to be the one."

"Me, too. Thanks."

"You didn't know it was him, huh?"

"All I could see from above the water was a hand. I had no idea who would be attached."

"Really rough. You sure you're okay? Anyone you want me to call for you?"

Theo nodded. "Yeah, actually, if you could call my dad and let him know I'm here, my mom's probably wondering why I was still gone when she got up." He grabbed a piece of paper on the table and scrawled his dad's cell phone number on it.

"I can do that." Detective Brown shuffled back out of the room, but popped his head back in the door. "You want coffee?"

Not really, but Theo figured it would make him seem more human. "Sure. Cream and sugar."

Detective Brown nodded and closed the door behind him.

Theo sat. And sat. And felt the chemicals that made up human emotion slowly leech from his system. He glanced at the door. How long could it take to get a cup of coffee?

A sharp knock on the door heralded the return of the detective. Theo sat back in his chair, exhaled, ran his hands through his hair. "Yeah."

Detective Gavahan swung the door wide, sat two cups of coffee on the table and swiveled the chair opposite Theo. He sank into the backwards chair, and propped his forearms on the seatback. He slammed the door closed with his foot.

"Walker."

Theo stared at the detective.

"I brought you coffee."

Theo watched the detective's face. "Thank you."

"You're welcome." Detective Gavahan returned the stare. He flipped something in his fingers.

Theo resolved to wait him out. If he had something to say, he could take the initiative. Theo had nothing to hide and nothing to say.

Detective Gavahan broke the silence. "What were you doing in Frick Park?"

"Walking. Thinking."

"You were walking and thinking at three in the morning?"

"I'm a night owl."

"A night owl." The detective grunted. "A night owl who chooses to walk in a dark, forested area known for drug problems and prostitution and more recently for the being the site of several killings."

Theo considered. "Yeah."

Detective Gavahan sipped his coffee, continued flipping the item in his hand. "I don't buy it."

"That's what happened." Theo wrapped his hands around the paper cup.

"What exactly did you have to think about that required you to be in the middle of fucking nowhere at three in the morning?"

Theo remained silent.

"Walker. Why were you in Frick Park in the middle of the night?"

"I told you."

"You haven't told me shit."

"I don't think I have to tell you what I was thinking about, Detective. I had nothing to do with Dr. Libitin's death."

"But you somehow managed to stumble on his body?"

What could he tell Detective Gavahan? Theo measured his words carefully. "I was in Frick Park to take a walk because I couldn't sleep. I hadn't talked to the doc in a couple of days, and I was worried. Ask Doug, the morgue tech. We were both worried. Frick Park isn't far from where I live. I can't exactly walk around Swissvale without one of the neighbors calling the cops about a prowler. The park seemed like a good alternative."

"And you just ended up at the doctor's body."

"Luck." Theo watched the metal object in the detective's hand flip over and under his fingers, like a magic trick.

Detective Gavahan's eyes widened. "Luck? Is that what you call it? Stepping on a dead man is lucky?"

Theo scowled. "It's not like that. How long would he have stayed in that pool if I hadn't found him? Would anyone have thought to look there? It's better that his friends and loved ones know." Theo stressed the "friends and loved ones" part.

"You just happened to stumble across the right pool."

"Yeah." Theo felt rumblings of anger. "What are you getting at?"

Detective Gavahan leaned over the back of the chair. "You knew he was there. You put him there."

Theo stared at the detective, his mouth hanging open. "Seriously?"

"You knew because you killed him."

Theo stared at Gavahan. "Why would I do that? He was good to me."

"Something about the good doctor we all questioned. It's more than a little strange to see the ME playing with the resident zombie. What could you possibly have in common?" Detective Gavahan sat forward, palmed the piece of metal, and pounded a fist on the table. "A love of corpses, that's what."

Theo waited for the rush of adrenaline to begin. It ran through his innards in a slow trickle. He sighed. "No. Dr. Libitin loved the science, loved solving the puzzles and helping bring closure to the families. He was a good man."

Detective Gavahan stayed silent.

Theo met his gaze. "He was a good man," he repeated.

"What about you, Walker? Are you 'a good man?'" The detective leaned back in his chair. "Don't answer that. It's not a fair question. You're not a man at all. You're a corpse."

Theo peered into his cup of coffee. If he felt rage, he might be tempted to toss the hot liquid in Gavahan's face.

He felt empty.

"You have anything else you need to say to me?" he said. "Because this is bullshit."

The detective's eyes narrowed. "This is bullshit to you? This is not bullshit. This is serious, Walker. You're in deep trouble."

Theo stared at him. "I haven't done anything wrong."

"I'm going to need you to give me a timeline of your actions last night from when you left your parents' house until you made the nine-one-one call." He pulled a pen and notepad from his jacket pocket and put the metal item he'd been fiddling with on the table.

Hornady stopped manufacturing a line of specific bullets in a hurry after the Event, or so he thought. A green dot on top of those bullets identified a round as a Z-Max bullet, created specifically to kill zombies. It started as a joke, like the racially charged ammunition of segregation, but then the Event changed everything, and out of political correctness or perhaps concern for the actual undead being killed, the manufacturer pulled them. After a sharp rise in demand, the ammunition disappeared into the collections of bigots and so-called historians.

Anyone in possession of the ammunition worked hard to find them and paid a steep price.

Theo looked closely at the bullet the detective placed on the table. The telltale green dot on the top of the round chilled Theo, made him pause and experience a stab of true fear.

Theo's gaze moved from the green tip on the bullet to Detective Gavahan's face. A smile hovered around his lips, but didn't materialize. He knew what he'd done, he'd seen Theo's gaze on that bullet.

He made his point.

Detective Gavahan tapped his pen on the notepad. "Walker? Trace your footsteps for me again."

"I've been here since five this morning. My story isn't going to change, because I told you already what happened. This is pointless." Theo's mind told him he should be frustrated, but all he felt was weary.

"It's not pointless. Let's start again. When did you leave your parents' house? What prompted your late-night walk in Frick Park?"

"I've told you and everyone else exactly what happened last night. There is nothing more I can add."

The detective's voice took on a condescending tone and he spaced his words out, as if speaking to a child. "Sometimes when we go through things a few times, something will come to mind. We should try that now."

Theo licked his dry lips. "I don't think so. If I'm not under arrest, I'm leaving. I gave you my statement. That's it." He stood to leave, and, as an afterthought, he reached over and flicked the bullet onto its side.

Theo expected his heart to race, but it maintained its slow thump as he walked toward the front door.

No one stopped him on the way out and he made it to the bus stop just in time to catch the 71A. Plenty of seats were available, so Theo dropped into one in the back of the bus.

The PAT bus rumbled its way from downtown through the east side of Pittsburgh. Theo did his best to keep his mind off the events of the night and morning, but Dr. Libitin's face emerged again and again from the muck in Theo's inner mind. Skeet's gloved hand swept brown goo off the familiar face over and over again.

Theo paused to note that although his body no longer subjected him to the torment of physical responses to

181

emotional distress, his mind maintained its ability to torment him with mental imagery.

All the punishment with none of the emotional release. Fantastic.

The Swissvale stop stood deserted, the street quiet, unusual for a Saturday afternoon. His father's car sat in the gravel driveway beside the house.

Theo turned the handle of the front door with care, pushed the door open with measured slowness, in an attempt to get into the house without notice. He slipped into the living room through an opening just wide enough for his body.

"Ted."

Theo started, an automatic response to an unexpected stimulus. His meager supply of emotion had been spent at the park, though, so he didn't feel even a tiny spike of adrenaline. "Hey, Dad."

"Where you been?" His father shoved a bookmark in the hardback he'd been reading. "Your mother wouldn't let me go to my golf game without figuring out where you were."

Theo frowned. "No one called?"

"You're supposed to call, son."

"I was at the station." Theo shrugged out of his jacket and hung it on the coat tree in the corner. "Detective Brown told me he'd call you."

"Oh." He seemed slightly mollified, but Theo knew his attitude would change. "What were you doing at the station?"

Theo dropped into a chair opposite his father. "Being questioned."

Bill Walker's sharp gaze fell on his son. Theo shrank inside.

"Questioned? About what?"

"I found Henry Libitin's body last night."

Bill stared at Theo for a long moment, then he placed his book on the table next to his chair. "Let's chat."

Theo told his father almost the entire story, leaving out the parts about him eating brains for Dr. Libitin, having psychic visions and contacting a killer via email. He also deliberately ignored the Z-Max round Gavahan taunted him with.

"So the gist of this is that you'd been helping out the doc and now he turns up dead so Gavahan's got a bug up his ass about you?"

"I guess so." Theo knew it wasn't quite that simple, but he couldn't bring himself to reveal the complications.

"Gavahan's a damn good cop but an arrogant prick. He'll give you a hard time. Ignore him. This will clear itself up." Bill got out of the chair and clapped Theo on the shoulder. "Let me make a few calls."

"No, Dad, please don't," Theo implored. "Really. I'm an adult. Let me handle it. Don't call in any more of your favors for me."

Bill peered down at Theo, his lips set in a thin line. "You sure?"

"Positive."

"All right." Bill nodded. "Keep me in the loop."

Theo nodded.

"I can still meet Cliff and Ed and get nine holes in. Tell your mother where I went."

Joyce's footsteps came down the stairs as the tires on Bill's car crunched the gravel driveway on its way out. "Where have you been?"

Theo rubbed his face. "I was at the station last night. I already talked to Dad. I'm going to get some sleep, okay? Dad went to get in a few holes." He stood and headed for the basement stairs before she could question him further.

"Do you want something to eat?"

"No, thanks. I'm just tired."

In the basement, he turned on all the heaters and his electric blankets, crawled into the nest of warmth and dropped off to a dreamless sleep.

A weight on Theo's chest woke him. He opened his eyes to find a pair of yellow cat's eyes staring at him.

"Hey, Ash. Could you move?"

The cat's feet kneaded the blankets and his eyes narrowed to slits. A rumbling purr escaped his throat and he butted his head against Theo's chin. Theo extracted a hand from the mess of blankets to rub Ash's head, then shoved him gently to one side.

He squinted at the clock. Six o'clock.

The buzz of his cell phone grabbed his attention. He fumbled off the mattress and dug the phone from his pants pocket.

"Hello?"

"Theo?" A female voice caught Theo off guard.

"Yeah."

"Hey, this is Shelby."

"Hey." Theo struggled to think straight. "Sorry, I just woke up."

"Oh, I can let you go..."

"No, no. That's okay. What's up?"

A muffled sound came over the line. Was she crying?

"I just found out about Dr. L."

Oh. "Yeah, it's rough."

"Definitely. I was just, uh, wondering if you want to meet for dinner or something."

Theo's eyebrows went up. "Um, yeah, that'd be great. I mean, it would be good to have some company."

"Okay. So in an hour?"

"Sure. Where?"

"You like Eat 'N Park? How about the one at Edgewood Towne Centre?"

Theo considered. Shower, transit. "Yeah, that works. I'll grab a quick shower and head over."

"Okay. See you."

Theo placed his phone on the bedside table, grabbed some clean clothes and headed for the bathroom.

He managed to avoid his mother until he was headed for the door.

"Teddy? Where are you going?"

He sighed. "I'm headed out to meet a friend, Ma."

"You haven't eaten."

"I'm eating with her," he said and immediately wished he could retract the statement.

"Her?"

"A friend from work."

Silence.

"Have a good time." Her tone was wounded.

Theo winced. "I will. Thanks, Mom." He made a mental resolution to look for an apartment.

His watch showed him he had time to skip the bus and just walk the several blocks to the restaurant, even at his normal pace. The surprise he felt at hearing Shelby's voice came back. No way he expected to be the person she turned to when her boss turned up dead. He felt guilty that he hadn't thought to call her and wondered how she heard about Dr. Libitin's death.

Suspicion reared. How did she know?

He shook it off. If Shelby knew, then Doug had to know already, too. Doug, who'd been concerned enough to take Theo to the doctor's house. Some kind of announcement was probably made at the morgue.

Theo looked for Doug's number in his cell phone and called. It rang several times, but Doug didn't pick up and when Theo got the automated voicemail message, he hung up. He wouldn't know what to say and leaving a message about this seemed too impersonal.

Shelby's car sat in the parking lot of the Eat 'N Park, so Theo bypassed the hostess and looked for her. She sat in a booth by herself, sipping a glass of cola.

"Hi," he said and slipped into the bench opposite her.

Tears gleamed unshed in Shelby's eyes. "Hi." She squeezed his hand. "How are you?"

"I'm okay."

"I heard you found him."

Theo studied her eyes. "Yes."

"I'm glad it was you. He would have been okay with that, you know, you being the last to see him." She sniffed.

Theo thought he would hardly be the last to see him, what with the autopsy and the funeral, but let the details pass. "Thanks."

The waitress came by and Theo asked for a glass of water, no ice, and a plate of scrambled eggs. Shelby ordered some kind of salad.

Shelby twirled her straw in the cola. "I'm glad to see you."

"Yeah, thanks for calling." Theo smiled at her.

Silence stretched between them, tinged with awkwardness. Theo squeezed lemon in his water, stirred it.

"Why did you call, Shelby?"

She wouldn't meet his gaze. "You were the last to see him."

He waited. "And?"

"How was he...how did the...uh..."

"How was he killed?" Theo finished the question for her.

She squirmed on the bench. "Yes."

"He was beheaded." Theo kept his tone low.

Shelby blinked a few times, then nodded. "It's related, isn't it?"

"Related?" Theo shook his head. "To what?"

"The Riser Killings."

Theo's mind went blank. Of course, he thought. Of course it is. He'd gotten too close. "Shelby," he started.

"It must be," she interrupted. "It's too much of a coincidence. I've been thinking about it all afternoon."

Theo replayed the scene in his own mind, the emergence of the body from the mud, Skeet's voice saying he had the head, that it was jammed under the rock. He closed his eyes and tried to erase the final memory of his friend's body floating in the filthy water.

"I don't know," he said, denying what was slowly dawning on him. "It seems too incredible. How could the killer know he was investigating the deaths on his own?"

"That I don't know," Shelby said, stabbing ice cubes with the straw. "But that's not my concern right now. What's done is done with Dr. L." Tears welled fresh in her eyes.

Theo put his hand over hers, ready for her to pull away. She actually turned her hand over and grasped his.

"What else then?" he said.

"If the killer knew Dr. L was looking into the murders, it stands to reason he knows you were, too."

The leap in logic boggled Theo for a second. Shelby's gaze was intense, her hands shook as she tore the straw paper into tiny bits.

The look on his face must have mirrored his thoughts, because her expression fell. She crumpled a bit onto the table.

"No, no," Theo said. "I believe you. I just hadn't considered it."

She sat up a bit straighter.

"But, Shelby, did Dr. L do anything outside the office? Something I might not have been involved with that someone else might have seen?"

"I don't know. I don't really think so. He spent nearly all his time at the office." She barked a laugh. "I know. I'm there a lot and I can't think of a time—aside from this past week—when he wasn't there, too."

"Did he sleep?" Theo spit the question out before he thought.

Shelby laughed, a genuine laugh that made him smile. "I don't know. I suppose it's possible he didn't. He was larger than life, wasn't he?"

Theo nodded. "Yes, he was."

The waitress came by with their food. "Eggs and toast, bacon cooked rare and a buffalo chicken salad, double the blue cheese dressing. You need refills on the drinks?"

Theo asked for coffee and the redheaded waitress plunked a mug down a minute later.

Shelby poked at the coffee mug. "It's too hot for coffee."

"No way. I'm always cold," he said, watching Shelby pour enough dressing on the salad to drown it. "Do you taste anything except the dressing?"

She glanced up at him. "Just the buffalo sauce."

"I see." He sprinkled a little pepper on his eggs and tucked into them. "Doesn't that defeat the purpose of eating a salad?"

"Depends on why you want a salad." She glared at him, then sighed. "I just want you to be careful."

"I will. I don't think I have anything to worry about, though. We haven't found any signs that he's killing undead. Just people who want to rise."

"Why is that? I mean, what's the point? You'd think if the killer had a problem with the undead, he'd target, you know, the *undead*."

"I haven't figured it out yet, but I will."

"No!" She looked around the restaurant, to see if she'd caught anyone's attention, then lowered her voice. "See, that's just it. You can't. You can't risk yourself." She stabbed a hapless piece of tomato.

"Come on, Shelby. Nobody else is going to do it. You know it."

"Tell me what you have so far. Maybe I can help."

Theo considered only for a second before launching into the entire story—his psychic visions, the reactions to eating the brain matter, the information about *The Pitt News*, and the email exchanges with the possible killer. He told her about Gavahan's problems with him and the Z-Max round he'd mocked Theo with. It all spilled out in one cathartic flow.

By the time he finished, just soggy lettuce lay in a pool of bleu cheese at the bottom of Shelby's bowl and toast crusts littered Theo's plate. His coffee cup was full again, for the fourth time. The sun dipped below the horizon outside the windows.

"Shelby, he was my friend. Dr. Libitin was someone who saw something in me and made me believe I was okay. He acknowledged and accepted the part of me that not even I've acknowledged—the zombie. It's who I am and not only did Dr. Libitin accept it, he found value in it. He was my only ally." Theo shook his head, knowing he should be feeling passionate about the situation, and sad, in a way, that he couldn't experience the emotions.

Shelby crunched a piece of ice. "Okay, obviously I want to tell you that you're nuts and to back off. This is too dangerous. I'd like to tell you to go to the cops. It's just as obvious that going to the cops would be pointless. You're not going to leave this one alone, are you?"

"No, I'm not. It's nice to see you heard me."

She waved a hand at him. "I heard you. It doesn't mean I agree with you. I think you should find a safer way of going about this. Maybe use a partner."

"A partner? You think Skeet would want to help me with this?"

Shelby stared at him. "You're incredibly dense."

Theo hesitated and stared back at her. "If it's not safe for me, imagine how unsafe it would be for you." He reached out and grabbed her left hand, flipped her wrist over to expose the RISER tattoo. The delicate lettering stood out in sharp contrast to the thin, pale skin of her inner wrist, like an advertisement. Kill me!

Theo once saw the tattoo as a mark of bravery, of choice. Now it looked more like a flag, a mark of danger.

The pale gray of his skin contrasted with the slight pink tinge of hers. The difference in their coloring underscored the fact that the girl sitting across from him still lived, still felt the emotions denied him. He felt a twinge of protectiveness toward Shelby and relished the emotion.

He gave her arm a gentle shake. "Until we know why the killer is targeting people with this mark, no one wearing it is safe."

CHAPTER 17

Shelby dipped her head. "Point taken."

He picked up the check. "I have to go. Let me think about how I'm going to deal with this. I'll be in touch with you tomorrow, okay? Maybe we can meet again."

"That's a good idea. I'll think about it overnight, too. Call me in the morning." Shelby pointed at the check. "What do I owe you?"

"Nothing. It's the least I can do in exchange for you listening to me ramble."

He stood, and Shelby slid out of the bench. She stood close beside him. He knew she was tall, but he still had an inch or two on her, a nice height difference. She reached out and put an arm around him in a half-hearted hug. He returned the gesture, and when he did, she wrapped her other arm around his waist and held tight, her cheek pressed against his. He felt her breath catch and her chest jerk in a sob. He embraced her fully with both arms, tight.

Her hair smelled like cherries.

After too short a time for Theo's liking, she backed out of the hug, tears on her cheeks. "Thanks, Theo. I don't know anyone else who will miss him the way I will. You're definitely the closest."

They walked to the front, and Theo paused long enough to pay. Outside the restaurant, Shelby walked toward her little hatchback. "Do you need a ride?"

"No, thanks. It's just a couple of blocks if I take the bridge. I like the walk."

Shelby nodded and Theo started toward the bridge before something occurred to him. "Hey, Shelby," Theo called. "You'll let me know about the arrangements, right?"

"Of course."

Theo stopped walking. "Who is in charge of that? I mean, who is going to carry out his final wishes and all? He wanted to rise, but given the circumstances, he'll be buried or cremated or whatever. I don't know if he...had family or..." It sounded pathetic to his own ears that he knew so little about someone who played such an important part in his life.

Buried or cremated. The neurons in Theo's brains fired.

Shelby smiled and dug in her cavernous bag. "He has a daughter. She's flying in to take care of him."

"Shelby." Theo hurried back to her. "Shelby, I need to ask you a favor. It's a big one. Huge."

Her keys jingled as she pulled them from her handbag. "What is it?"

Theo searched her face for some sign of hesitancy, found none. "Who will do his autopsy?"

"I'd have to guess Linda Baler. She's second in command—or first now, I guess—and most qualified."

"I need some of his brain."

Her expression clouded. She narrowed her eyes. "Shit, Theo."

"Shelby, I might be able to see what happened. I might be able to see who killed him."

"This is really risky. I could lose my job, and if they find out I'm bringing it to you and for what... What would they do to you?"

"I don't know, but I'm willing to risk it. Dr. Libitin knew about the visions. If he suspected he was meeting with the killer, maybe he looked clearly at his face so I could see it, too. I'd bet he tried to form memories I can see, too."

Shelby fidgeted with her keys. "This is dangerous stuff, Theo."

"The visions are powerful, and so far they haven't led me wrong. I just have to interpret them. I know I'm close to understanding. This could be what we need." Theo grasped Shelby's hand. "I'm asking a lot. You know what's at stake and so do I. Please?"

Her brow furrowed. "I don't know, Theo. I don't even know when they're going to do the autopsy."

"I bet they'll do it soon. They'll need to issue a statement about his death." He squeezed her hand. "Please, Shelby. Try."

"I'll see what I can do. I can go back in tonight to check the schedule and see if they set aside a time." She squeezed his hand back. "I'll try. No guarantees."

He put an arm around her shoulder in a half-hug. "Thank you."

She leaned in with both arms around his waist, her cheek on his shoulder. "We'll be okay. I'll miss him."

He wrapped his other arm around her, took comfort in her living warmth, a moment of gratitude for friendship. "I will, too."

She unwrapped her arms from around him and he released her. She sank into the driver's seat of her car. "I'd better go. I'll make some phone calls and ask to be present for the examination. I'm not sure if they'll let me."

Theo nodded. "Do what you can. I know this could break the case for us."

She pulled the driver's side door shut and started the car.

Theo made his way across the parking lot toward the pedestrian bridge over the busway and train tracks. The fading light of the summer evening lent a beautiful glow to the church on the corner.

He took a detour into the church. Rows of pews stood empty, so he sat.

A church was probably a safer place to think than Frick Park, given the circumstances.

Dinner with Shelby showed him one thing. Her safety, and the safety of his remaining few friends and family, was the only important thing. His life, what was left of it, didn't matter, not in comparison.

Theo lost his only friend in the Event. Dale was a true zombie buff. He could quote Romero and Raimi like no one else. Ironically, he died from radiation poisoning during the worst of the solar flares and never rose. Theo missed him in his way.

He had no one else to miss. He'd never had a girlfriend. His few experiences with girls were awkward and very short. The thought of never being able to remedy that situation frustrated him. Death stole his life and his chances at a new one.

The only good thing about his death was his new job. He couldn't work in retail again. Back at the beginning, no retail stores would hire the undead—they drive away customers—so his father had to get him the job with the forensics lab.

His job saved him, gave him a purpose; it enabled him to make connections with other people.

He couldn't give up those connections.

He couldn't let a killer take another of them away.

"Can I help you?"

A priest stood at the end of the pew. "Uh, no. I'm just thinking."

"Think away. It's a good place for introspection." A kind smile accompanied his words and he moved on to the altar where he lit candles.

"May I light one?" Theo said.

"Of course."

Theo walked to the altar, took the lighting stick from the priest and lit one white candle in a sea of white candles. He passed the lighter back. "Thanks. A friend of mine passed away recently."

"I can include a name in the daily prayers, if you'd like."

Theo considered Dr. Libitin. He had no idea if the medical examiner was a religious man, but knew he wouldn't have a problem with positive energy being sent into the universe on his behalf. "That would be great. His name was Henry Libitin."

If the priest recognized the name, his face didn't betray it. "Henry. I'll add his name to my list and pray for peace."

"Thank you." Theo took one last long look at the candle he'd lit for Dr. Libitin. As the priest touched flame to the candles around it, Theo's throat closed. He turned to leave.

"Stop in again." The priest awarded Theo another smile.

"I will."

The warmth of the day faded with the light, and Theo stepped up his pace to get home. The driveway sat empty.

"Mom? I'm home."

In the kitchen, he found a note on the table that his parents went to a movie and dinner with friends.

So much the better.

He grabbed a Coke from the shelf under the microwave, popped the tab and took a swig. He went to the computer table and typed in the information to access his phony email account.

More spam, more offers to increase his manly girth.

Ha. Unless those supplements included human brain matter, that wasn't happening.

Three emails from the bottom, he found the one he'd been looking for.

> Hi again Pat,
> I enjoy meeting with my clients at Ryan's Pub, which is directly across the street from the main playground area of Frick Park. I'll be there Sunday at eight. Ask the hostess to direct you to me.
> Regards,
> Alice

Theo's heart beat a tiny bit faster. Frick Park. This has to be the killer. She wants to meet with people interested in rising, at a location in close proximity to where many of the bodies were found.

Too good to be a coincidence.

Theo pushed back from the computer, Coke in hand. He sipped from the can, thoughts deep in logistics.

Shelby had a point. This was hardly a safe situation. He had to think it through and be sure he had the right plan in place to handle anything that might go down.

Most likely "Alice" couldn't risk being identifiable at the restaurant, so probably waited for her prey to go in the restaurant and come back out looking confused. Maybe she followed them back to their vehicle, waited for the right moment, waited for the light to be just dark enough to make identification difficult, but not so dark that a woman wouldn't take a walk in the park.

Or she waited for the victim to get in his or her car, then someone subdued the target and dragged him or her into the park.

Theo noted one major problem with his brilliant plan: his death. One look would tell Alice Theo wasn't interested in talking about rising. He'd already done it.

He would need help. He'd need someone living to set this up for him.

He only knew one living human well enough to ask even a simple favor from, one it just so happened he'd suddenly developed an aversion to putting in harm's way.

Shelby.

His cell phone buzzed in his pants pocket. He stood to retrieve it.

"Hello?"

"Hi, it's Marjorie."

He ran a hand through his hair, then immediately felt foolish. "Hi, Marjorie."

"How are you?"

"I'm good. You?"

"I'm great. Hey, do you want to get together?"

Theo stopped pacing. "Uh, now?"

"Sure. I'm headed home and I'd love to stop off for a bite to eat. You like The Raw Bar?"

"I already ate this evening." Theo mentally kicked himself.

"Oh." Marjorie actually sounded disappointed.

"But, uh, I could come along and get a drink or something. You know, just to keep you company."

He could almost hear the smile over the line. "I would love that. Meet me there when you can."

Theo popped the phone back in his pocket.

Holy shit. Two girls.

He allowed himself a moment of strutting around the living room before he grabbed his jacket and headed back out to the bus stop. Maybe he'd look into an apartment and a car.

The crowd outside the Raw Bar parted to let Theo in. The restaurant catered to zombies, serving raw meats and various other items appealing to the undead. Unfortunately, that also meant it attracted groupies and undead posers. The bouncer did his best to keep the living out of the bar, unless they were guests of the undead, but a few living dressed in tattered clothing and sporting cosmetic contact lenses loitered by the front.

They looked ridiculous.

Theo wondered about Marjorie's choice of restaurants on the ride over. He liked the food at The Raw Bar, but usually didn't appreciate the attitude of the other patrons. The typical customer eschewed the living in favor of the dead. These zombies demonstrated what Theo considered discrimination toward the living.

But the food was good, so maybe Marjorie was just hungry.

Once inside, Theo looked around for her. He spotted her in the corner, chatting with another zombie. He made his way toward the back where she sat, nodding to a few zombies he recognized from the support group last week.

Natalie sat at the bar, head close to a man in a plaid flannel shirt. They appeared to be arguing. Natalie jabbed the man in the shoulder, two hard pokes, and he put his hands up, palms out in concession. He stood and walked toward a door off to the side of the bar, painted the same color as the walls. Natalie peered around the room, and followed him, her limp pronounced. Flannel Shirt opened the door and allowed her to pass through first.

Marjorie appeared beside him and gave him a brief hug. "Theo. Come sit."

He took a chair opposite her. "Hey, Marjorie."

The woman standing next to Marjorie assessed him.

"I'm sorry to interrupt," he said. The other woman sported ultra-short silvery gray hair, but her face appeared much too young for the color. Either her hair changed when she died or she colored it. Tall and thin, her deep green eyes set off delicate features. Only her tattered ears and the hue of her complexion showed evidence of her death. Theo couldn't help but appreciate sex appeal. The skin-tight black leather pants and silver halter-top didn't hurt.

She raised one eyebrow and extended a hand. "Hi, Theo. I'm Delilah."

Her hand felt cool and dry when Theo accepted it. "Nice to meet you."

She nodded. "I haven't seen you here before."

"No, I don't come often."

"You should change that. Can I get you something to drink?"

Theo stared.

Delilah had a husky laugh. "I'm the bartender."

"Oh, um, what do you recommend?"

"You like beef?"

"Yeah," Theo said.

"I'll be right back." She stalked away, her lanky legs eating the distance between them and the bar, where she lifted the counter and went behind.

Theo stared.

"I've known Delilah since the Event. She's a First Gen." Marjorie spoke with a soft voice.

"She's, uh," he started.

"She's beautiful, I know." Marjorie glanced back at the bar. "And a really wonderful undead."

Theo tore his gaze off Delilah. "So how are you?"

"I'm good." In front of Marjorie sat a plate of finger foods, sliced raw beef on lettuce leaves, calves' brain in shot glasses with some sort of sauce, and various other items Theo couldn't identify. "Help yourself."

"No, thanks. I did eat earlier."

"Here you go. My specialty." Delilah shared a glance with Marjorie and placed a glass in front of Theo. "Pureed beef in tomato juice with a shot of spun serum." Delilah headed back to the bar.

Theo peered at the chilled drink. The mixture was deep red in color with a metallic scent. A thin layer of clear liquid floated on the top. Theo stirred the serum into the meat puree and took a long drink. The thick drink slid down his throat, refreshing him, giving him an instant energy boost.

"How is it?" Marjorie said.

"Wow. Really good." Theo raised his glass to Delilah. The shapely bartender nodded in satisfaction.

Marjorie sipped on a shot glass of brain. "How are things at work?"

"Crazy. I'm not sure when I'm going to be allowed to get back out there with my crew. I guess I might be on lab duty for a while."

Marjorie tilted her head. "Why? What's going on?"

Theo put his glass on the table. "You haven't heard?"

"Heard what?"

"Oh, God." He put his hand on the table. "Marjorie, I have some bad news."

She reached across the table for his hand. "Tell me."

"Dr. Libitin is gone."

"He left the medical examiner's office?"

"No," Theo squeezed her hand. "He's dead. I found him last night."

Marjorie withdrew her hand from Theo's. "You what?"

"I know, it's insane. I was walking in Frick Park and found his body."

"You found him?" Marjorie shook her head. "How is that possible?"

"I couldn't believe it myself. I just talked to him. Doug and I went to his house, looking for him." Theo held Marjorie's cool hand in both of his. "I'm so sorry to have to tell you like this. I figured you'd know."

Her gaze searched his face. "How would I? I mean, I haven't been at work today, and I'm not technically employed by the morgue."

"Shelby knew. I assumed she would tell you. It's been on the news."

"I haven't seen Shelby today. And I don't watch television."

"Oh, geez, see, I'm so stupid. I'm sorry." How could she not know? The news was all over Pittsburgh. Did she live under a rock? Theo mentally shook himself. To each her own.

Marjorie sat up straight. "It's okay, not your fault. But wow, what a day you must have had. Tell me."

Theo related the events of the evening and morning to Marjorie. "And I think Gavahan thinks I had something to do with it, but he has to know that's ridiculous. Even he has to know that."

The camouflaged door beside the bar opened and Natalie emerged alone. Her eyes shifted around the bar, like someone either afraid or on speed, and color shone high on her cheekbones. She walked straight for the exit, limp less pronounced than it had been. Theo watched her, puzzled at the change, but unable to put his finger on why.

"Another?" Delilah's voice came from over Theo's shoulder.

He looked down to find his glass empty. "Yeah." He held it up to her. "That's awesome."

She exchanged a smile with Marjorie and walked back to the bar.

"Did you see Natalie? She looked a little off," he said.

"Was she with a dark-haired guy?" Marjorie sipped another drink.

"He was wearing a flannel shirt, yeah."

"They've been dating on and off. Problems."

"Oh." Could arguing with a boyfriend or girlfriend have that effect on a zombie? He shrugged it off. "So anyway, I had dinner with Shelby—"

"You had dinner with Shelby?" Marjorie interrupted.

"Yeah. She was really close with the doc. I was, too. She called and wanted to talk."

"Oh." Marjorie's face smoothed and she reached across the table for Theo's hand. "How is she? I'm sure she's devastated. Should I stop by her apartment tonight?"

"I think she'll be okay." Theo grabbed a slice of beef liver topped with some sort of mousse. "She may have been going back to work anyway."

Marjorie frowned. "Back to work? On a Saturday evening? That's not like Shelby."

Theo's heart thudded. "Oh. She's working on a favor for me."

"A favor at work? Something to do with the killings?" Marjorie leaned over the table. "What's going on, Theo?"

"There have been more killings. All the victims wear the tattoo. The connection is there, but it's tenuous. Dr. Libitin was sure the tattoo linked the victims." Theo shook his head. "Now he's dead. I think he found something, he knew something, and the killer had no choice but to eliminate him."

Marjorie said nothing. Theo looked up at her, expecting to see shock on her face, but saw only anger.

"Theo, seriously? I can't see how the murders could be a conspiracy to kill potential risers. It's ridiculous. If someone has a problem with the undead, they'd just kill zombies. It seems like a really inefficient way to do away with a problem."

Theo blinked, a tinge of irritation at her mistrust and disbelief coloring his reply. "I can't figure it out, either, Marjorie, but it's no coincidence that every single murder victim in Pittsburgh in the last week—and there have been a disproportionate number of them—wears the tattoo. Something is going on."

She shook her head. "I just don't see it. The evidence isn't there."

Theo knew the evidence was there. The visions pointed to one mastermind, even if he couldn't see the motive. The motive wasn't important—it was the black shadow in the visions, that black aura flitting in and out of sight in the last moments experienced by the dead.

But only he knew it. He and Shelby and Dr. Libitin. Only Dr. Libitin died for it. Of that, Theo was sure.

"Marjorie, you have to trust me. I know, without a doubt, that these killings are connected and were committed by one killer. There is no indication he's going to stop."

"How do you know? What are you not telling me?"

He couldn't stand to look in her eyes and see the contempt and derision he heard in her voice. He saw and heard those things time and again, both before and after his death, in the faces and voices of people who mattered and those who didn't. He didn't want to hear them from Marjorie.

He made a decision.

"Because I have a gift, or a curse, I'm not sure which."

"What are you talking about, Theo?"

He chose his words carefully. "I get visions from the dead. I see their final moments. Not exactly *see*, but more like *feel* the moments leading up to their death. I've seen the last moments of most of the victims of the Riser Killer, and I know the same person is killing them all."

He couldn't stand to look at Marjorie, to see the horror on her face. Silence sat between them, pregnant with tension that Theo knew should be there, but couldn't feel.

CHAPTER 18

"How?"

She spoke softly, and he dared to look. Not horror, but curiosity clouded her eyes.

"What do you do? Lay hands on them or something?"

"Not exactly." His tongue tied itself in knots. He wasn't sure he wanted to share the "how."

"Then what? How do you do it?"

He squirmed in his seat. "Listen, just take my word for it."

The noise of disgust he heard made her skepticism clear. "Is that what you need from Shelby? She's bringing you something from the morgue?"

"Yes. If I can get a vision from Dr. Libitin's last moments, I'm sure I'll figure this out. He knew about my...ability. We were working together on this. He would have assumed I would try with his...when he died, so maybe he made sure to get a close look at the killer's face. I know he tried."

"Theo, you're being evasive. I don't understand what you're talking about, and, frankly, you sound insane." Marjorie's voice carried the contempt Theo hated so much. It tore at his heart.

"I'm not comfortable saying more right now. Once this is settled, I'll tell you everything, I promise." A vibration in his pocket startled him. He pulled his phone out and found a text message from Shelby: "L is on the tbl now. Will have what u need by tmrw."

A viscous wave of adrenaline suffused Theo's midsection. Shelby had followed through. He'd have Dr. Libitin's brains in hand tomorrow. This would be over. He just knew the doc would have been sure to seal the image of his killer in his mind when he died. He knew Theo would see it.

The thought of eating his friend's brains made his stomach feel hollow. The cool, slippery feeling of gray matter sliding over his lips would be a reality tomorrow.

"Theo?"

He forced his mind back to reality, away from the metallic tang of human tissue. "Listen, I'm sorry about all this. Shelby is getting what I need and hopefully this will all be over."

Marjorie's smile did not reach her eyes. She brushed her hair, that long, black wash that Theo longed to tangle his fingers in, back over one shoulder. "Okay. I'll take your word for it for now, but I want an explanation soon."

Delilah stepped next to the table. "Another. On the house." She placed a glass in front of Theo.

Marjorie ran a finger along the back of Theo's hand. "We have to work together. No one else understands what it's like. The First Generation undead experienced the worst of it."

Delilah nodded. "Truth."

"What do you mean? 'The worst of it?'" Theo heard the skepticism in his own voice.

Delilah's low, raspy voice carried an edge. "We broke new ground, Theo. We were the first. A lot of us died—permanently—in the beginning because the living were afraid of us. That hasn't changed. We'll never be accepted back into society."

Theo peered at Marjorie in the low light of the bar. She was watching Delilah, but Theo couldn't read her expression. "Everything new is met with hesitancy. It's part of what makes us human," he said.

Delilah smacked the table with a resounding crack. "That's just it. We're *not* human anymore. We're something else entirely and we'll never be accepted. That's why we shouldn't bother to integrate."

In some ways, he could see where the bartender was coming from. Those who survived the first wave did so either because they were smart enough to hide or because they had family to protect them. Now, most undead maintained a low profile. If they worked, they worked in a field that didn't put them in direct contact with general society. He worked mostly with a tiny group of science-oriented people, and, to a lesser extent, the dead. Marjorie worked with the newly risen. The other zombies he knew were in similarly insulated positions, like Hugh and his all-undead crime scene clean-up crew.

Marjorie reached across the table and placed her hand on his. Her soft fingers stroked his palm and clouded his thoughts.

But that didn't mean they would never be accepted. Acceptance would begin at home, where people who loved the undead were forced to acknowledge their relatives were still just part of the family. Slowly, as more people rose and went about their business, society would adapt. Adaptation remained a great feature of humanity.

"I don't know. I think, in time, things will iron themselves out and we'll be fine. I don't want to cut anyone off just because they don't understand. They will. Life will go on, and death will go on, and sooner or later this will all sort itself out and we'll have our place right alongside everyone else where we should be. We're no better or worse than the living. Just different." He met Delilah's gaze. Her pale face was set in hard lines. She really believed it.

"You're wrong. So wrong, Theo. If we don't take care of our own and make our own way, we'll go under. We're better than they are. We lived through death. We should not have a place 'right alongside everyone else.' We belong above them."

His phone rang. He flipped it open, squinted at the caller ID in the low light. It read "Gavahan, Dec."

What the hell could he want? Whatever it was, Theo didn't want to hear it. He muted the phone, slipped it back in his pocket.

"Anything important?" Marjorie said.

"Nope." He searched her face, looking for something he couldn't put a finger on, something to show that Delilah's words didn't reflect Marjorie's feelings. He couldn't read her.

He pulled his hand out from underneath hers. "I don't know. We're all still just human."

Someone at the bar called for Delilah. The leggy, silver-haired bartender stood, but turned back to Theo. "I'm sorry to hear it, Theo. I thought you would stick with us." She stalked away

A tiny flash of anger exploded and extinguished in Theo. He looked at Marjorie. "Us? It's 'us' versus 'them?' No, Marjorie, it's just us. Just people."

She grabbed her bag from the corner of the bench. "Delilah had a really rough rising. She might be a little out there, but I think it's with good reason." She stood next to his bench, effectively blocking him from getting out. "She knows a lot of zombies, Theo. She's seen more than you or I have, and she's connected. Don't dismiss her."

Theo watched Marjorie push through a crowd near the dance floor. She disappeared with a swirl of that thick, black hair. Something twisted in his guts, a flash that dissolved as fast as he noted it. He'd wanted her for so long, since the first time he laid eyes on her at the morgue last year. Did he just screw up any chance of being with her?

The bar had steadily filled with patrons while he'd talked with Marjorie, and Theo peered into the hazy room. Zombies stood at the bar, occupied the tables, and hovered around the dance floor. Delilah dispensed drinks, her sequined top reflecting the multicolored lights, talking and laughing with everyone who ordered a drink.

Delilah is connected? What the hell did that mean? Connected to what?

What was behind the door next to the bar? The big man in the flannel shirt still hadn't appeared.

Theo slid out of the booth and Delilah looked up. He met her gaze and she flashed him a smile. A zombie in jeans and a black leather jacket leaned over the bar to say something near her ear. She nodded, and led the way around the back of the bar to a door painted to blend in with the wall. He took a step toward the camouflaged door when his cell phone vibrated again with a message from Shelby. "Got it. Call u l8r."

Excitement moseyed through him, followed closely by a chill, and he headed for the exit. The brains, the memories, the dying moments, of Dr. Libitin, his friend. His human instincts told him this was the break he needed to discover who and why these people were dying.

His undead half just waited in quiet anticipation to be fed.

The massacre on the small screen just wasn't cutting it. He sat in his basement room, trying to pass time.

Why didn't Shelby just say she'd meet him as soon as she got out of the morgue?

Where the hell was she? Did she go home and to bed? Why wouldn't she just call?

He flipped his cell phone over in his hand, checked it for a missed message, knowing that he didn't miss anything.

Theo looked at the clock again. Two AM. Too late or too early to call her. His parents rolled in around eleven, checked on him and went straight to bed. He'd been taking his frustration out on the *Call of Duty* zombies since he couldn't sleep.

Could it even be called frustration? He didn't feel the accompanying physical symptoms of anxiety, just a mental nagging that something big loomed on the horizon and he didn't want to wait.

The Riser Killer could be out now, looking for another victim, and he was powerless to prevent it.

If he could get to that sample, however, he would solve this thing. He knew it.

If he could figure out the identity of the killer, it would solve the problem of asking Shelby to stand in for his alter ego of "Pat" at the meeting with "Alice" on Monday. Theo felt certain Dr. Libitin would gift him with an image of "Alice."

But he had to get to Shelby first.

He tossed the remote onto the throw at his feet for the fourth time, picked it up, put it on the bed.

Ash yawned with reproach.

"Sorry, dude. Can't sleep. Not stopping you, though."

The cat tucked his nose under his front paws.

Theo turned off the lights, burrowed under the now toasty electric blankets, and stared at the ceiling for the next few hours.

When he heard his mother putzing around the kitchen, the clock read sixty thirty. He decided to give up and just get up.

"Morning, Teddy. This is early for you," Joyce said when Theo emerged from the basement.

"Can't sleep."

"Is it too cold down there? We can move you back up to your old room." She poured a glass of orange juice.

"No, it's fine. Just preoccupied."

"Anything you want to talk about?" She moved around the kitchen, wiping counters and folding the dishtowels.

"No. But thanks for the offer." His mother always reminded him of June Cleaver; so proper and naive. He'd begun to suspect her attitude and lack of interest in the outside world were carefully constructed facades. Every now and then he saw a flash of something in her, and he sensed she fought hard to keep the outside at bay. He wouldn't spoil it for her. "Thanks for the OJ."

"Any time," she called over her shoulder as she walked out of the kitchen.

Theo glanced at the clock on the microwave. How late was late enough to call Shelby?

He occupied himself for the next hour or so playing solitaire on the computer and checking his fake email account for more information from Alice. Nothing.

When the clock finally read eight o'clock, he went back downstairs and dialed Shelby's number. He waited anxiously through three rings, then four, before her voicemail message picked up.

"Shelby loves messages. Leave her one."

Theo chuckled. Her voice made him smile and the message was just so *Shelby* he couldn't help himself.

"Shelby, it's Theo. Call me as soon as you get this." He hesitated, not sure how much was too much over the phone. "Uh, everything's better when it's fresh."

He cringed as he snapped the cell phone closed. Despite the honesty of the statement, it seemed callous to refer to the brain matter of a friend in such a way.

Solitaire proved an ineffective distraction. His father walked through the living room, wearing his lawn mowing clothes, tucking earbuds into his ears, and warming up his vocal cords.

Theo spared a thought for the neighbors.

"Hey, Dad, where's the hedge trimmer?"

His father stopped short. "What?"

"You know, the trimmer? For the hedges?"

"In the shed."

Theo set his phone to the highest possible vibration setting, slipped it in his pocket, and followed his father outside. He grabbed the electric trimmers and went at the hedges with as much gusto as he could muster. His father's operatic accompaniment cheered him, even if Mrs. Prentiss next door glared from her porch swing.

The July heat and activity level soon limbered him up and he made quick work of the neat row of boxwoods surrounding the Walker property. He checked his phone for missed messages and found none.

"I'm done with the lawn, son. Gonna go grab a shower, unless you want to get one first."

Theo hadn't even broken a sweat. "No, I'm good. Go ahead."

Bill wiped his face with a stained handkerchief. "Thanks for the help, Ted."

"You bet."

Theo retreated to the basement. He dialed Shelby's number, and was again rewarded with the voicemail message. He snapped the phone shut before leaving another message and tossed it on the carpet. Where was she?

His cell phone rang and he almost fell off the mattress trying to get to it. The caller ID read "Gavahan, Dec."

Fucking Gavahan. He threw the phone back on the floor, ignoring the rings.

Should he go to Shelby's apartment? He wasn't even sure where she lived, except somewhere in Squirrel Hill.

In the same building as Marjorie.

He dialed Marjorie's number. If he got ahold of Marjorie, she could walk to Shelby's apartment and knock on the door. Maybe Shelby's phone was off, or she left it in her car. Who knew? But Theo had to find her. His patience was wearing thin...as was his need.

Marjorie's phone rang several times before also going to voicemail.

"This is Marjorie Frey of Community in Death. I'm not available to take your call, but leave me a message or connect with me on our website at Community in Death dot zom."

Theo paced his room. Where the hell were they?

He would have to go to Shelby's apartment, but he had to find it first.

He dialed another number.

"Hello?" Doug's voice finally broke the chain of voicemail.

"Hey, man."

"How's it going? Are you okay?" Doug's voice sounded thick.

"Yeah, I'm all right." Theo realized he hadn't spoken with Doug since they left the doc's house two days before. It seemed like more than just two days. "You?"

Doug cleared his throat. "I'm hanging in there. I still can't believe the whole thing. You finding him that way...it's just unreal, you know?"

"I know, I do. It's been a real shitstorm." Doug had no idea Theo had sat in an interrogation room for hours on end. He didn't know about the Zombie Killer rounds Gavahan used. Shitstorm about summed it up.

Noises of assent came across the line.

"Do you happen to know where Shelby lives?" Theo said after a moment of silence.

"Shelby Gusky?"

"Yeah, the only Shelby I know."

"Uh, yeah, in Squirrel Hill. Why?" Doug said.

"I know in Squirrel Hill, I mean an address. I've got to find her."

"I can get you one. I'm at the morgue. I can look it up real quick."

"Please. I'd appreciate it." Theo said a thousand mental thank yous to the gods.

"Yeah, okay. Hang on. What do you need Shelby for?"

Theo hesitated. "She promised to do me a favor, and I need to talk to her. I can't get her on her cell, so I thought I'd stop by her apartment."

"She was here at the morgue until really late last night. We autopsied the doc…" Doug's voice trailed off. "Anyway, she left in a hurry, didn't even stay to go out with the rest of us. I think this situation with the doc must really be eating at her."

Theo found Doug's choice of words interesting. "No doubt. It's eating at all of us."

"True. Here's the address." Doug rattled off a street address familiar to Theo.

"I know where that is. No problem."

"If you see her, tell her we're thinking of her. She should come out tonight; in fact, you should come with us."

"Thanks. I'd like that."

"See ya later. We'll be at Fuel and Fuddle around six thirty or seven." Doug said by way of good byes.

"Teddy, do you want some lunch?" His mother's voice echoed down the stairwell.

Theo took the steps upstairs two at a time. "No, thanks, Ma. I'm headed out."

She put her cheek out for a peck, like she did so often when he was alive, then dropped her chin. Old habits die hard. He put an arm around her anyway. "Thanks, Ma."

Her mouth turned upward into a smile. "Have fun."

"I will," he said, despite the uncomfortable mix of anticipation and dread that'd begun to trickle through his innards.

Theo got off the bus at Forbes and Murray. He walked the few extra blocks down Murray and turned onto Douglas.

His phone rang, and he fished it out of his pocket. GAVAHAN, DEC. It went back in his pocket.

The apartment was about a half block down. Once outside the glass double-doors, Theo checked the names listed on the intercom. Shelby's name, written in pink marker with an orange flower for flair, indicated she lived in apartment 6B. Marjorie's name, in neat, black, block letter, appeared next to 6A.

Theo pressed the button for 6B.

Nothing.

He pressed again, the harsh drone of the buzzer sounded, but no one answered.

She had to be there. She promised to call.

He pressed again, and again, with no answer. Finally, out of frustration, he pressed the button for apartment 6A.

Nothing.

He exhaled with a whoosh and stared at the glass doors. The right door was out of alignment with the left. He glanced around at the street, but no one appeared to be paying him any attention. He grabbed the door and pulled it open.

Once inside, he peered around to be sure no one noticed that he came in unaccompanied. The tiny lobby was deserted. A bank of silver mailboxes stood off to the left side, a hallway to the right. A sign for the elevator hung near the hallway, so he made his way toward it.

It took a minute or two to come to the first floor, but the elevator was empty when the doors opened. He entered and pressed the button for the sixth floor.

The doors opened on a hallway identical to the one on the first floor—ugly patterned carpet, gray-blue walls. The doors were painted a darker version of the walls and marked with gold numerals and letters. Four apartments per floor.

The door for 6A, on his right, was shut tight. The door for 6B, on his left, stood ajar.

CHAPTER 19

Theo knew he should feel anxiety at the sight of the opened door, but, of course, he didn't. For a second, he rationalized that Shelby just stepped out for a minute, but just as quickly realized he would have seen her, either on the street or in the lobby. She didn't seem like the type to leave her apartment unlocked and just take off.

He peeked at the edge of door. Yeah, the three deadbolts attached to the frame would confirm she normally took security seriously.

Should he knock? Yell through the crack? He stared at the slice of dim light between the door and the frame, waffling between impulses. Finally, he turned to 6A and knocked. Knocked again. "Marjorie? Are you home? It's Theo."

He waited.

"Marjorie!" He took a chance and yelled.

A door down the hall, 6D, opened. A gray-haired woman in a pink sweatshirt leaned through the door. "Quit 'cher hollering. She ain't there."

"Are you sure?" he said.

"I'm sure. I'm old, I ain't stupid. She came in last night, made a ruckus, and left again. She hasn't come back yet, else I'd hear that damn music she plays. Some new age shit. Irritating as hell."

Theo jerked his head toward Shelby's apartment. "How about this one?"

"I don't know about that one. She's usually quiet." 6D shook a finger at him. "Quit hollering," she repeated, before slamming her door.

Theo sighed, looked back at Shelby's apartment, and made a quick decision. He slipped through the door and closed it behind him with just a gentle click.

"Shelby?" he called, trying not to alert 6D to the fact he'd let himself in. "Shelby?"

No answer. The apartment felt empty, as if it waited for Shelby to come back. He could see into the galley-style kitchen on his right, but not around a corner at the far side of the room.

"Shelby?" No answer. She wasn't here.

Theo turned to leave, then stopped before he touched the doorknob. He pulled his phone from his pocket and looked at the last text message from her the night before.

"Got it. Call u tmrw."

He peered around the tiny living space, a room smaller than his basement bedroom. An orange-cushioned papasan chair sat in the corner, adorned with a lime-green stuffed Cthulhu.

His heart melted just a bit.

A stack of bright floor pillows sat next to the papasan, the only piece of furniture, and a small television hung on the opposite wall. The kitchen, separated from the living room by a bank of counters, sported a stack of bright pots and pans next to the stove.

He walked the short distance from the front door to the little hallway beside the kitchen. One door led to a bathroom, the other to Shelby's bedroom.

The bathroom was neat and clean, towels folded on a bar, a rainbow bathmat arranged beside the shower.

A surprisingly frilly and feminine spread covered the full-size bed in the next room. The pink lace caught Theo off-guard. He wanted to be aroused by the mental image of Shelby, nude, on the bed. But no. Nothing.

He shook it off and checked out the rest of the bedroom. Nightstand piled with books, closet door closed. Pink shag rug beside the bed. Not much else. He took the few steps back into the living room.

His gaze went to a small side table beside the front door. Her yellow messenger bag sat atop it, the strap dangled behind. Theo folded the flap back and opened the top wide.

Several notebooks sat near the front of the bag, and he shoved aside other items looking for an obvious container for the brains.

Nothing. He retreated to the bathroom, opened the medicine cabinet, scanned bottles of face moisturizer and Tylenol. He even shook a few bottles to be sure they contained pills.

Nothing there either.

Back in the main room, he walked around the counters that divided the kitchen from the living space. He tapped on the counter, considering.

Maybe she'd come home last night and left Dr. Libitin's brains in the apartment. Her bag was here. But if she did, he should get them now. Time was critical. But where would the sample be?

Where would Shelby leave a brain sample?

Duh, he thought, disappointed in his own idiocy. He turned around and opened the refrigerator.

There, behind the half-gallon of milk and a jar of pickles, sat a brown paper bag. He grabbed it, forced himself to move slowly and deliberately. The bag felt light; the perfect weight.

Theo closed the fridge before he reached into the bag. His hand made contact with a cold plastic item, which he withdrew from the paper bag.

Inside the small specimen cup glistened a gray chunk.

Theo's heartbeat sped just a bit. Anticipation of eating the brain called forth the zombie, and his salivary glands kicked in. He noted this response from an emotional distance, but acknowledged a nagging apprehension about the sensation.

Every zombie he knew, himself included, worked hard to overcome the primal instincts of the zombie, the need to feed on human flesh, the overwhelming urge to feast on the essence of life. Society, the living and undead, saw the zombie appetites as something to be suppressed. Society would turn on the undead if they thought they were on the lunch menu.

The First Generation zombies were the only generation to have given in to that need. Under violent circumstances, most of them turned on their attackers. After the process was better understood, the newly risen were offered other sources of food and medications to suppress the need. The newer zombies didn't even know what they missed.

Theo never did anything right. He couldn't even rise like a normal zombie. He woke from his death with the cravings of a zombie, the undeniable voracity to consume the living, to take into himself the very thing that had been taken from him, but his hunger had no outlet. The few other zombies he knew of who'd been denied food in those first days came out of it warped, not right. Some had to be locked up or simply put down with a devastating blow to the head.

Theo finally felt like a true zombie. He understood what the zombies agreed to give up to fit back into society. He'd finally fed. Now he understood what it meant to truly have that appetite satisfied. Human flesh enabled him to be more human—to feel, to think clearly, to mate. Since he began eating, the desire to continue strengthened.

Theo studied the small plastic container in his hand, the blue cap and clear plastic cup with the chunk of soft tissue gleaming wetly. The zombie at his core flared to life.

He took off the cap and held the cup to his nose. Eyes closed, he inhaled the scent of fresh brains, metallic and sweet. He ran his tongue around the inside of the cup, not touching the chunk at the bottom, heightening the promise of what was to come. He forced his thoughts to Dr. Libitin. He couldn't lose sight of why these brains were here. He had a crime to solve, a killer to catch.

This eating had a purpose.

He tilted the cup back and let the soft mound slither into his mouth. His nose buried in the cup, he inhaled to capture the scent while his tongue rolled the brain around behind his teeth. It fit into the curve of his palate and he savored the sensation of relaxing his tongue and allowing the brain to fall. He nibbled the front edge of the morsel, grinding a bit of it into pulp, then rubbing the gelatinous goo against his teeth.

The cup clattered to the floor, and Theo grasped the edge of Shelby's kitchen counter. Images flashed behind his eyelids even before he swallowed.

The home felt familiar to Theo, but the strong, creased hands at the ends of his arms did not.

Surprise was an insufficient word to explain what he felt when he checked his email. He'd turned away from his computer to pull a few files from his work bag—he often took his work home—and heard the telltale chirp signaling a new message. He almost hadn't looked, he was off the clock, his work phone on the charger in the bedroom, but figured, hell, one more.

The sender's email address, z011774 at a common provider, gave him no details. The message was simple: "Come to Frick Park now for information about the Riser Killings. Fern Hollow to Falls Ravine."

He sat in front of the machine, watching the blinking cursor, for a long moment before clicking the reply button.

"I'll be there."

He'd carried the Ruger since he testified in a gang killing and then received death threats from a defendant's family. Up to this point, he'd never needed to use it. Once a month, he took it to an indoor shooting range to be sure he could hit where he aimed, but otherwise, it stayed in his work bag. He'd even taken to leaving the loaded clip loose in the bag, instead of carrying a loaded gun.

He hung his lab coat on the back of the door, pulled a dark sweater over his head and snapped the clip into the Ruger.

No one tried to contact him, no one approached him. There'd been no instructions in the email as to how to make final contact, so he assumed the sender knew him and would be waiting somewhere along the trail. He avoided all the marked trails and instead hiked through the thick undergrowth and followed deer paths whenever he could in the hopes of getting a look at the sender before they saw him.

Eerie silence permeated the forest, even as a sense of dreadful anticipation filled him. The dread belonged to Theo, and he shook his head, trying to rid himself of the foreboding.

He knew what this walk ended with. Flashes of the rock used to weigh down his body moved through his consciousness, and he screamed in his head, "No, Dr. Libitin!

Don't! Turn around—walk away!" before remembering it was too late.

Theo let go of the counter and sank to the floor, giving himself over to the vision, not fighting, letting himself be immersed in the final moments of his mentor.

He moved as quietly as he could through the undergrowth, choosing to follow a rough deer trail rather than the well-marked path. Perhaps he could avoid having his presence known until he was ready to reveal himself. The cool scent of pine surrounded him, cleared his sinuses and he pushed a branch aside.

A large form crashed down beside him, and he jumped back, arms swinging wide. The telltale flash from the ass end of a whitetail deer careened through the trees, and Henry relaxed somewhat.

Moonlight filtered down through the trees up ahead, and he crouched to the bed of pine needles. A small clearing lay ahead, and he wanted to scout around the perimeter before entering.

He moved through the low branches, watching the clearing. A pool of water dominated the area, and the sound of a small waterfall masked his movements. He continued in his deliberate circle until he reached a point where he would have to scale a rock face to get around the waterfall.

Instead, he sat to wait. The heft of the handgun under his sweater reassured him.

Henry didn't wait long. Through the tree branches, he could just make out a dark shadow, moving without caution, but not entering the clearing. He felt certain the shadow across the water hid the Riser Killer.

It seemed they played a game of cat and mouse, but he was unsure which role he occupied.

The black shadow flitted to the left of him, growing closer. Unease flickered through him. He was backed against the rock face, and, in effect, cornered.

He scanned the rocks and waterfall for some means of escape. He could perhaps get around behind the waterfall, but it would put him in a very precarious position on exposed, wet rocks.

From the corner of his eye, he saw the black shadow step from behind a tree, uncomfortably close. If this person harbored no ill intents, he would have announced himself.

Dr. Libitin took the chance on the rocks.

He leapt from the bank onto the first rock, caught his balance and hopped to the next. He checked for the whereabouts of the shadow, only to find it no longer a shadow, but clearly a dark figure standing on the bank where he'd been a moment ago.

His heartbeat hastened.

He turned back to the rocks in front of him, judging the best one for his next leap forward. He brain raced with the decision, unable to judge clearly in the throes of naked fear. He chided himself mentally—he was acting irrationally. This person wanted to meet with him, not harm him.

He made the leap onto the big rock near the center of the pool, just within arms' reach of the waterfall. He spun to confront this shadowy person playing games with him and took a faltering step back at the proximity of the black figure. It—she?—was just mere feet away from him, and his backward step landed on the edge of the rock, which tilted down toward the water.

Dr. Libitin fell backward into the water as the end of the rock canted down. "Shit!" The exclamation escaped his mouth when he hit the water. The frigid temperature made his bones ache, and on Shelby's kitchen floor, Theo moaned.

A soft laugh echoed in Dr. Libitin's ears. A soft, feminine laugh. The shadow was a woman. He looked around, sliding in the muck, the heavy, muddy water slowing his actions. Fear mounted that the woman was merely a decoy and someone nearby would make the final blow.

"Doctor," she called in a singsong voice. "Stop struggling."

"Who are you? Why did you bring me out here?" He spoke to cover the movement of arm reaching behind him for the Ruger.

"You're too close. I don't want to do this. You are worthy." She held her arms behind her back, her chest a clear target against the moonlight that turned her into the dark silhouette. "So many are not. I cannot let you stop me."

217

The gun was gone. Panic gripped the doctor like a straightjacket. He fought against it, feeling in the mud for the gun.

"Who the fuck are you?" he screamed, as his hand bumped a metal object. He wrapped his fingers around the butt of the gun and stood in one motion. "What do you want?"

"Purity, Doctor. Purity and recognition."

"What the fuck are you talking about?"

She tsked. "Profanity, Doctor. It does not become a man of your stature. You would have made a fine addition." She shook her head, as if sad, a long dark mane swinging out from her sides.

He squinted at her, the petite frame and black hair jogging his memory, but could not put an earthly name to this ethereal form. Death came for him as a woman.

He swung his arm around, searching for her, ready to fire at the apparition on the rock, but his arm stopped short when a gleaming sword swung from above and, quite painlessly, lopped his head off.

Theo screamed.

CHAPTER 20

He banged his head on Shelby's kitchen floor over and over, until the final crushing view of Dr. Libitin's killer receded into the pain.

He lay on the floor, panting, willing the overwhelming emotions to go away, to have the unfeeling zombie return to the forefront. A sob escaped his mouth, his chest hitched in the convulsions of crying, but no tears ran down his cheeks. The horror of Dr. Libitin's last moments leached from Theo's tissues, moving from chest to arms and legs and finally evaporating.

Theo couldn't be sure how many of the emotions were Dr. Libitin's and how many were his. The jolt of adrenaline from eating the brain was his, augmented by the shock and betrayal of putting a name to the doctor's killer.

Marjorie.

He rolled onto his side, squeezed his eyes shut, his mind working overtime to make sense of what he'd seen. He breathed deep, trying to set the world right again, to put people back in the places they were supposed to occupy.

Marjorie.

Her place in his world was gone, obliterated in just a few minutes of someone else's memories. The neat little place he kept her, and all the places he hoped she'd occupy, smashed like a bullet through a skull.

A moan escaped his lips. So much blackness. Not just the blackness of her hair, but her eyes and her soul. Through the eyes of the dying, Theo saw her soul, and it was empty.

He retched, a fruitless attempt by his body to empty his stomach of its contents. He'd eaten nothing but Dr. Libitin's tissue in the last twelve hours or so. Gagging heaves wracked him until he pushed himself to a sitting position on the cracked linoleum floor.

Still breathing hard, he focused on pushing the emotions of the vision to the back of his mind. He stared at the lines in the linoleum, tracing them to different intersections.

Why hadn't he seen this before? He always saw black shadows and darkness in the visions. He hadn't connected the dots in time and his friend paid the ultimate price. He should have seen it, should have recognized the feeling in the vision as another zombie, then he might have...

Might have what? There would have been no way he would have suspected Marjorie, sweet, beautiful Marjorie of the black hair and eyes, someone who would have been out of reach before they both died. Dying gave him something in common with someone like her, gave him a chance. He would have wanted her if they were still alive, and wanted her more in death.

Could he have seen it? Did he miss something in the clues provided to him through the visions? He struggled with the memories, other people's memories, their last moments of existence. So much information, all a blur, how could he piece it together? All the visions...he didn't even know which memories and emotions belonged to whom.

He crushed his fists into his eyes in a futile effort to block the mental image of Marjorie swinging the sword from above his head, the black hair spread around her like the wings of a demon.

He opened his eyes, peered around, trying to get his bearings again. Shelby's apartment came into stark relief. The clock blinking on the microwave read two o'clock. He'd been on the floor for quite some time.

Shelby.

Where was she? He scanned the apartment with a growing sense of urgency. It appeared neat, there were no signs of a struggle, but it suddenly seemed *off* to him.

He'd told Marjorie last night that Shelby was getting him what he needed to crack the Riser Murders open. Marjorie knew Shelby had something important for identifying the killer.

They were best friends. Would Marjorie hurt her best friend?

An image of Marjorie, sword raised, with those black demon wings came unbidden into Theo's mind.

Yes, Marjorie would hurt her best friend.

He decided to look again for signs that something was amiss. From his seat on the floor he opened the dishwasher. A couple plates and bowls took up a little space, but it was mostly empty. He couldn't tell if any of the dishes were from a breakfast or not.

Back in the bedroom, the pink lace coverlet caught his attention again, but for different reasons. The bed was neatly made, no piles of laundry decorated the floor. Shelby hadn't gotten up in a hurry to go anywhere, she took the time to make the bed and be sure her things were put away.

Or she never slept in it.

The bathroom was similarly arranged, bottles of girl stuff lined up on the counter, towels folded over the rack. He grabbed a towel and felt on the underside— dry. Either she'd showered very early in the morning or she hadn't showered this morning at all. He ran a thumb over her toothbrush, making a mental note to buy her another one. Dry.

The orange papasan in the living room sported a throw over the back, also folded.

He looked around, frustration gnawing at his edges, knowing something obvious was just out of reach. It wasn't until he turned a slow circle that he caught it.

Her purse. On the tiny table next to the front door, sat her bright yellow canvas bag slouched on the table. Theo opened it, pushed a few things around. Her keys were in the bottom, right next to her purple cell phone.

His heart sank.

Shelby took that phone everywhere. He picked it up, pressed a button to make the screen illuminate. Different icons filled the screen, and he found the one for her recent calls, scanning the list for familiar names. He pulled out his own phone.

"Hello?"

"Hey, Doug. Have you seen Shelby?"

"Today? Why?"

"I can't find her."

"Why are you looking for her?"

"I'll explain everything later. Do you have any idea where she is? It's really important I find her."

"No, man, I haven't seen her since we all left the morgue last night."

"Did she say where she was going?"

"Home, I think. We were all pretty beat. Rough time, you know?"

"Yeah, I'm sorry about that. Do you think Shelby was headed home?"

"That's what she said. Now you've got me worried. I'll make some phone calls, see if anyone else knows where she went. Did you check with Marjorie?"

Theo glanced at the door. "Yeah," he lied. "I did. Marjorie's not answering her phone either."

"Maybe they're out together for lunch or something. Let me know if you hear from Shel, okay?"

Out to lunch.

"Theo? Let me know if you hear anything, all right, man?"

"Yeah, yeah. I will." Theo tapped the red button that ended the call.

He slipped Shelby's phone into his pocket with his own, then grabbed her keys and wallet from the bag. He let himself out of her apartment, after a quick look down the hall to make sure 6D wasn't watching, and locked it behind him. He took the stairs rather than risk waiting for the elevator and having 6D catch him still hanging around the hall.

Back out on the street, he stopped, unsure of his next step. His priority had to be Shelby.

Theo took a chance. He pulled his cell phone from his pocket and dialed Marjorie's number.

Four rings, then voicemail.

He used Shelby's phone to call, thinking Marjorie wouldn't blow off a call from her best friend.

Voicemail again.

Either she ignored it or she knew it couldn't be Shelby on the phone.

Theo didn't like where that line of thinking led him.

He headed back down the street toward the bus stop at a slow jog, trying to figure out his next move.

Marjorie was the Riser Killer. He had no doubts. Dr. Libitin gifted him with that final image. He'd seen shadows and glimpses of the killer from the other visions, but maybe because none of the other victims actually *knew* Marjorie, the images left in their brain matter were less concrete. Dr. Libitin knew her, he recognized her, and his brain was able to retain an image of something already familiar. That would also explain why Theo was able to see other details from the other victims—children or johns. Those were images already indelibly inked in the brains, not a fleeting look at a person one time, in a moment of great distress.

It made sense, in a sad, sorry way.

The bus pulled up in front of the shelter and Theo followed a teenager aboard. He took a seat near the middle door, both phones in hand, waiting for a callback or something, some sign that Shelby was just taking a break.

Marjorie's motive made no sense at all. She killed people who wanted to rise, become a part of their community. Increasing undead numbers meant society had to pay attention to them, meant businesses and lawmakers would view them as a valid part of society. More zombies equaled more opportunity, a better chance of reintegration.

What had Marjorie said at The Raw Bar, though? She didn't believe in reintegration. Zombies were superior. "We belong above them."

But why kill them? It would be impossible to exterminate the living, because the undead had to start somewhere. Killing the living would mean no more undead. The undead could be killed and as far as anyone could tell, they would eventually die of natural causes. Permanently. So without the living, the undead would eventually die, too, and poof! Humanity would be extinct.

So what the hell was Marjorie doing?

The bus stopped at the corner near his parents' house, and Theo stumbled off, his mind so occupied with how he would go about finding Shelby and Marjorie, he walked right past the unmarked police car sitting at the corner. It wasn't until he made it part way down the street that he felt the presence behind him. He started, but resisted the urge to turn around. Instead, he picked up his pace, determined to get to the house before whomever it was decided to pester him.

As he walked faster, the footsteps on the sidewalk behind him increased their speed. A tiny flutter of nervousness tickled Theo's diaphragm, a remnant of his feeding.

The walkway to his front porch was only feet away when a hand grasped his shoulder. Theo's adrenaline bubbled and he turned, ready to lash out.

"Whoa." Detective Gavahan stepped back, hands up. "Yo."

Theo sneered, the slug of adrenaline fueling his ire. "Are you just here to grunt at me or is there a reason for this harassment?"

Detective Gavahan's eyes narrowed. "No need to get shitty. I just want to chat."

"Like the last time?" He pointed at the detective's sidearm. "What are you packing in there now? More Z Max?"

Gavahan glanced down at the Smith and Wesson in his hip holster, ran a hand over the grip. "No. Plain old forty cal cartridges."

The two men faced off, Gavahan's bigger frame squared at the shoulders, Theo's smaller, thinner body turned sideways as if seeking an exit.

Theo broke the silence. "I've got things to do if you're not arresting me."

"I'm not arresting you." Gavahan shifted his weight from one foot to the other. "I want to talk to you."

"You mentioned that. I'm not buying it." Theo breathed heavily, trying to dissipate the remaining adrenaline. And to think he'd once longed for this.

Gavahan looked around, eyes resting on each of Theo's neighbors out doing yard work or just bullshitting on their front porches. "Not here."

"I'm not going anywhere with you."

"Don't you live here?"

"Yeah." Theo didn't like where this was going.

"Well, your place."

"No."

"What'd you mean 'no?'" Gavahan shook his head. "This is not something I can discuss in the street."

"I'm kind of busy right now." Theo turned to walk away. Gavahan grabbed his arm again and Theo opened his mouth to chew the detective a shiny new asshole but stopped when the big man leaned in close to Theo's ear.

"You were working with Henry Libitin on something before he died. It's something to do with his death. You need to tell me what it is."

Theo shut his mouth.

Still too close for Theo's comfort, Gavahan continued. "I don't like admitting this, but I think you're one step ahead of me. Remember Blaine? He says hello."

Theo took a step back, out of Gavahan's grasp. "Blaine? Who are you talking about?"

"Blaine of the pastel shirts at the William Pitt Union."

Lightheaded. Holy shit.

Gavahan's gaze stayed on Theo's face. "Yeah, that Blaine."

"Oh."

"I need to know what you know, Walker."

Theo sucked on his teeth, considering. He really didn't know what his next step would be, had no idea of where Shelby or Marjorie could be, no way of finding out. Pittsburgh was a big place; he couldn't exactly just walk around knocking on doors. If Gavahan got to *The Pitt News* through some other direction, maybe they could meet in the middle.

"Okay," he said. "My house." He led the way to his parents' house, wondering the entire time what it would take to keep Gavahan quiet about the fact he still lived with his parents.

"Teddy," his mother called when he walked in. "Teddy, how was your day? Can you make sure your laundry is in the basket? I'm doing whites this afternoon."

Theo despised the amused smile on Detective Gavahan's face.

His mother rounded the kitchen corner and stopped short at the sight of the tall, dark, and handsome asshole standing in her living room. "Oh, hello. Who's your friend, Teddy?"

Theo didn't even get his mouth open to reply when Gavahan stepped forward and took his mother's hand in a gentle grasp. "You must be Mrs. Walker. I was barely out of the Academy when I started hearing stories about your cookies. It's a pleasure to meet you, ma'am."

Theo stared. His mother giggled. She *giggled*.

"Thank you. You are?" she said, eyebrows high on her forehead, a goofy grin plastered on her face.

"Detective Decebal Gavahan, ma'am. Your husband is a legend in the department. Almost as much a legend as your cooking."

Joyce peered up at Gavahan, clearly flattered by the attention. "Young man, you are flirting with me."

Theo made a conscious effort at keeping his mouth shut when Gavahan just smiled.

"Can I get you some coffee, Detective?" Joyce bustled off toward the kitchen.

Gavahan appeared to consider. "I have a couple things to discuss with your son, ma'am. Maybe after."

"Well, that's fine, Detective. You two go ahead and talk shop. I'm used to it. You can come in the kitchen, if you'd like."

"Theo? Kitchen?" Gavahan said.

"No." He led the way toward the basement.

Gavahan ducked his head at the bottom of the stairs and stooped to fit under the drop ceiling. Theo pulled an old desk chair out from behind a folding table and rolled it into place next to his bed.

"Jesus, it's hot down here." Gavahan unfastened the top couple buttons of his shirt and plopped into the chair.

"I like it hot."

"Obviously."

The men sat in awkward silence for a few minutes.

"What the fuck do you want?" Theo finally said.

Gavahan didn't respond right away. He sat, his mass hunched in the broken chair, peering around the dim basement. "I need to know what you've got."

"Why?"

Gavahan snapped his head around to pierce Theo with an angry gaze. "Because I have some fucking psycho killer out there and I don't have a clue who it is or why they're killing. Because this freak murdered our medical examiner. A damn fine medical examiner." Gavahan's hands bunched up in fists and he pounded on his knees. "The best medical examiner Pittsburgh's ever had."

Theo, surprised at the vehemence in Gavahan's tone, agreed. "What makes you think I know more than you?"

Gavahan barked a laugh. "Jesus, no one was more surprised than I was when I went to *The Pitt News* and pretty boy Blaine told me he already had a cop—a zombie cop—in the office asking about the ads." The detective leaned over, elbows on knees. "You shouldn't pass yourself off as a cop, Walker. First offense is a misdemeanor."

"Whatever. How did you know about the ads?" Theo's pulse picked up just a bit.

"I interviewed Naomi Flores's family. Her sister told me Naomi'd mentioned something about seeing a funny ad in *The Pitt News*." Gavahan shook his head. "I went out on a limb checking the college paper, but once Blaine told me you'd been there, I knew I had something."

"Maybe." Theo considered what he knew about the ads. He still had no concrete evidence—not even psychic evidence—connecting Marjorie to those ads.

Theo studied Gavahan's face. Lines etched into his forehead were new, as were the suitcases under his eyes. Grief and exhaustion alternated in his face.

Gavahan stared right back at him. "Listen, Walker, we're not friends. But if you know something, anything to help me nail this fucker, I'll take back a lot of what I've said about you. I'm not always a good person, but I'm a damn good cop. They tell me you're good at what you do...whatever that is. Help me."

Theo took a deep breath. "I think the killer put ads in the paper for victims."

CHAPTER 21

Gavahan's brows met between his eyes. "Excuse me?"

Theo rummaged next to the bed for the copy of *The Pitt News* he threw there at some point during the week.

God, had it only been a week? Yeah, give or take...about a week for his life to turn upside down.

He found the paper, shook it open to the page where he'd circled "Alice's" ad, and handed it over to Gavahan. "That ad, right there, was placed by someone looking for people who want to rise. 'Alice' meets with them and kills them. In fact, I'm supposed to meet with 'Alice' tonight."

He flipped through the pages of the *City Paper*, then handed it over, stabbing at the paper. "And there, too."

Skepticism knitted the detective's brows together. "What does this have to do with the doc?"

"We've been calling this the Riser Killer or the Riser Murders. Someone's taking out potential risers."

Gavahan's jaw twitched. "What in hell for?"

"I haven't figured that out yet. But Dr. Libitin knew there was a connection between the victims. Aside from the fact they all wore the tattoo, the only commonality we could find was that these victims are all what might be considered a burden on society."

"Burden?" Gavahan held his hands out, palms up.

"Here." Theo handed him the list of victims and basic information he'd made the night he discovered the ad in *The Pitt News*. "Look. Meth dealer, gang leader, prostitutes, welfare moms. A retarded girl. Someone with little compassion might look at these people as trash, you know, a non-contributing member of society, someone who takes more than they give."

Gavahan grunted. "That's pretty shitty."

"Murder is shitty, too." Theo heard his own echo and thought back to the conversation with Dr. Libitin. He felt a stab of regret knowing he'd never see his friend again. "I don't think this killer cares about being nice."

"True." Gavahan held out the list. "Where did you get this?"

"Dr. Libitin."

"Why did the ME share confidential details of our investigations with you?"

Theo averted his eyes from the detective. "He thought I could help."

"Why?"

It was a simple question, a fair one for Gavahan to ask, but it made Theo sweat. He got the feeling Detective Gavahan wouldn't settle for the same explanation he gave Marjorie.

The thought of Marjorie quickened his pulse. Where was she? Did she have Shelby?

"You're not going to like this."

"I'm sure." The detective's voice remained low and even.

Theo hedged his bets. "I'm a psychic."

Gavahan's eyebrows shot up. "What?"

"You know, a psychic. I get visions. I can relive the last moments of someone's life right up until death. Dr. Libitin knew and he used my ability to find clues." Theo struggled to get the words out. He'd never felt so ridiculous in his life—either life. He knew how it sounded, especially without the full story.

"Uh huh." Gavahan nodded, crossed his arms over his chest. "And what did your visions tell you?"

"They told me these people were all seeing and feeling the same things before they died. The same person is involved in their deaths."

"Why didn't you—or for that matter, the doc—come to us with this?"

"Yeah, sure. You think I'm not already sick of the way people talk about me? And I'm pretty sure the doc wasn't willing to lose his credibility until we had something to back up the evidence in my visions."

Gavahan exhaled loudly, frustration evident. "People are dying, Walker."

"I didn't see anything concrete until Dr. Libitin's death."

"His death? This vision happened when you found him? You didn't say anything when we had you at the station."

"No, it happened this morning. And what would I have said to you at the station?" Theo struggled to keep his voice low. "'Oh, hey, put that fucking zombie ammo away and let's talk about my visions?' Please."

"This morning? What were you doing this morning?" Gavahan's eyes narrowed. "How do you get these visions?"

Too late, Theo realized his mistake. He swallowed hard. "Can you just take my word for it?"

"I'm opening myself to all kinds of problems just coming here. I've been trying to get in touch with you for two days now. I have information you want, you have information I want. I need to know what you know, and that includes how you're getting this information."

"Shelby Gusky is missing."

"Who?" Detective Gavahan frowned. "The morgue girl?"

"Yeah. I saw her last night for dinner and she promised to have something for me today, something that would help me with the visions. That's where I was, her apartment. She wasn't there but her door was open. All her stuff was there, you know, her purse and keys." He pulled her purple phone from his pocket. "I have her cell."

"Apart from unlawful entry and a possible theft charge for taking that phone, I don't see a problem. So she's not in her apartment? Doesn't mean she's missing. Maybe she was in the laundry room."

"No, I stayed for a while." Theo grew increasingly uncomfortable under the detective's stare. "What? I told you. She had what I needed to get the vision from Dr. Libitin. I had no choice but to go into her apartment. Like you said, people are dying." He sighed. "I know who the killer is and

I'm certain she took Shelby because she thought Shelby would lead me to her."

Gavahan's eyebrows shot up. "You know who's doing this?"

"Yes."

The detective threw his arms up. "Do tell, Mr. Psychic Zombie."

"Marjorie Frey."

Gavahan's eyes opened wide. "The counselor chick? She's a zombie! Why the fuck would she kill people who want to become zombies?"

"Shh. Lower your voice." Theo glared at the detective.

"How long have you known this?" Gavahan hissed through his teeth.

"Just since this morning. Shelby left something at her place for me. Something Marjorie didn't know about."

"Walker, sooner or later you have to tell me what the hell you're talking about."

Theo leaned toward Gavahan. "Listen to me. I don't think we have a lot of time, and I need your help. Shelby lives across the hall from Marjorie. She's in trouble because of my fucking mouth. I told Marjorie something last night that put Shelby in danger. You have to listen to me. We have to find her."

Gavahan's jaw twitched and he rubbed his chin. "Didn't you say you're supposed to meet with this 'Alice' tonight?"

Theo fidgeted. "Isn't there some way to speed this up?"

"Are you sure the person placing the ads is Marjorie?"

"It has to be. I don't believe in coincidences. She wants to meet at Ryan's Pub. She specifically mentioned Frick Park. That's where most of the bodies have been found." Theo looked away. "Plus, my visions indicate that some of the victims responded to an ad. It's too much to ignore."

"There are those visions again. Don't think I'm going to let this go, Walker." He looked at his watch. "What time are you supposed to meet with this person?"

"Eight. Except I need Shelby to do it."

"Why's that?"

"Because this person is going to be looking for someone who wants to rise." He pointed at his chest. "That's obviously not a concern for me."

"Shelby was going to go in your place? Doesn't sound like a terribly good idea."

"Who else? The only other person I considered asking was Marjorie, and, gee, that wouldn't have worked out either."

Gavahan leaned back, put his hands behind his neck. "Listen, I have to get out of this basement. It's fucking stifling down here."

"And what? What are we going to do? I'm sure Marjorie has Shelby. She could be dead by now." Panic trickled into Theo's chest.

"We're going back to see Blaine."

"So get your boss. I don't have a warrant, but I have a badge. Time is critical. Make the call now."

Theo watched Gavahan in action, grudgingly impressed. He didn't just *order* Blaine to pass over the information about the person placing the ads, he *commanded*.

Blaine, dressed today in a mint green polo shirt and tan chinos, looked near tears. "Fine. Fine. I'll get it, but I'm calling you when I get in trouble for this."

Gavahan leaned over the counter. "Blaine, no one needs to know. Chances are this person will never come back to *The Pitt News*. If this is someone else, there's no way for them to know we asked."

Blaine squinted at the detective. "You'll keep it between us?"

Gavahan actually sketched an X over his chest. "Cross my heart."

"Okay." Mollified, Blaine turned to the computer monitor next to him. He tapped a keyboard for a minute, then scribbled a name on a piece of paper. "This is the name and contact information for the person. I can't say for sure if the name is genuine, but the phone number has to be, since we contact the advertiser via text message when it's time to renew."

The college kid slid the paper across the counter at Gavahan. "You're welcome."

Detective Gavahan smiled as he took the paper. "Thank you, Blaine."

Theo grabbed for the paper, but Gavahan took his elbow and led him out of the office. "Not here."

They made their way back out and downstairs to the lobby of the William Pitt Union. Gavahan glanced at the paper, his face turned stony. He handed it to Theo.

Marjorie Frey. And when he recognized her cell phone number, his stomach dropped like a stone—a clear contrast to the elation he'd felt only days ago when he saw that number appear on his own phone.

"Goddamned cocksure piece of work. She never thought anyone would connect her to those ads." Gavahan spoke under his breath as they crossed the lobby.

"She also never thought anyone would connect the victims to the ad. Who mentions a classified ad about rising to their friends and family? It's like a cry for help—'Hey, I'm suicidal!'" Theo resisted the urge to shred the paper.

"Remember, Walker, we still don't have concrete evidence linking the victims to the ad. That's your arena, and even though the dead walk, I don't think judges have changed their mind about admitting psychic evidence."

Theo followed the detective through the big double doors at the front of building. "You're taking this rather well."

"What do you mean?" Gavahan unlocked the car doors with the remote as they approached the unmarked sedan illegally parked at the curb.

"You know, the whole psychic angle." Not to mention the zombie, but Theo opted not to point that out.

"I won't tell you how I reacted when Blaine told me you got to him before I did." Gavahan slipped behind the driver's seat.

Theo snapped his seat belt on, expecting Gavahan to start the car. "Where are we headed?"

"I don't know. There's no way to know where our suspect might be right now, and I can't arrest her without something more than your visions."

"We have to find them. Shelby's in trouble."

Gavahan shifted in his seat to look at Theo. "What do you see in these visions?"

"I see the last minutes of someone's life, just before they die."

"How?"

Theo squirmed. "I'd rather not say."

Gavahan's gaze didn't leave Theo's face. "If we have something of Marjorie's, could you get a vision? Something personal of hers?"

Theo knew what Gavahan was getting at. Psychometry. Sometimes the police actually took information from psychometrists, people who could get impressions from physical objects. Skeet mentioned a woman, Elaine something or other, who came in and helped find missing persons.

"No. It doesn't work that way for me."

"Then what? What do you need?"

"The person has to be dead. Maybe it's a side effect of my own death. It's like an imprint of their last moments."

Gavahan slapped the steering wheel. "All right. Let's get down to the station."

"What's at the station?"

"Chief Niemic."

"Oh." Theo knew Chief Niemic from his father's days at the bureau. Nice enough guy. Kind of standoffish. "And we want to see him why?"

"Because if he okays bringing our suspect in, we can put patrolmen out to look for her."

"Oh."

"You're still not going to give me the details of this psychic ability of yours, are you?"

"No."

Gavahan huffed. "If I knew what you need, I could try and get it."

Theo almost smiled. "Dr. Libitin and I did what we could with all the victims he felt might be linked to the Riser

Killer. There's really nothing for me to do, unless someone else turns up dead."

"Listen, Walker, I've reached out this far. You have to meet me halfway here." Gavahan made a sharp right that left Theo grabbing for the door handle. "Zombies shouldn't be part of the force. The public still doesn't trust your kind, and it undermines our authority. But here I am, asking for your help." His voice grew hard. "Now help me before we find another body."

"We have to find Shelby first. It's my fault she's involved. After I know she's okay, I'll tell you everything and I will help you." Theo pitched his voice to be equally stony, hoping the detective wouldn't call his bluff.

"Finding the killer has to be our priority."

"Finding Shelby will find Marjorie. I'm sure of it."

Gavahan sighed. "You're really stubborn for a dead man."

"No, sir, I have no leads other than what Mr. Walker has offered. The fact we reached the same conclusion through two different avenues of investigation tells me the information Mr. Walker offered is good."

Chief Niemic watched Theo while Gavahan explained the situation. Theo tried to sit still.

"And how did Mr. Walker come to this conclusion?"

"Confidential informant."

Theo snapped his head around to look at Gavahan, who appeared relaxed in the rigid, high-backed plastic chairs. His expression was mild, and Theo admired his ability to stay so cool.

Confidential informant? Theo tucked that away for future use.

His attention went back to Chief Niemic, whose gaze still rested on Theo.

"Son, I'm going to put my name on the line based on your 'confidential informant.' I'm going to tell a judge that an undead woman has been running around my city shooting and beheading our citizens, including our own medical examiner." He leaned across the desk. "Are you willing to let me do that?"

Theo considered the brains he ate, the visions he had and the deaths he'd witnessed. His "confidential informants" were the dead themselves. "Yes, sir."

"Okay. Let me make a quick phone call to Judge Richards. He can sign the warrants for the apartments and we'll circulate descriptions of these young ladies for an all-points." He picked up the handset from the phone on his desk. "Go on. Start writing up the descriptions."

Gavahan stood. "Thank you, sir."

Theo followed him into the cubicle area that served as an office for the homicide team. Gavahan walked to a cube and grabbed an extra chair.

"Since they both work for the city, we'll have photos on file. That's one good thing." He tapped a computer mouse to activate his computer and clicked into a program with templates for informational posters. "You better hope you're right."

"I'm right." Theo watched the detective pull up employee photos for both girls and insert them into the sheet. Across the top read the words "have you seen."

"What are we doing with those?" Theo said. "Passing them out door to door?"

"We will if we have to. Mostly these are going out to officers. Vehicle patrol will get this bulletin on their computer. Those on foot will get it on their phone. Every cop in the city will have these faces in front of them. We'll find them."

Theo shook his head. "It's not fast enough."

"What else would you suggest, hotshot?"

"Tell me what you know about the victims. Were they all killed where they were found?"

Gavahan pulled up a file. "We think so. Some at Frick Park, the others elsewhere. The evidence at all the locations suggested they were killed and left. None of them were transported after death."

"For those that died somewhere other than the park, were they killed at locations that made sense for the victim?"

Gavahan frowned. "You mean did the victims who weren't found in the park have a reason to be where they were killed? Yes."

"Maybe Marjorie took Shelby to Frick Park. She didn't kill her at her apartment, so obviously she took her somewhere. Why not the park?"

"Pretty obvious, isn't it? Don't you think she knows we'd look there?"

"Don't most killers stick with an MO? Creatures of habit and all?"

Gavahan gave Theo an appraising look. "Yeah, usually."

"So why wouldn't Marjorie take Shelby to Frick Park?"

The detective shrugged. "It's possible. The park is a big place, though. What makes you think we'll find them if we just start walking?"

"I don't know, but I can't just sit here." Theo's temper began to awaken.

"Help me finish with these and we'll figure out our next move," Gavahan said.

Theo helped supply some basic information about the girls and Gavahan sent the bulletins out to all the police communication devices. He clicked another button and a printer behind Theo hummed to life.

"We'll take a few with us in case we can pass them out." Gavahan grabbed the papers from the printer. He handed one of each to Theo.

Marjorie's beautiful face, surrounded by the black shroud of hair stood out in stark relief against the white backdrop of her work identification photo. Theo shuddered, the memory of the emptiness of her black eyes looking down on Dr. Libitin, cut him to the core.

Shelby's smile beamed from her photo. The warmth of her personality shone in her sunny smile and crinkled eyes. Theo's heart stopped for a long moment.

He couldn't live if something happened to her because of him.

Gavahan tapped his shoulder. "Come on. Let's go get the search warrants from Chief Niemic."

The chief was on the phone when Gavahan and Theo reached his office. He pointed at a packet of papers on the corner of his desk. Gavahan gave him a casual salute and took the papers.

Theo caught the chief's gaze and mouthed a silent "thank you."

Chief Niemic gave Theo a slow nod.

Outside, Theo realized how cold he'd become and slowed his pace to soak up more sunlight. "Where are we headed?"

"Marjorie's apartment." Gavahan unlocked the car door with the remote.

Theo jogged to the car. "Let's go."

CHAPTER 22

"Which one is it?" Gavahan said.
Theo pointed at Marjorie and Shelby's apartment building. "There."
Gavahan pulled into a handicapped parking space on the street and slid a parking permit on the dash. Theo trailed him through a light rain to the apartment building.
In the lobby, Theo perused the potted plants while Detective Gavahan spoke with the landlord, Marvin Gour, and tried not to look like he was eavesdropping. Officers Martin and Minet stood back by the door, jostling one another.
"The papers are all in order. Judge Richards signed them this morning." Gavahan loomed over the short, rotund landlord.
"Let me see." Mr. Gour held his ground against the detective and put his hand out. He took the warrant and shuffled through the papers. "All right. I guess this is legit. Let me call and see if she's there."
"No. We're sure she's not there, but in case she is, I'd prefer to go unannounced. If she hesitates to open the door, we're just going in."
Mr. Gour shrugged. "You're the boss."
"You have keys?"
Mr. Gour held up a full ring.
They took the elevator to the sixth floor, four men and a zombie crammed into the tiny, mirrored elevator. Theo noted with keen amusement that none of the men made eye contact with one another and they acted as if Theo wasn't even there.
When the doors slid open, Gavahan put an arm out to block them and let Mr. Gour out first. The roly-poly man led

the way to Marjorie's apartment. He knocked. "Hello? Miss Frey?"

Knocked again. "Miss Frey, are you in there?"

No answer.

Theo watched down the hall toward 6D and waited for the pink-clad woman to make an appearance.

"Just open it."

Mr. Gour rolled his eyes as he inserted the key in the lock. He jiggled it and swung the door open. "Miss Frey?"

"We'll take over from here." Gavahan moved past Mr. Gour, missing the black look the landlord shot at him. Officers Martin and Minet entered next. Theo brought up the rear. As he passed into Marjorie's apartment, the sound of a door opening caught his attention and he looked down the hall. 6D watched the proceedings with wide eyes. Theo grinned and waved.

The temperature in Marjorie's apartment was stifling. Even Theo found it claustrophobic. Gavahan closed the door behind them, removing the only source of light.

The outline of heavy, light-blocking drapes over the windows was the only thing clearly visible. "Find a switch or something," Gavahan said.

Theo fumbled along the wall, feeling for a light switch.

"They're back here," Mr. Gour said and illuminated the room.

The black and white color scheme and austere furniture were a study in contrasts to Shelby's apartment. The sharp lines of the modern, black loveseat and chair did nothing to soften the sterile white walls and beige carpet. An MP3 docking station sat on a small metal stand. Otherwise the tiny room was empty. The layout appeared to be the same as Shelby's, in mirror image, so the tiny kitchen stood to Theo's left. The counters, impeccably clean, were bare.

"Okay, Minet, start in the kitchen. Martin, here in the living room."

The officers pulled gloves on, moved into their assigned places and began lifting cushions and opening cabinet doors.

"Theo, you want to check the bedroom?" Gavahan stood in the small entryway, his cell phone in hand. "Standard evidence collection procedure. Let me know what you find."

Theo walked around the corner of the kitchen tugged nitrile gloves onto his hands. The bathroom, equally devoid of personality, offered nothing at a glance. He turned into the bedroom, eyes closed, simultaneously anxious and full of dread about what he might see.

The twin-sized bed, positioned against the far wall, was covered with a plain white duvet. Two pillows, in white cases, lay stacked one atop the other at the head of the bed. A plain wood dresser sat opposite the bed, the top clear of any knick-knacks or items that might give a clue as to the personality of the owner.

The only concession to Marjorie, as anything other than a cardboard cutout, was the electrical cord running from a wall outlet under the duvet. An electric blanket.

"Can I open these curtains?" Martin's voice brought Theo back to the task at hand. He dropped to the floor to look under the bed. Nothing, not even a dust bunny. He felt under the duvet, but found nothing. The closet door swung open in silence, revealing the clothes Theo was accustomed to see Marjorie wear. He hesitated only a second before pushing aside the tan chinos, white shirts and feminine sweaters to get a look at the back of the closet.

A thin shelf ran the length of the closet, hidden by the clothing. At one end, a nondescript wooden box took up space. Near the center, a long, thin box sat. Theo shoved the hanging clothes as far down the rod as he could, making room to get closer to the boxes in the back.

"What do you have there?" Gavahan's voice came from close behind.

"Not sure yet. There's a shelf."

"Anything on it?"

"Wooden boxes."

"Bring 'em out."

Theo retrieved the long box first. It was about three feet in length, and he had to step sideways to bring it out of the closet. Gavahan took it and placed it on the bed. Theo reached back for the smaller box and bumped a black leather jacket on a hanger. It fell to the floor with a thud, a misshapen lump apparent in the jacket.

He handed the box to Gavahan and bent over to grab the jacket. It felt weightier than a leather jacket should. Whatever it hid was heavy. Minet stood in the small bedroom next to Gavahan, taking up much of the space. He held a digital camera.

Theo placed the jacket on the floor next to the bed.

"We didn't find anything in the living room or kitchen. She's the damn neatest person I've ever seen. It's not like a home."

Home would imply a life. No, Theo thought, she doesn't *live*. Humans live. The undead do not. She would not lower herself to *an actual life*.

Gavahan lifted the lid of the long box and Theo leaned over, anxious to see what it held. Minet snapped photos.

Nothing.

It sported a padded satin lining, but nothing else. A case of some sort? For what?

A frustrated sound escaped his lips.

"Calm down, Walker." Gavahan inspected the case. "What do you make of this?"

"My brother has a case like that for his haidong sword."

"His what?" Gavahan looked to be smothering a laugh.

"Haidong gumdo. It's a Korean martial art form with swords." Minet explained. Theo could have sworn he heard him finish his statement with "jackass." He watched Minet with interest. Maybe Gavahan wasn't universally loved.

"Swords?" Gavahan repeated and Theo took another look at the case.

"Could be."

"No sense in speculating. We don't know what it's for. Could be for some sort of calligraphy supplies." Gavahan studied the box.

Calligraphy? Theo looked at Gavahan, then back at Minet, who shrugged.

"What's in the other box?" Theo said.

Gavahan opened it. A matte black Glock model 17 lay gleaming against a white cloth. A box of nine-millimeter cartridges accompanied the pistol. The anise scent of gun cleaner wafted from the box.

Minet whistled. "Is that what we're looking for?"

"Yes." Gavahan's jaw twitched. " However, there are no laws against owning weapons, not even for zombies. Anything else?"

Theo held the jacket up. "This jacket's packing something heavy."

"Check the pockets."

He laid the jacket on the bed and patted it until he found the item. He felt around on the inside, but discovered that the lining of the jacket had been slit open and a sizable plastic container stored inside. Made from semi-transparent plastic, it sported a green lid. It appeared to be full of a dark substance.

"What is it?" Minet stood over Theo's shoulder, camera at the ready.

"I'm not sure." He held the plastic tub up to the light, but the contents were unidentifiable. "Can I open it?"

Gavahan gave a curt nod.

Theo twisted the cap on the top and lifted it off.

The smell hit him first, but with a much different result than it elicited from the two other men in the room. While Gavahan fought with the same gag reflex Minet gave in to, Theo's blood boiled.

"What the fuck is that?" Minet said between dry retches.

"Human flesh."

Minet stumbled out of the room. Gavahan's face went from red to greenish.

"This combined with the sword case makes it pretty obvious, doesn't it?" Theo felt the stirrings of anger. "Is that enough?"

"Enough to bring her in. Not enough to convict her for murder." Gavahan gestured to the container of meat in Theo's hand. "Are you absolutely positive that's human flesh?"

"Oh yes," Theo said, with a smile he wasn't quite quick enough to suppress. He turned to Minet, who'd come out of the bathroom. "What time is it?"

The cop checked his watch. "Quarter after seven."

Theo turned to Gavahan. "I'm supposed to meet her at Ryan's in forty-five minutes."

"If she's out there with Shelby, what are the chances she's going to keep the appointment with you? Unless, of course, she's already killed Shelby."

"The gun is still here. Unless your perp is in the habit of killing people with swords, you've got nothing to worry about." Minet shuddered and pointed at the container. "Of course, that changes the game."

Theo's stomach squirmed. "Gavahan, I have to find her. This is the only chance we have right now."

"Let's go." He waved a hand toward the human remains. "Leave that here."

They left Martin and Minet back at Marjorie's apartment to catalog the Glock and the case and wait for the coroner's office to come for the flesh. Mr. Gour muttered under his breath as he escorted Theo and Detective Gavahan out of the building. Theo's best interpretation of the landlord's quiet rant was something along the lines of a "no weapon clause in the lease" and "freak magnet."

"If she's not there?" Gavahan said as they pulled away from the curb and turned onto Murray Avenue. Misty rain covered the windshield and the detective turned on the wipers.

"I'm going into the park." Theo clicked his seatbelt into the clasp.

"How do you plan on finding two people in a park that's over six hundred acres?"

Theo's frustration got the better of him. "I don't know. I don't fucking know, but I can't sit around here waiting anymore. It's my fucking fault Shelby's out there with Marjorie. I have to do something about it, goddamn it, whether you're helping me or not."

Gavahan's eyebrows went up.

"If you're not coming, then we're done. I'll go by myself." Theo turned to the window.

They drove through Squirrel Hill and into Edgewood in silence. Things were starting to fall into place for Theo. The gun in place, the missing sword. He thought back to the cases Dr. Libitin outlined for him and the visions. The beheadings occurred when Marjorie planned a kill. She beheaded the ones who answered her ads. She shot the others, probably the ones she killed on impulse. Maybe she even went hunting for them, waited where she knew she might find people living on the fringe of society, like the blowjob in Frick Park.

Given what Theo knew of her attitude toward the living, he guessed she was exterminating people she felt didn't deserve to rise. Lower social demographics, criminals, a mentally retarded girl... Marjorie was cleansing the unworthy from the pool of potential risers.

Gavahan pulled into a spot behind Rosie's Ice Cream and jammed the car into park. "Listen, Walker. I have to worry about safety first. There may be nothing we can do for Shelby at this point, but there's no sense in getting one or both of us killed." He gave Theo a sidelong look. "Or killed again. Anyway, the best you can figure is that she's had Shelby since last night or this morning, right?"

Theo ground his teeth and nodded.

"What makes you think she hasn't killed her already? Our suspect doesn't seem like the type to beat around the bush."

"Shelby is her friend. Marjorie didn't want to have to kill Dr. Libitin—she said he was 'worthy.' I think she's going to have an even tougher time killing her best friend." Theo got out of the car and slammed the door.

He walked around the corner toward Ryan's Pub without bothering to check if Gavahan followed. The footsteps behind him told him the detective wasn't far behind.

When he got to Ryan's he asked the woman at the front counter if Alice was available.

"I'm sorry, are you meeting someone named Alice?"

"Yeah."

"I haven't seated anyone waiting for a party. Would you like to be seated and wait?"

"Yes. If someone comes in looking for Pat, that's me."

She nodded and grabbed two menus. "Right this way."

"Can we have a back corner?" Gavahan said.

She started to point at a table near the front. "Your friend will be able to see you here..." Her words were cut short when Gavahan flashed his badge. "Okay. Corner in the back."

"I'll take a water." Gavahan squeezed into a chair that allowed him to have his back to the wall.

Theo took the chair next to him, which gave him a clear view of the front door. "Coffee, please." He pulled his cell phone from his pocket to check the time when the waitress dropped the drinks on the table. Twenty minutes until the meeting.

"Uh." Gavahan sipped. "What does it mean that she has human remains in her apartment?"

Theo leveled his gaze on the detective. "She's eating."

"Obviously." Another drink of water. "But what does that mean? You know, what happens to you guys if you do that? I thought it was a no-no among your kind."

"It is." Theo stirred his coffee, considered his words. "It probably means, I mean from what I've been told, that she's more powerful, more alive, than the rest of us. Or at least those of us who are abiding by the rule." Theo thought about the Raw Bar and wondered what Delilah actually put in that drink.

"Uh huh." The detective fiddled with a straw paper. "Where did she get it?"

Theo froze, his coffee mug partway to his mouth. He set the mug back down. "I don't know. None of her victims were mutilated."

"None that we know of." Another sip.

Was Marjorie killing others and eating them? She had to be. Where else could she get human flesh? The mass in the container smelled rank—it had been there a while.

If she killed to get fresh meat, why would she store foul product? Theo's head spun with the implications.

"What are you going to do if she shows up?"

Kill her. "I figured I'd play it by ear."

"Remember we're in a public location. No one gets hurt."

Theo ignored the detective, instead concentrating on the rising pull of the zombie. He led a tame existence, particularly since his death, since he tried to stay off the radar of people like Gavahan. The drive he fought now, a byproduct of the last week's tension, the current anticipation of spilled blood, and anger at Marjorie hiding human flesh, was new to him. The zombie, brought to life partly by the scent of real food, whispered in his ear, tugged at his common sense, brought his primal instincts to the forefront.

Gavahan's voice faded into the background. He concentrated on listening to the blood circulating through every patron in the restaurant, on feeling the essence of the living. He could sense the heat radiating from the living bodies, fought the urge to take it for his own.

Dangerous ground. This was not the right place to entertain the zombie. He'd never done it before—he always deliberately kept his emotions in strict check—and the power of his darker half both frightened and excited him. He felt his capabilities, knew what he would be if he gave in and ate.

"Walker." Gavahan nudged his hand.

Theo spun back to the table, just barely avoided hissing at the detective.

Gavahan's expression changed from concerned to wary. "What the fuck is wrong with you?"

Theo tamped the zombie down with as much force as he could muster, despite his growing desire to let it loose. The pressure loosened his tongue. "I'm worried. I'm scared for my friend. If you would kindly shut up I'd like to concentrate on what I'm going to do here."

The detective's eyes narrowed. "Fine."

A voice cut through the crowd. "Pat? Is there a Pat here?"

Theo stood. "That's me."

A waiter traversed the maze of tables to get to Theo. "Alice just called. She asked me to tell you she's not going to make it."

The zombie roared to life and Theo shoved the waiter aside to get to the door.

"Hey!" The teenager grabbed a chair behind him to remain on his feet.

Gavahan's voice barely reached through the thundering in Theo's head. "Sorry, he's a little upset. Walker. Walker!"

The zombie howled, struggled to gain control.

CHAPTER 23

Theo fought the zombie struggling just below the surface, but barely. He knew the fastest way to find Marjorie and Shelby was to let the zombie lead.

Someone grabbed his arm from behind just before he crossed Braddock. He turned, snarled.

Gavahan raised both hands, stepped back. "Jesus Christ, Walker. Knock it the fuck off. We're on the same side here."

Theo shook his head, trying to maintain control. "I have to go find her."

"I'm coming with you."

"You are not."

"Theo, I have the only weapon between us."

"I don't need one." Thunder cracked and the light rain picked up into a shower.

Gavahan's expression changed. "You'll never cover enough ground."

"So we'll split up. You have the weapon, remember?"

The detective took his phone from his pocket. "Give me your number. If you find her, call me. I'll call you if I spot her. Do not do anything until I get there."

Theo rattled off his number and put Gavahan's number in his own phone before turning the sound off.

He wouldn't use it. He knew that.

Detective Gavahan shadowed him across Braddock. At the tennis courts, Theo veered right, listening to the zombie, and Gavahan took the left trail. Theo stopped and watched the detective's back until it disappeared in the trees.

He closed his eyes and called for the zombie.

The strength of the drive to feed staggered him. Could this be a byproduct of having eaten so much? A kind of withdrawal? Theo had no experience with it, since he'd never fed even in the early days. What must those first zombies have gone through after eating, some with total abandon, and then being cut off abruptly? What must Marjorie go through on a day-to-day basis if she continually fed?

It explained her attitude. Human flesh: zombie heroin.

He put the thoughts out of his mind and listened to the zombie. The undead part of him sensed life in the undergrowth, the small animals that made Frick Park their home, several larger sources of life. He felt Gavahan's presence, a tiny beacon in the huge park, moving away from him. In seconds, it was gone.

He could feel living beings on all sides of him, but only a few humans. Could he sense other zombies? No way to know for sure. If he could, he would find Marjorie, but she could probably sense him as well, and her senses were no doubt heightened since she'd fed recently.

He concentrated on what the zombie reached for and headed toward the strongest beacon.

The leaves coating the ground were slick with rain and mud. He slid his way through the trees, trying to move as quietly as possible, grateful for the sound of rain to cover his noise.

He felt them before he saw them, and knew immediately the people to his right were not his prey. He crouched down among the scrub and approached. A man sat cross-legged on a ratty tarp, a woman, naked from the waist down straddled his crotch. The woman bounced up and down on the man, making guttural sounds. She whined, stilled her movements, and put an arm out to him.

A syringe lay on the filthy canvas. As Theo watched, the man picked up the syringe, licked the dirt from the needle and plunged it into her vein.

Junkies.

He passed them by, stretching his zombie senses. Rabbits and squirrels scurried from in front of him, as though they felt his reach. A faint presence pulled him further right, down through Falls Ravine.

He hiked through the wet weeds and leaves, sliding down hills, stopping occasionally to check his bearing on the flicker of life. The rain increased to a steady drizzle, and lightning occasionally lit the sky. His body cooled under the precipitation and he worried about his chances of moving quickly enough to get Shelby out of a dire situation.

The tiny beacon of life drew him forward in stealth, and he reached a small clearing. He tried to judge how far he'd come and estimated he was somewhere near Clayton Hill Trail. Maybe he overestimated his pace. The sliver of human life still felt a long way off. Was he on the wrong trail?

He stretched the zombie sense as far as he could, given the chill rain and his own exhaustion. It was still there, flickering against the emptiness.

Something told him that flicker was important.

He kept moving.

The rainclouds blotted the glow of the rapidly setting sun. The lack of light would impede his search and increase the odds of Marjorie finding him first. All she had to do was sit and wait. She knew someone would come looking for her. She knew it would be him.

The human remains in her apartment shocked him. Was she killing to eat? If she was feeding off her victims, they were victims not found. None of the bodies associated with the Riser Killer were mutilated other than the injury that killed them, and those injuries were solely mortal blows to the head.

Was she killing to feed?

He stopped to rub his hands together and warm them when a sound ahead caught his attention. He dropped to the pine needle carpet beneath him and listened with all his senses.

The human still felt a ways off, but something moved in the trees. He couldn't feel anything with his zombie sense, but he heard footsteps and a dragging sound.

If he couldn't sense life, it was something dead.

He lay on his stomach and moved forward on his elbows, slowly and deliberately. If he couldn't sense her, she couldn't sense him. He guessed zombies were dead even to other zombies.

From his poor vantage point on the forest floor, he could only make out a vague shape moving around a tree. When the figure turned a corner, he glimpsed a darker shadow. His mind brought back visions of the black shadow, the shade of death, that each of the victims saw as they died. Carly Harris, the first he ate from, saw only black as she was gunned down. Naomi, the retarded girl, saw a black wave, unidentifiable in her slow innocence. A blowjob before the world turned red and black.

He gasped, tried to clear his mind without breathing. Flashbacks of the other deaths toppled upon him, one after the other. Unicorns and wildflowers, hot semen, the tang of a methamphetamine lab, a little boy laughing on a swing...all the memories...they all ended in a black shadow.

With supreme effort, he willed himself back into his own skin. He peered at the figure circling the tree, saw a whisper of shiny black, and knew without a doubt the Riser Killer—Marjorie—stood before him.

He crawled closer, confused as to why she continued to circle a tree. He painstakingly pushed part of a bush from his line of view and froze.

Shelby sat, tied to the tree. Ziploc bags encased her hands and were duct taped to her arms above huge slashes in her wrists. Her blood pooled in the bags. Theo reached out with his zombie sense and realized the tiny beacon of human life he'd felt, the one he thought was so far away, emanated from Shelby.

She was dying. Right in front of him, the life ebbed out of her and into those bags.

The phone in Theo's pocket vibrated. He pressed it hard against his thigh to muffle the sound, unsure of Marjorie's hearing after feeding. When the vibrations ceased, he took it from his pocket, yanked the battery out and dropped both the battery and phone to the ground.

Marjorie circled the tree again. She stopped in front of Shelby and knelt to check the bags. She whispered something. Shelby turned her face away, giving Theo a clearer view of his friend.

Her ghostly pale skin indicated time was of the essence. A sob escaped Shelby's mouth, and the tiny gleam of her life essence flickered. The zombie roared.

Theo rose from his hiding place just as Marjorie stood from checking Shelby's wounds.

"Theo—" She managed only his name before he rammed his shoulder into her midsection. He drove her back into a tree and they rolled together onto the forest floor. He landed on top of her, knocked the wind out of himself.

Marjorie was unfazed. She stood, pushed him off and ran.

Theo forced himself to his feet and chased her.

They moved through the trees, her black hair flying out behind her like demon wings. Theo, unaccustomed to the wave of adrenaline the chase brought, took full advantage of the chemical windfall. A burst of speed put him within arms' reach and he grabbed her hair.

She screamed and hit the ground. Theo went to his knees beside her, his hands still tangled in her hair.

She punched him hard in the chest and scrambled to her feet. Theo wheezed and rose to meet her when she launched herself at him, fingers going for his throat and eyes. They went down together. She wielded more strength, but he had the weight advantage, and wrestled her underneath him. He grappled with her, grasped her wrists, and forced them to the dirt.

"Stop, Theo! You're hurting me!" She sobbed.

"Stop? You're hurting more than just me, Marjorie! You're killing people!" He leveraged her strength with his body, lying almost prone on her.

"I haven't hurt anyone, Theo, I couldn't."

"What the fuck did you do to Shelby? She's your friend! And all those other people? You killed them. You cut their fucking heads off or blew their brains out!"

"It wasn't me. I found Shelby like this. I'm trying to help her." Marjorie's voice lowered to a whine and it set Theo's teeth on edge.

"Don't lie. I know it's you. I've seen you, felt you in their memories. You're a fucking psycho, Marjorie."

She stilled beneath him, he felt a shift in her, and her quiet voice spoke volumes. "I'm quite sane, Theo. Those people needed to die. Not everyone should be allowed to rise. Only the best of us get to come back. The people I kill are not worthy of another chance. Chances must be earned and those people were seeping wounds on the face of humanity. Evolution needs a little help now and then." A wide, red grin split the fair skin of her face. "We will purify the undead and take our rightful place in society."

"You'll take your rightful place in prison, you fucking lunatic."

She looked up at him, those beautiful black eyes narrowed, emphasizing the decomposition around the corners. Her mouth opened wider than Theo thought possible and she screamed, an incredible shrill, banshee scream. She thrust him off, leapt to her feet and hissed at him. She took off running back toward Shelby.

The zombie in Theo burst free. He howled, embraced the power of the undead. His vision turned dark red, and he followed the black void that was Marjorie.

Marjorie's energy sucked in all light around it, a psychic black hole. It consumed more than its share of life from the very air, and sent back a deep, crackling evil.

As Theo raced back to where he'd found her, he noted the pale glow of Shelby's life essence. Diffused white light surrounded her; the scent of her life intoxicated and incensed him. With effort, he turned the rage of the zombie on the chasm of Marjorie's existence.

She dove to the ground just beyond where Shelby slumped, dying. Theo launched himself on her as she turned to face him, sword raised. He impaled himself on the sword, felt the cold steel puncture his midsection. A blast of ice cold stabbed through his midsection, and he screamed his agony.

He slid down the sword, forcing Marjorie onto her back on the forest floor, her hands pinned around the sword hilt by his body.

"Theo, no!" was all she managed before he bit into her neck, exploding in a vicious fury, fueled by the final memories of a dozen people, including his friend, the only man who ever accepted him as a zombie. The image of Dr. Libitin's head floating free in the water filled his mind as Marjorie's flesh filled his mouth. He tore chunk after chunk from her neck, biting, mauling, chewing through the skin, tendons and vertebrae until he'd sated his rage.

He lay on the ruin that was Marjorie for long minutes, until the zombie began to recede. When his vision cleared and he was able to see the colors of the world around him again, he sat back, the sword hilt falling free of Marjorie's once again dead hands.

Theo looked down at Marjorie, shock replacing the zombie. He'd chewed right through her neck, separating her head from her shoulders. The gore left from his attack surrounded her corpse. He spit again and again, attempting to exorcise all remaining tissue from his mouth, wiping at his face frantically.

He grabbed the hilt of the sword embedded in his body and pulled it back out with a cry of anguish. Once the freezing metal slid free of his body, he remembered.

Shelby.

He threw the sword and spun around, looking for the white light that indicated Shelby's essence. A mere candle flame remained.

"Shelby." He knelt next to her, tried to remove the duct tape from her arms without hurting her further, stanch the flow of blood from the slashes. "Are you okay?"

Her eyelids fluttered once and the light went out.

"No!" He ripped the tape from her arms, took her hands from the bags. Blood spilled all over the ground. The zombie sniffed the blood, the fresh meat, and began to emerge. Theo screamed, jammed the zombie back into the recesses of his psyche, and put pressure on Shelby's wounds.

He needed help. He couldn't save her here by himself. He patted his pockets for his phone, before he remembered he'd taken the battery out and tossed it.

"Help!" he screamed. "Help us!"

Shelby's wounds no longer bled. Her skin, so pale it seemed translucent, felt cooler than it should. Theo shook her, pulled her onto his lap, stroked her hair. "Shelby. Shelby, wake up. Stay with me."

Theo sat, cradling his friend, for long moments, trying to keep her body warm and collar the zombie at the same time. His gaze travelled to Marjorie's body again. Her face looked away from him, tilted too far away from her body. He saw the remnants of her neck, the places where he'd torn her apart, and the zombie grudgingly retreated, pleased for the moment at the devastation it had wrought upon its prey.

"Walker! Walker!" Gavahan's voice came through the rain.

"Stay back." Theo swallowed, tasted rancid blood. He stood, wiped at his face, but only succeeded in smearing the blood covering his entire torso. "Gavahan, stay back. Just call for an ambulance. Please stay away."

The detective burst through the trees behind Theo and stopped short. Theo turned to him slowly. Gavahan's face, bright red from exertion, paled so fast Theo was afraid the big man might pass out. He took a step toward the detective, but Gavahan stumbled backward. "No!"

"Are you okay?" Theo put his hands up, palms out.

Gavahan shook his head, shook it again. He peered at the mess of Marjorie's body. "No," he said again before he turned and retched.

Theo waited for the sounds of puking to abate.

"What the fuck happened here?" The detective wiped his mouth with a handful of wet leaves.

"I found them."

"I see that. And then you...what? You *ate* that one?" He gestured at Marjorie's remains.

Theo stayed silent.

Gavahan blinked several times, appeared to come to some sort of decision. He pulled his phone from his pocket. "This is Gavahan. I need an ambulance yesterday at Frick Park. We're just off Clayton Hill Trail."

Theo sat next to Shelby and took her hand. "I'm so sorry, Shelby. So sorry." Her long lashes rested against her cheeks.

Gavahan produced a pocketknife and cut the zip ties that bound Shelby to the tree. "Lay her down."

Theo lowered her from the sitting position onto her back, her head in his lap. "Hang on, Shelby. Please hang on."

The zombie nosed its way to the surface, and Theo released it, needed the answer it could provide. No interest at all in Shelby.

She was dead.

~

Soft knocking on the door of the room where Shelby's body lay roused Theo. "Come in."

Gavahan slipped through the door. "We need you to come to the station."

"No."

"I don't want to have to order you." The detective rubbed his face with both hands and leaned against the wall. "Come on, Walker."

"No."

"Stubborn son of a bitch."

Theo cracked the slightest smile. "Yes."

Gavahan echoed the smile. "I can't delay this much longer."

"Do you believe that it was self-defense?"

"Absolutely."

No hesitation in Gavahan's response. Theo's anxiety abated just a bit. "Then what's the problem?"

"Formality, you know. Yes, it's clear it was self-defense. I saw the puncture marks. She speared you clean through. But, Walker," he said. "You, uh, chewed through her neck."

Theo shrugged, checked his watch. The sun should be rising soon. "I didn't have a weapon."

A sound of exasperation slipped through the detective's lips. "Fine. But when they send someone else down to bring you in, don't come crying to me."

"Okay."

"They found a broken sword in the dumpster outside her apartment building. It was wrapped in a towel. The piece of blade you found at the Melwood site fits what's left of the broken blade. Pretty conclusive, if we can prove the one in the dumpster belonged to her, and preliminary prints are good." Gavahan picked at his cuticles. "Did she say why she did this?"

Theo shifted in his metal chair. Less than comfortable, but comfort didn't matter now. "Kind of."

"Care to elaborate?"

Theo sighed. He took Shelby's cold hand in his, stroked the back. Her skin, cleaned of blood, held the dull and pasty appearance of death. He pressed his lips to it in a soft kiss, then positioned her arm back on the gurney beside her body. He turned to Gavahan.

"Aside from the fact that Marjorie was certifiable, she believed zombies are superior to humans. She was cleansing the undead pool before the unworthies got a chance to rise." He shook his head. "It's almost too bad we'll never know what happened to her to make her like that. I wonder if she snapped when she died or if it was something from even before."

"Do you know anything about her family?"

"Not a thing. Just that she's not originally from Pittsburgh. Out west, I think she said once. Maybe San Diego."

"I'll do some checking. We have to notify next of kin anyway. She had nothing in her apartment that identifies her or anyone who might be missing her." Gavahan tilted his head to look at the girl on the gurney. "Why didn't she kill her?"

"Shelby was her best friend. My guess is enough humanity remained in her to not want to kill someone she loved. Plus, Shelby is worthy of rising." He turned back to his dead friend.

Gavahan nodded, went on about statements and questioning.

Theo only half-listened. He had the zombie on alert for any sign from Shelby of something, anything.

A hand gripped his shoulder. He turned to see Gavahan standing close behind him. The detective did not remove his hand. "Listen, I'll try to keep the questions to a minimum for now. Sooner or later you'll have to make yourself available. We still need to figure out where the human remains in her apartment came from and, maybe more importantly, why she had them. But for now..." He cocked his chin at Shelby's inert form. "I get it."

Theo put his hand out to Gavahan. "Thanks."

The detective accepted Theo's shake without a flinch. Progress.

Detective Gavahan closed the door behind him when he left. Theo returned to his metal chair and took Shelby's hand again.

He must have fallen asleep at some point, because when he woke, bright sunlight poured through the windows. Shelby's hand still lay motionless in his.

He leaned over, rested his forehead on her hip.

He felt no surprise when her hand squeezed his.

Acknowledgements

To my Seton Hill University contingent: you are the best, most enthusiastic and wonderfully twisted cheering section I could hope for. Candy and Diane... you keep me going. The Biskits...thank you for the advice, the laughs, and the vodka. Bladow! Scott...the absolute best mentor and colleague I could imagine. Thank you for seeing the potential in this story and not letting me stay under the couch.
You all rock my socks off.

To RJ and the Editorial Department team: this is a better story because of you. Thank you.

To Tekla H: thank you for not freaking out when my son brought in twenty spelling sentences all
featuring the word "cadaver."

To my family, Zombie Squad Delta: you are the reason I can do this. It's very simple. Without you, there would be no me.

About the Author

Nikki Hopeman loves the kind of horror that leaves her quaking in the back of the closet, the kind that won't let her close her eyes. Life before writing includes a bachelor's degree in microbiology, and positions as a cancer research tech, a veterinary technician, floral arranger, blueberry picker, parade pooper scooper, and VW Beetle mechanic. She holds an MFA in writing popular fiction from Seton Hill University. When she's not writing, she can be found in the tattoo chair or on her Harley Davidson. Nikki shares her home in Pittsburgh with her husband, two sons, two crazy corgis, and an angry hamster. She can be reached at www.nikkihopeman.com.

CPSIA information can be obtained
at www.ICGtesting.com
Printed in the USA
LVHW040043110420
653056LV00002B/163